THE EAGLE OF ULTIMATE POWER

Richard Rogers

Copyright © Richard Rogers, 2013
ISBN 978-1-291-36590-0

DEDICATION

For Tom and Dan, my action heroes.

Contents

Chapter 1 When things can't possibly get any worse (but then they do) _____ 7

Chapter 2 The Wink of a Shadow _____ 23

Chapter 3 The Flick-Knife and the MP _____ 39

Chapter 4 Out in the Night _____ 59

Chapter 5 Free Fall _____ 79

Chapter 6 The Detectives and the Stolen Wallet _____ 93

Chapter 7 The Voice of the Eagle _____ 103

Chapter 8 The Disguise and The Bear Pit _____ 121

Chapter 9 Danger in the East _____ 131

Chapter 10 Shots in the Dark _____ 143

Chapter 11 The Missing Body _____ 163

Chapter 12 The Death of Dreams _____ 177

Chapter 13 The Eve of Battle _____ 191

Chapter 14 A Moment of Madness _____ 205

Chapter 15 A Whole Lot of Questions _____ 221

Chapter 16 The Return of a Friend _____ 239

Chapter 1 When things can't possibly get any worse (but then they do)

Daryl Green, or Dags as he was commonly known, was a thug and a thief and a bully. His CV, if he had had one, might have said in proud bold letters that he was a trainee gangster, specialising in robbery, grievous bodily harm and bad jokes of limited appeal. Last September he had been one of the new intake of Year 7 students at Newlands Secondary School, though 'student' might have been stretching the meaning a little too far in his case. An ugly foul-mouthed slimeball was how Tom Parks preferred to think of him, and at this particular moment, Tom would have loved to have crushed him beneath his heel like the cold-hearted slippery slug that he was.

But there was a problem with this. Several, in fact.

First, Dags was bigger and harder than Tom, which meant that Tom was unlikely to win any fight that might arise from this very unpleasant meeting. Second, Dags was accompanied by his loyal foot soldiers, Micky Clarke and Steve Warren. These two could have been twins, judged only on appearances, both with straight black hair and dark brown eyes, standing shoulder to stout shoulder, both unsmiling. Third, and most disturbing of all, Tom was trapped in a corner of one of the school yards. A quiet corner. And it was at a time after the last school bell when everyone's thoughts, both students' and teachers' alike, were focussed on getting home as quickly as possible, rather than rescuing some poor soul who might be about to lose his front teeth.

"Hello, pretty Parks," said Dags, snorting with laughter.

The answer was obvious, and as Tom had pretty well given up hope of ever enjoying life again, he didn't hold back.

"Hello, Ugly," he said, smiling sourly.

The bully's square face began to twitch. If he wasn't ugly before, he certainly was now. Tom saw his squinty eyes home in on the large poster tube sticking out of his carrier-bag and didn't need an A Grade in 'Bad People' to work out what was coming next.

"Okay, wise-guy, what've you got?" growled Dags. "And no tricks."

Micky and Steve offered half a grin each (probably, Tom thought, because it needed two of them to manage a whole one). They clenched their fists, hungry for battle.

"It's just a project," he said in his most boring voice.

He'd become very good at that voice over the last two years in which his life had become so deeply boring that he'd been certain it couldn't possibly get any worse. But now, of course, it had. His Election Project, however, was one of the few things that still excited him. It shouldn't have, because it was schoolwork and schoolwork wasn't cool, but it did nonetheless (and maybe that showed how truly boring his life had become). What it meant, though, was that this was something he wasn't going to give up in a hurry.

"Oh yeah," sneered Dags. "What's it about then?"

"The General Election. Parliament. That sort of thing."

Tom glanced up cautiously at Dags, wondering if he knew anything about General Elections or that the next one was only two months away. But there was no way of knowing what might be going on inside that dense ugly head of his. Tom could only hope that he believed him and was as uninterested in politics as everyone else seemed to be.

"Hand it over," said Dags, holding out his hand.

Tom drew back.

"There's only a poster of the Houses of Parliament and some stuff I've written," he said. "It's not interesting. Believe me."

"*Hand it over*," snarled Dags, "or else!"

"Look, Dags, there's no money, no mobile - nothing!"

"Get him!" shouted Dags, snapping his fingers at the other two who promptly started forwards.

"You're too thick to vote!" Tom suddenly shouted angrily, edging backwards, then cried out for help.

A moment later his backpack struck the brick wall behind, bringing him to a sudden halt. Micky graciously bowed aside, letting Steve come through to strike the first blow. Steve skipped forwards and coiled his arm back in one agile movement. But then, as Tom turned his face away from the inevitable punch, something dark slipped across the ground between them.

Suddenly his attacker crashed downwards, smashing his head against the smooth tarmac with a loud crack. He cried out in pain, blood spluttering from his mouth.

Micky leaped past the sprawled body, eyes ablaze.

Another dark movement shot across the yard like the shadow from a bird passing overhead.

Micky jerked in mid-air, losing his balance. His arms waved frantically and the look in his eyes turned to icy terror. An instant later he smashed into the wall, then collapsed in a groaning heap below.

Cowering down, Tom looked round in astonishment, while Dags snarled like a rabid dog. Dags kicked Steve's legs out of his way, then started forwards, eyes filled with hate.

A dark movement crossed the bully's ankles - Tom glimpsed it through the gap in his arms which he held protectively over his head - and while Dags kept moving, his feet did not.

As Dags fell he strained round to see what had snagged his feet. But when his head swung forwards again he was too late to stop his face smashing down on top of Tom's bent knee. His teeth bit through Tom's trousers into his flesh and his lip split open. He gave a muffled grunt, while Tom let out a cry big enough for the two of them. His head rocked back and he toppled to the ground.

Tom's knee felt as if it was on fire, but he forced himself back up the wall, then limped away past the wounded bodies sprawled around him. He took no more than a few steps, however, before another voice brought him to a stuttering halt.

"What the hell's going on here?" snapped Mr Denton, the PE teacher, wheeling round as he passed through the yard. "Stop right there, Parker!"

"It's Parks," said Tom, trying to straighten up.

"And what have we here?" said the teacher, suddenly showing great interest as his eyes ran over the others dragging themselves off the ground. "Well, if it isn't Dags and his merry men! And it looks like you've come off worse, for once."

Dags scowled, grimacing from the pain in his mouth, then spat a thick mixture of blood and saliva at the feet of the teacher.

"Right," snapped Mr Denton, "I want all of you in my office in 5. And get yourselves cleaned up on the way," and turning on his heels, he strode off again.

Tom limped quickly after him, not wanting to be around when the others revived, and on entering the teacher's office was pointed to a row of four chairs hastily assembled in front of the desk. He waited there while the teacher sorted out his work from the day, moving books in a steady stream between the desk and the shelves and his tatty leather briefcase. When the door banged open again, the gang swaggered in, shirts hanging out, blood streaking their clothes and faces.

Mr Denton nodded towards the row of chairs at the end of which sat Tom. Reluctantly they shuffled across the room and slumped down on the chairs. Micky sat next to Tom, glaring at him with a mixture of hatred and deep suspicion. The teacher dropped a stack of exercise books into his briefcase, snapped it shut, then with a weary sigh moved round to the front of his desk.

"Right. Any of you sorry lot need to see a doctor?"

The gang shook their heads, looking away defiantly, while Tom tried to keep his hand from straying towards his throbbing knee.

"Okay, then," he went on, "who's going to tell me what happened?"

No one spoke.

"Dags?"

The boy shrugged his shoulders and mumbled something.

"What was that?"

"Dunno."

"Don't know, *what*?" said the teacher pointedly.

"Dunno, *Sir*," said Dags, a hateful glower in his eyes.

It was the same look that the teacher had seen in his face all too often. There were one or two of his sort in every year. They came and went, leaving a trail of destruction behind them. But Mr Denton wasn't put off so easily. He hadn't been a teacher for twenty years without learning a trick or two, and life wasn't worth living if you gave in to his sort.

"Look, it's obvious you got beaten up out there," he said as if it didn't matter at all. "All I want to know is-"

"That ain't true!" shouted Dags, his mouth twisting with rage and pain, caught on the teacher's hook. "He never touched us. None of us. He couldn't beat us, the little punk. We're better than him any day."

"What about the blood, then? And what were you doing on the ground? Having a lie down after a hard day's work? I don't think so."

"He never laid a finger on us! He's not good enough!"

"*Not good enough?* What's *good* about you, Dags, eh, tell me that? There were three of you against *him*" - he pointed a firm finger at Tom, his eyes remaining fixed on the bully.

"So, tell me, what were you after? What was it you wanted? And how *did* you end up like you are now?"

"I'm fine, just fine," said Dags, grinning foolishly, a fresh trickle of blood seeping from his lip.

Mr Denton hadn't expected a miraculous confession and knew only too well that the gang had been out to get whatever they could from the defenceless Parks. But how defenceless exactly was Parks? Dags and the other two might not have the sharpest brains around, but they were tough enough to take on any student their own age without breaking into a sweat and plenty of those a lot older than themselves. So, what did happen out there? The teacher had taken Tom for one or two PE lessons and was unimpressed with his commitment or abilities. He was like so many other students nowadays who didn't connect with sports or team work and simply faded into the background, hanging around miserably until the ordeal was over and they could move on to their next lesson.

"So, tell me, Parks, what happened?"

Tom squirmed, glancing up nervously at the teacher, trying not to look across at the gang. His fingers fidgeted with the handles of the carrier-bag leaning up against his chair.

"Well?"

"Dunno, Sir," said Tom, lowering his eyes to the floor.

There was a long pause and when he spoke again, his voice was much quieter. "They fell over," said Tom.

"They *what*?"

"They fell over. I saw it."

"You're telling me that there was no fight?" said the astonished teacher. "That you didn't touch them? That they just *fell over*? That that's how they got these injuries?"

Tom nodded, keeping his head down.

"Yeah," said Micky brightly, seizing on the excuse, "it's true, ain't it?"

Dags glared at him. In the toilets on their way there he'd told the other two to keep quiet and let him do the talking if they didn't want a whole lot of trouble. Micky took the hint, backing off.

"Yeah," said Dags, picking up on the theme, "it was an accident. We fell over. It happens, don't it? It was probably the ground. You could be in a lot of trouble if you don't get that fixed, *Sir*."

A clever grin spread across his blood-smeared mouth, giving him a ghoulish appearance. Mr Denton silently counted down from ten, wishing he could wipe that grin straight back off his face. He didn't like bullies, especially the arrogant ones.

"There's nothing wrong with the ground out there," said the teacher, "I saw it. And as no one here's telling me the truth then you're all just going to have to come back here tomorrow and go through everything again. I'll be contacting your parents. The Head'll be told too. Okay, get lost, the lot of you!"

The chairs scraped back and the gang shuffled away. Daryl was still grinning, having no fear of either Mr Grange, the headteacher, or his own mother who, if he saw her at all, was more likely to pat him on the back and start ranting against the school. And the thought that he might be excluded from school was only an incentive, offering him the opportunity to roam more freely and exert his power more broadly. Steve and Micky followed him out of the office, darting wary sharp-eyed glances back at Mr Denton and Tom.

Tom hesitated, taking as much time as he could to gather up his carrier-bag, not wanting to leave the safe confines of the office. He knew only too well what was likely to be waiting for him outside.

"Wait there," said Mr Denton eventually as he neared the door. "I can give you a lift home. What's your home number?"

A wave of relief swept over Tom. However, it was soon replaced by a new fear as he wondered what his father would have to say when he learned of what had happened. As the teacher picked up the phone on his desk, he winked in a friendly way at Tom, then spoke briefly with his father.

"Okay, let's go," he said, dropping the phone back and hauling his briefcase off the desk. "Got everything?"

"Sure," said Tom, glancing down at his carrier-bag and smiling to himself.

As they drove out of the school gates Mr Denton glanced across at Tom and noticed him rubbing his knee.

"Are you all right?"

"Dags bit me," said Tom, promptly adding, "when he fell."

"Right," he said, raising an eyebrow in surprise, then smiled. "Maybe you should get a jab for that. He might not clean his teeth."

"His breath stinks," said Tom, smiling too.

After checking the directions for Tom's house again, the teacher asked if he had any interest in sport.

"A bit," said Tom.

"What in?"

"Netball," he said hesitantly, remembering the few occasions he'd enjoyed playing it at primary school.

"Ever tried basketball?"

"No."

"Want to?"

"Maybe."

It was kind of the teacher to show an interest in him, but Tom knew that what really held him back was not having any friends to go with him to these activities. Ever since he had moved up to Secondary School he'd lost contact with the dwindling number of friends he'd known before, becoming like a ghost, drifting in and out of the bustling crowds of children, unseen, unheard and unhappy. It left a terrible empty feeling inside. Once he had managed to tell his father about it, but he had managed only a few fumbling words of advice before rushing off again in his usual hurried way. Nothing had changed for Tom.

"Maybe *may be*," said Mr Denton with an encouraging look. "There are coaching sessions on Wednesdays straight after school for one hour, if you're interested."

Tom shrugged vaguely, watching the road ahead.

"This is the right way, isn't it?" said the teacher as they swung down a steep hill.

"Yeah."

Mr Denton glanced across at him, trying to gauge the mood of this quiet thoughtful boy. He had wanted this opportunity to talk to him alone and, as they were nearing his home, he decided to press ahead with his questions.

"So, they fell over, did they?" he said with a disbelieving look. "But it's not like they fell over each other. They weren't all piled up in a heap. I saw them. And Dags and Warren looked as if they'd taken a good hard punch in the mouth."

"I never touched them," said Tom, frowning. "They came at me and then…and then…"

"Then what?"

"*I don't know*," he said, struggling with his thoughts, "but they fell over. They did. It wasn't me."

"And Dags bit your knee?" said the teacher, shaking his head. "You know, I wouldn't blame you if you'd stuck up for yourself. God knows, they need teaching a lesson. But I'd really like to know what did happen back there. You do understand, whatever you tell me doesn't have to go any further?"

Tom nodded, but remained silent.

The trouble was that every time he tried to put in words what he had seen, it sounded so foolish. Everyone knows that a shadow can't trip up people. And if it wasn't a shadow, then what was it? The thought sent a shiver up his spine.

"They just fell over," he said again.

"Okay," said the teacher with a deep sigh, then turned into the road where Tom lived.

Penrose Avenue consisted of a terrace of 2-storey Victorian houses, the kerbside lined with cars parked bumper to bumper. Mr Denton drove past Tom's house, No.38, until he found a space, then they walked back. They stood in the porch and the bell rang out and soon the door opened. Tom's father, Alan, wiping his hands on a small towel, ushered them both inside.

"Are you all right, Tom?" said his father.

"Yes, sure, dad, I'm okay," he said, hiding his limp and slinging his bags down in the hallway.

"Perhaps we could talk privately for a moment," said Mr Denton.

"Oh, yes, of course," Alan said after a moment's hesitation, then looked towards the front room. "Come in here."

The front room was strewn with papers and books and magazines. Dirty mugs and plates dotted its surfaces and an untidy pile of DVD's sat around the television like presents under a Christmas tree. This was the sort of family room Mr Denton recognised straight away; he had two teenage daughters of his own.

The teacher explained that he needed to get home shortly, then spoke about what had happened. Alan nodded, listening closely, a weary look on his face. The teacher told him what he knew about Dags and the gang and about his own concerns, then asked that if he or Mrs Parks discovered anything more about the matter that they would let the school know. Mr Parks explained about his divorce, but assured him that he'd pass on the information. And of course, if he found out anything more, he'd let the school know straight away.

"Tom's never really settled at Newlands," Alan went on. "But then he took the divorce a lot harder than Clara. At least that's how it seemed to me. I don't think he's ever been his real self since then."

"And is that Clara I can hear?"

The teacher cocked his head towards the ceiling from where a dull bass beat pounded out.

"Yes," said Alan with a laugh. "She's growing up fast. A real handful. I'm not sure how much of a help I am."

"We can only do our best," said the teacher, giving him a friendly slap on the shoulder, then excused himself. On his way out of the front door, he added, "You might want to check if anything of Tom's has gone missing."

"I will," said Alan, "and thank you."

Tom listened for the sound of the front door closing, looking out from the bay window of his father's bedroom. He watched Mr Denton trot back to his car and drive away. Moments later, as his father started up the stairs, Tom hobbled back along the landing to his own bedroom at the back of the house. He settled himself back on his bed, carefully lowering his knee down. He puffed out a long sigh, dreading having to go through his story again, even if it was with his father.

But the story was easier to tell the second time around. After all, he wasn't lying, only skipping over the bit he didn't really understand. Nothing was stolen, either, which pleased his father, though his face fell again when he spotted the torn and blood-stained trousers. Another pair would have to be bought, he supposed, unless by some miracle his own sewing and stain-removing powers suddenly improved. They looked at each other for a moment, then laughed, shaking their heads.

Moments later his father dashed off, remembering the cooking that he'd left unattended, and Tom was left to reflect on how much better his mother was at all those practical sorts of things.

"So, who's been a naughty little boy, then?" said Clara, biting off the tip of a burnt sausage half an hour later.

Clara was two years older than Tom and seemed to have no features in common with him. Her hair was naturally blonde, his mousy brown. Her eyes were green, his light brown. Her nose curved up to a slender tip, his was just plain small and did nothing fancy at all. Only their slim mouths were similar, but then hers was covered in a generous layer of sparkly pink lipstick. And she really knew how to talk, too.

"Cut your sausage," said her father, glancing up, "and stop waving it around in the air."

She nodded vaguely, then carried on as before, while Tom glared crossly at the two of them, realising that his father must have already told her about what had happened.

"Come on," she said, "tell me how you beat up Dags and those two other half-wits. I'm just *dying* to hear this one."

"I didn't beat up anyone," said Tom, giving a potato a sharp poke with his fork. "They were just after my stuff and then...then they fell over."

Clara giggled, shaking her head, her fine hair tickling her cheeks. "That's what dad said, but it sounds even funnier coming from you. They just 'fell over', did they? *Just like that.* It's amazing! I'd like to know how to do that trick."

"Don't worry," sneered Tom, "no one's *ever* going to go for you."

Clara's eyes narrowed, but before she could respond their father told them both to cool off and stop playing with their food or there really would be trouble.

"I still think there's something fishy about it," said Clara, staring at Tom, but then quickly went on, "Okay if I go over to Jess's tonight, dad?"

"As long as you're back by nine."

"Sure," she said brightly, then flashed a sly smile at Tom. "I did the vegetables, so you can do the washing-up."

"All right, Tom?" said his father.

"Sure," he said miserably, then, after his father looked way, took the sausage on his fork and made a rude gesture at Clara.

Clara blew him a hateful kiss and the rest of the meal passed by in stony silence.

After the washing-up Tom was at a loss to know what to do. He had planned to look over his project work, but that was before Dags had tried to take it off him, and now, somehow, his enthusiasm for it was gone. He got as far as pulling out the magnificent poster of the Houses of Parliament, but soon pushed it aside and wandered off into the back garden.

The garden was small, consisting of a patio, a square of grass, a thin flower bed along each side wall, and, along the back wall, a shed, a pear tree and the gate leading into the alleyway beyond. He remembered the tortoiseshell cat he'd seen occasionally spying on him from the back wall. His only pet, Robbie, a hamster, had died over a year ago, and the thought of the cat as a replacement appealed to him. He didn't think his dad would like it, though. But then, if the cat was to hang around for long enough, then maybe it could simply blend in with the family and no decision would have to be made. But the cat didn't show up. He tried meowing, hoping that might attract it, but the only response was from a dog barking angrily further down the terrace.

Back in his bedroom, he ran his fingers idly along the books lining his shelves, but none of them caught his interest. On one of the shelves stood Robbie's empty lifeless cage and next to it a framed photo. In the photo the whole family were together, arm in arm. Everyone smiled. It was one of those rare moments captured before the divorce. It was taken three years ago, but seemed a lifetime away. He moved on to his desk in the corner, then sat down and flicked on the computer. The rest of the evening was frittered away playing computer games.

The next time he looked up was when the front door slammed shut and Clara called out that she was home again. Seconds later she shut herself away in her bedroom and the thundering bass beat of a heavy metal band kicked in.

The computer went off and Tom stood at his window, looking out into the rapidly darkening night. The light from the kitchen window reached out over the patio and grass. The opposite terrace, across the alleyway, was silhouetted like a cardboard cut-out against the amber glow of streetlights. A slither of moon slunk behind a smoky cloud.

He drew the curtains, then went to bed. He tossed and turned, his fingers returning to the hardening scab on his throbbing knee. His mind was filled with questions about what had happened in that quiet corner of the school yard. He relived it again. His arms wrapped tight over his head, he glimpsed the shadow tripping Dags, actually taking hold of his ankles. But such thoughts were madness! Things like that didn't really happen - *couldn't* happen - and he was certain that he really would go mad if he kept on thinking them. Long torturous minutes passed before, finally, exhausted, he drifted into a fitful sleep.

Not long afterwards, the duvet at the foot of his bed lifted slightly and something darker than the darkness itself slipped down onto the bare floorboards. It moved across the room, making no noise at all, not even a whisper. It spread as smoothly as oil, parting round the legs of the dressing chair and the clothes spilled on the floor, then coming together again on the other side. It moved purposefully, reaching out like the fingers of a hand searching, at the same time drawing itself in behind.

It came to the skirting board beneath the window and rose effortlessly up the papered wall. As gentle as a draught, it didn't scratch or tear. The curtains rippled, then slowly pulled apart, the wooden curtain-rings chattering quietly to the ends of the rail.

A figure stood, silhouetted against the glass.

It looked out at the night, deep in thought, untroubled by time.

Almost an hour later footsteps came towards the door.

The figure slid down out of sight.

The door opened slowly and Alan's head poked cautiously inside. Then he stepped into the room. His shadow, cast by the landing light, fell towards the window where it was troubled for a moment by another shadow before settling again.

He walked lightly across to the bed, then listened to the sound of his son's breathing. It was calm at last. He went to adjust the duvet lying at an angle across his body, but then decided against it, not wanting to disturb him. He leaned closer, looking at his face. The worries of the day were written there.

"Never mind, son," he whispered, "those bullies will get what's coming to them. You saw them off and I'm really proud of you. Don't worry, there's better things ahead, I know there are. You've just got to be patient. Just remember, tomorrow's another day. I love you."

He would have liked to have kissed him, but the days when he had his permission to do so were long gone. Like Clara, Tom was growing up fast, and the most he could hope from them nowadays was a mumbled please or thank you tossed to him in passing. He was just happy to have him home, safe and sound. He crept out of the room, drawing the door gently shut behind him.

The figure returned to the window.

It looked out beyond the clutter of the town into the darkest depths of the night sky.

Something was coming, coming soon. Something that would affect Tom whether he liked it or not. Something of grave importance - something that would change the future of this nation - something that could even destroy it. Something that *must* be stopped.

The figure looked over at Tom.

He was so young.

It was unfortunate, but the young, too, were sometimes caught up in the evils of war.

Chapter 2 The Wink of a Shadow

The following Monday, almost a week later, Tom popped into Cuttles Newsagent on his way to catch the bus home after school. But when he emerged from the shop, Dags and his gang stepped out from round the corner and blocked his way.

"Hello, pretty Parks!" said Dags, a brown scab glaring from his grinning lips. "I've missed you."

Tom had known this moment would come, when Dags would want his revenge for his humiliating defeat. Mr Grange's lecture to the gang, however threatening, was never going to change them. They'd passed him several times in the school yards, keeping their distance but eyeing him up, reminding him of the unsettled business, that a time of reckoning was coming...and that time was now.

"Hello," said Tom cautiously.

"Hello, *Sir*," said Dags pointedly, his fists clenching and unclenching as he waited for Tom to address him properly.

Tom wanted to sneer and say, "You really don't have to call me 'Sir'," but managed to hold his tongue. However, an anger was rising inside him, a righteous anger. He didn't much care about the cheap mobile and the small change inside his backpack and it was only dirty PE kit inside the carrier-bag, but what really got him was how this bully dared to defy all authority and come straight back to him to cause trouble again.

"What do you want?" he said bluntly.

"What've you got?" he snarled.

Tom lifted up the carrier-bag. "Stinking socks, stinking shorts, stinking shirt, stinking trainers. Anything you fancy?"

Instantly Dags's fist swung round and Tom felt a bolt of pain shoot up his arm. The carrier-bag dropped to the ground, spilling out the PE kit.

23

Steve and Micky laughed, but stopped suddenly at the sound of the newsagent's doorbell.

A small boy stepped out of the shop, glanced up at the others, then scuttled off round the corner.

"Right," said Dags, returning to business, "hand over the backpack."

"Get a move on!" said Micky.

"Yeah!" said Steve.

The gang were hungry for the kill, but Tom, whose head had suddenly lowered, didn't respond.

Tom's eye had been caught by a movement on the ground. A dark movement. And now he was watching a shadow…his own. It stretched forwards, though he wasn't moving a muscle himself. It rippled over his carrier-bag and PE kit, then headed straight towards the gang.

"*Hand it over!*" shouted Dags furiously, getting ready for his next strike.

At that moment the shadow's arms split and shot out like grappling hooks, wrapping around the ankles of the gang.

"What the hell are you staring at!" screamed Dags, his eyes darting about fearfully as he remembered his last painful defeat.

Suddenly darkening, the shadow pulled tight.

The gang rocked on their feet and waved their arms frantically about them as if caught in an earthquake.

"Dags! Help!" cried Micky and Steve.

"Get off us, Parks!" shouted Dags. "*Now!*"

The newsagent's doorbell sounded again and out stepped the owner himself, Mr Cuttles. His eyes sharpened the moment he caught sight of the gang.

"You again!" he said. "Always you! And what are you up to now? Haven't you had enough warnings? This time I'll phone the school *and* the police. And don't think any of your miserable excuses will help you!"

"Shut your face!" yelled Dags, trying to stay upright. "We ain't done nothing. Keep away from us."

Mr Cuttles stepped forwards, ready to take hold of Dags's grubby collar, but at the same moment the shadow loosened its grip and slid back. Dags twisted round and ran stumbling away, while Steve and Micky fell into each other's arms, fumbled apart again, then lolloped off after their leader. At a safe distance away, they jeered and chanted in hollow triumph, then quickly disappeared out of sight.

"Good riddance to bad rubbish," said Mr Cuttles, then turned to Tom. "Are you all right?"

"Yeah," said Tom vaguely, staring at the ground.

His shadow, now, appeared completely normal. It had a head and body and two arms and two legs and, when he turned sideways, a hump for his backpack. He tried moving about and it moved with him, exactly as it should.

Mr Cuttles glanced back at his shop, wanting to return, but the boy still seemed to be not quite himself.

At that moment a small slit opened up in the head of Tom's shadow, letting the light through. The momentary glint looked exactly like a wink. Tom smiled hesitantly.

"Fine, then!" said Mr Cuttles, pleased to see the smile, then went back inside his shop.

Eventually Tom remembered what time it was and went on to the bus-stop, though all the while keeping a careful watch over his shadow. And from that time on he thought about little else. He went over his run-ins with the gang and his sightings of the shadow and, of course, the wink. Now he was certain that what had happened to Dags's gang had all been the work of his shadow and yet, the more he looked down it and it remained perfectly normal, and the more he went over and over the extraordinary events in his mind, the less real it all became. The truth, it seemed, was as hard to pin down as a shadow itself.

The next day Mr Denton came across Tom in the school yard and reminded him of the basketball on Wednesday, then, a little later, Ms Newby, his Form teacher, drew him aside, taking him into an empty classroom. She asked if there had been any more trouble with Dags. Tom would have loved to have told her about his shadow, but was certain that if he did he'd end up shut away for miserable long hours with the Educational Psychologist, a prospect that didn't attract him.

"I saw Dags down at Cuttles," he said, "but he ran off."

"Good," she said. "It sounds like he's got the message."

But neither of them truly believed that. Earlier that morning Tom had spotted Dags's gang skulking away from him. The sight of it had both astonished him and made him very happy, but at the same time he knew that it wouldn't be long before they were muscling up to some other poor victim and taking whatever they could.

That evening Tom thought of telling his father about his shadow, but as ever he was caught up in his chores. Tom didn't blame him for that, after all, someone had to cook and wash and tidy, especially now that his mother wasn't around. Yet still he longed for his father to stop and ask him how he was. If they ever did get round to talking about his shadow, though, Tom thought, there was still the problem that his father didn't believe in anything supernatural. He'd probably only laugh at Tom and tell him not to be so silly. And the only other person Tom could confide in was Clara, and there was no way he was going to do that: he valued his life too much! Sharing that precious information with her would provide her with enough ammunition to keep him pinned down and begging for mercy for months ahead.

On several occasions he tried again to get his shadow to come to life, but with no success. And so, as the week wound on, his thoughts of it grew less and less. And then, on Thursday, along came a special announcement in his History lesson, giving him something completely different to think about.

"Is everyone listening?" said Mr Harris, waiting for the class to quieten down. "Now, before I tell you what's going to happen, can anyone remind me what this project is about?"

There was laughter because everyone knew the answer to that question; they'd spent over half the term working on nothing but the project.

"The General Election," several voices shouted out.

"Good! I'm glad something's sunk in after all that work," said Mr Harris, smiling to himself. "Well, as part of the project, I can now tell you that we are going to have a very special visitor to the school."

A murmur spread round the class.

"Of course," he went on, wandering away from his desk, "I'll need you to be on your best behaviour. It's extremely rare that someone so important comes to Newlands and we don't want anyone spoiling it and giving the school a bad name."

"But, Sir," piped up one boy, speaking for the whole class, "*who is it?*"

"'Who is it?'" teased Mr Harris, pretending to ponder the question deeply. "Hmm? What a good question. Well, our special visitor is no ordinary man. In fact, he is a Member of Parliament. *Our* Member of Parliament. So, who knows his name?"

There were one or two groans at the thought of the visitng MP and no hands were raised.

"I'm a little disappointed," he said, shaking his head, but then straightened himself up and looked out over them with a determined look in his eyes. "But never mind! His name is Mr van Reiner and what really matters is that straight after the Easter Holiday you're going to get to know him a lot better. That is when he's coming here. *And* there are going to

27

be television cameras and news reporters too. It'll be quite an event!"

Suddenly, at the thought of the cameras and reporters, a buzz of excitement swept round the room.

The teacher smiled to himself, waiting for quiet again.

"But why have I invited Mr van Reiner to come here? Well, as we all know, the General Election is only two months away. And it is then, as we've already learned in our project, that the people of this country will vote for their next Government. But - *and this is crucial* - how does anyone know who it is they should vote for?" He paused, giving them a moment to think about the question, then continued. "Well, the easiest way is to *talk* to the prospective candidates - to those people who want our votes. We should ask them what they're going to do if they get elected and make sure that they really are the right people to govern over us. And *that* is exactly what we are going to do. We are going to put our very own questions to Mr van Reiner and he is going to have to answer them. It will be exactly the same as Minister's Question Time in the House of Commons when written questions are presented to the Prime Minister and he has to answer them in front of all the other Members of Parliament. Except that this time the questions will be our very own and we will be the very important people listening carefully to the answers. But there's still something missing," he added. "Can anyone tell me what it is?"

"We'll need a bigger room," a loud voice called out from the back.

Everyone laughed, including Mr Harris.

"Good point," he said, "and that's why our Question Time will take place in the main hall. But that wasn't what I was thinking of. Anyone? No. Well, what we need to think about are the questions we want to ask. And that's not as easy as it might sound. But imagine this..." Fixing his eye on them, he adopted a far more serious tone. "This, is *our* chance to find out what Mr van Reiner's going to do for us. And not just for us. For our school and our families, too, and for our town, and for the nation itself. We can ask anything we like. We can ask about the things that interest us, and the things we'd like to see made better, and the things that make us angry that we want to see put right. *We can ask him absolutely anything.* And that," he concluded, taking a deep breath, " is exactly what we're going to think about right now."

And for the rest of the lesson they discussed the questions they'd like to put forwards, agreeing which were the best and noting them down. Then, at the end of the lesson, Mr Harris handed out information sheets for their parents. On the sheets were permission slips which needed to be signed and returned no later than the first day of the next term (which, he reminded them, was only three weeks away). Along the bottom of the sheets was another section with space for any questions they or their families might think of later. These had to be in by the same day, too.

When the bell sounded, the class moved on, but few of them thought about anything else for the rest of the day.

At the end of the week and the start of the Easter Holiday, the handover of Tom and Clara from their father to their mother took place. On the Friday evening the children packed their bags in the same sombre routine that had become all too familiar over the last two years. As the time for them to go approached, their father called out to make sure that they were ready, then said his goodbyes. Several minutes later the doorbell rang and the children went out of the house on their own. There had been a time, just after the divorce, when their mother would have come rushing up to the front door, brimming with excitement and enfolding them in her arms, but that had soon come to an end. From then on it had always been her new boyfriend, Georgie, who came to collect them. A younger, handsome man with flowing black hair, and charming, too, he always called out to their father and offered friendly greetings. Mr Parks, however, showed no interest in venturing out from the house while he was there. After all, Georgie was the reason that his wife had left him. Instead, he would wait until the Mercedes had pulled away, then quietly settle himself once again in the then silent lifeless house.

The Mercedes cruised across town, heading from north to south, until it arrived in the affluent suburb of Cedarwoods. But from then on, for Tom at least, it became a matter of survival. It wasn't that he didn't love his mother or that Georgie wasn't fun to be with, it was just that their lives didn't seem to connect together as a family any more. First there would come the over-the-top welcomes on their arrival, then the gift-wrapped presents (wrapped by the shops, of course, because their mother with her busy lifestyle never had enough time to fit in that sort of thing), then the tour of everything new and luxurious in the 5th floor apartment. Then they would sit down together and enjoy a sumptuous dinner prepared by Georgie (who really did know how to cook), which would be accompanied by endless talk of their mother's business (how interesting did she think dental products could be?). Eventually she would remember to ask how they were getting along at school (as if that was all there was to their lives), and then, inevitably, excuse herself so that she could tackle the essential paperwork and calls for her business.

That was it. Always the same.

And for the rest of the week the children would be cut loose with enough money to keep themselves occupied in the shops about town, which was heaven for Clara and hell for Tom. Clara loved the gift-wrapped presents presented to them on their arrival and Georgie's sparkling white smile and most especially the offer of endless shopping time, which was why, he supposed, she found little to complain about. She would phone up her friends and arrange to meet them in town, while he could either remain alone in the apartment (which his mother frowned on) or, as inevitably happened, wander around after Clara and her friends. But to make matters worse, Clara was given control of the money. So, whenever he wanted any of it, she would insist that he did whatever she wanted first. He had to wait here or go there or run off to find her something or disappear for 20 minutes, all in return for the money that was rightfully his!

It was hell!

On this visit, the hand-back came a week later, at the end of the Easter weekend, straight after the Sunday service at his mother's church. After the last wavering hymn and a final swing of the giant incense ball, the priest proclaimed that death and hell were defeated and that Jesus Christ was risen indeed. The congregation responded with a loud 'Hallelujah!' which Tom joined in with heartily, relieved that at last his own personal hell was coming to an end.

His mother stayed on after the service, as she always did, chatting enthusiastically with various members of the congregation she'd never met before or would even recognise in the street, while Georgie returned Clara and Tom to Penrose Avenue. Georgie tried to make them laugh on the way home (always having more success with Clara than with Tom) and did his best once again to be friendly with Mr Parks. Then the front door shut, their father smiling with relief.

On the Bank Holiday Monday, he took the opportunity to do the week's family food shopping. In the afternoon he tackled what should have been a simple piece of DIY. However, the broken door-handle proved more difficult than he had expected and for much of the time dark mutterings and loud thumpings could be heard by the children when they cautiously stepped past him. In the evening he proudly presented a roast dinner, though it struggled to compare with anything that Georgie could have made.

"Nice beef, dad," Tom said bravely, chewing on the great stringy dry lump filling his cheek.

"God, it's awful!" said Clara, coughing out a grey mass on the side of her plate.

"Okay, okay," said their father, valiantly chewing on, "I get the message. I'll cook it for a bit longer next time."

"About a week," said Clara.

The room went silent.

The children glanced up nervously at their father.

Then, thankfully, they all burst out laughing.

For the rest of the week, Clara spent much of the time out and about with her friends, while Tom enjoyed the comfort of having his own belongings around him once more. The time passed uneventfully except for the Wednesday when he spotted from his window the tortoiseshell cat on the back wall of the garden. He tore down the stairs and ran outside, then listened, breathlessly, to its sad mewing. It was as if it was pleading for help, but when he urged it to come down, it only paced nervously back and forth. Finally it jumped down out of sight into the alleyway. Tom kicked a plastic flower-pot lying on the grass, which unexpectedly took off and spun over the back wall. He wished it could have landed on the stupid cat's head (though really he wanted only for the cat's return).

Then, on the Friday, when his thoughts began to turn towards the Summer Term looming ahead, he remembered his Election Project and the visit of the MP to the school. *And what had he done with the information sheet with its permission slip?* Suddenly he was back in his bedroom and frantically searching. His backpack and carrier-bag were turned inside out and his drawers were scoured, until finally he discovered the precious piece of paper folded neatly away in his bedside table. He sat on the floor next to the table for some moments afterwards, the hand holding the sheet trembling.

But his father was out, and when Tom calmed down again, he had a moment of inspiration. In the History lesson he hadn't thought of any questions himself, but had wanted to. But now, as he looked down at the sheet in his hand, he saw the section at the bottom for any other questions they might think of later. And he wondered if he could discover a really good question by looking up information about the Member of Parliament on the internet.

He went over to the table by the window and flicked on the computer. He searched for Mr van Reiner, Member of Parliament. Several hits came up instantly. He scrolled down the list and quickly spotted the MP's own website. He clicked on the mouse. The screen flickered, hesitated, then, a second later, presented a large image of Mr van Reiner himself.

The MP stared out at Tom. He was sitting at a mahogany writing desk in an office lined with expensive leather-bound books. He wore a smart dark suit and leaned forwards studiously, his slender fingers folded together. He had dark hair, swept back, and handsome watchful eyes.

Suddenly, making Tom start, the MP tilted his head slightly then started talking.

"Hello," he said in a well cultivated voice, sporting a warm smile, "and welcome to my website. I am Derek van Reiner, Member of Parliament for Bellington North, and I'd like to tell you what I *will* do for you. It's simple really. I will get this country back on its feet and put the 'Great' back into Britain.

"But how?"

"Well, I always back winners and *they* do the rest. But ask yourself, how often does the present Government waste time pouring taxpayers' money after losers when there is no hope of success and no thought of the cost? *All too often.* But that is not how *I* do business. With my many years of experience in commerce and finance, I *know* what winners looks like and I know how to make them succeed.

"So, let's get back to work. And let's work *together*, because *together* we can make Britain 'Great' once again.

"I am Derek van Reiner. A vote for me is a vote for your country."

The light classical music that had been playing in the background faded and the MP jerked back to his original position, the online movie preparing to play again. One more mouse click put a stop to that.

Tom leaned closer to the screen, staring at the glinting gold cufflinks of the MP. Zooming in on the image he studied their shape. They were blurred and set at an angle, but he could just make out the swooping bird set on top of a circle. He panned up, coming to the MP's face. The MP's eyes looked unusually mean, close up. He zoomed out again, then tracked down the page, discovering more pictures of the MP, this time static press and publicity photographs of him shaking hands with other politicians, important dignitaries and business people from this country and around the world. There were plenty of smart suits and colourful national costumes as well as backdrops of magnificent state buildings and rugged sweeping scenery. The captions read like a Who's Who of governments and global businesses with plenty of gushing words about the lucrative contracts that were of such great benefit to all.

Impressive as it was, Tom still found himself unable to think of the one good question that he would like to ask. So, leaving the computer, he returned to other things, and it wasn't until after dinner that evening that he remembered the sheet again and pressed it in front of his father.

"Hang on, hang on!" said his father, who had just flopped down in his armchair in the front room. "I've got to sign this form, have I? But what's it all about?"

Tom explained as best he could about the visit of the MP and the Question Time, and then his father dutifully signed the form, at the same time spouting unhappily about not wanting any child of his being used to boost the profile of a politician by giving them extra air-time before a General Election.

"But you do get to ask your own questions," he went on with great interest as he came to the bottom section of the sheet. "We could have some real fun here."

"What do you mean?" said Tom, more than a little wary of that playful tone in his father's voice.

"Let's put it this way," he said. "There are plenty of questions you could ask that *no* MP would ever want to answer. Get it?"

Tom nodded vaguely, not really sure what sort of questions his father meant.

"Anyway, you said you'd looked him up on the internet," said his father. "What did you find out there? Nothing useful, I bet."

"He seems pretty important," said Tom, then added with a smile, "Oh, and he says he *will* make Britain 'Great' again."

"He will, will he?" said his father, laughing to himself. "I doubt that very much. There've been plenty of rumours about him over the years and some of them more than that. There was a lot of dirt dragged up about him to do with some nasty goings on in night clubs and casinos and some pretty shady businessmen, too. People you wouldn't want to meet on a dark night. 'Gangsters, bruv', that's how you'd say it today, wouldn't you?"

"Almost, dad," said Tom grinning. "It's *gangster bruvs.*"

"Oh, I see," said his father vaguely. "Anyway, I don't think anything came of the investigations back then, because he's still around today. I wouldn't trust him, though, and he's certainly not getting my vote. But now, I wonder what nice little question we could dream up for him?"

Tom shrugged. "Don't know."

"How about: 'Why didn't you get caught and put in prison?'" His father laughed wickedly. "That might stir things up a bit, eh?"

"*Dad!*"

"Okay, maybe it is a bit over the top." His father put on a more serious face again. "How about this one, then. 'Mr van Reiner, what would *you* do if you had *all* the power in the world?' That should tempt him out of his protective shell."

Tom considered it carefully, then nodded in agreement. "It sounds really good."

"Write it in, then," said his father, handing back the sheet, adding with a final chuckle, "I only wish I could be there to see his face when you ask it."

"Thanks, dad," said Tom, and as soon as he finished the writing he ran upstairs where he folded the sheet neatly away and put it inside his backpack, ready to take back to school on his return.

It was a wet weekend, the April showers turned on full. It wasn't until the Sunday afternoon that the clouds finally parted long enough for Tom get his bike out of the shed and take off around the park. Refreshed by the burst of cool air in his lungs and the sunlight on his back, he took in several circuits of the playing fields and ornamental gardens before skidding to a halt next to one of the old fashioned metal benches. He leant his bike up against the end of it, then sat down.

As soon as he got his breath back, he leaned forwards and studied his shadow that was lying in sharp outline on the path in front of him. He hadn't thought about it for most of the Easter Holidays and felt all the better for it. But even so, as he considered it now, he couldn't help wondering.

"Shadow, if you're there," he said quietly, after making sure that no one was watching him, "I wonder if you could sort out Dags again. It's the Summer Term on Monday and I could do with the help. It worked really well last term."

He paused, hoping for some reaction from his shadow, and while he did, other thoughts came to his mind.

"Next week we've got a real MP coming to our school," he said. "That's a Member of Parliament, of course. His name is Derek van Reiner. My dad hates him, but we've thought of a good question to ask him when he comes. Clara's been her usual self - a real pain. She's got Jess round now and all they do is *yap yap yap*. I really needed to get out. Mum's was pretty boring. She doesn't do *anything* with us any more. I don't think she even wants us there. Georgie's all right, except he fancies himself too much. He does try, I suppose, but then he has to help mum with her business and that takes up most of their time. Oh, there's this cat," he said, brightening for a moment, "but it won't come down from the wall. It might've got bullied when it was small or something. You could grab its legs," he said, smiling to himself, "just long enough for me to pick it up and stroke it. I think it'd stay then."

Tom's voice dried up as he ran out of things to say, leaving the air empty except for the trilling of a robin and the hum of the traffic hurrying alongside the park. Soon it felt as if it was time to get back, but when he looked down one last time at his shadow, it winked back at him.

It took his breath away. But then, as he looked at it more closely, he saw the droplets of water on the ground there, glistening and winking in the sharp sunlight, throwing out sparks of brilliant blue and yellow, taunting him remorselessly.

He sighed heavily, thinking again that everything about his shadow must just have been a silly dream.

He cycled away, scything from side to side of the path, weaving his way home.

His shadow, however, remained behind, sliding up onto the bench.

37

It sat there, deep in thought, considering all that Tom had told it and some of the things he'd left unsaid too. It thought about the cat, smiling knowingly to itself. Then, as if in prayer, it bowed its head.

Some minutes later it vanished - or moved so quickly from there that it couldn't be seen - and as Tom pushed his bike through the back gate from the alleyway it was there again at his feet as if it had never been gone at all.

Chapter 3 The Flick-Knife and the MP

When Tom awoke on the first Wednesday of the Summer Term his eyes fluttered open, then suddenly he shot bolt upright as if stabbed with a very sharp pin. This was the day of Mr van Reiner's visit to Newlands school. This was the day when Thomas Parks himself was going to stand in front of the rest of the school and all the television crews and press photographers assembled there and put his question to the MP. *This was the day!* The rush of blood to his head made him giddy with excitement and for the next hour or so his morning chores passed in a hazy blur.

"Sock it to him, son," his father said with a wink and a slap on the back before he went off to work.

"Yeah, and don't mess it up," added Clara, chewing her gum and rolling her eyes.

Tom left the house shortly afterwards, his carrier-bag, swollen with the trappings of his Election Project, swinging heftily at his side. He happily ignored the light shower of rain on his short walk to the bus-stop, displaying a definite spring in his step, and his excitement only increased as the school came in sight. There, already assembled at the front gates, was a large crowd of students and parents. All eyes were taken by the media vehicles parked across the hard courts in front of the school. The vehicles were splashed with the colourful logos of the media companies and on their roofs were various arrangements of aerials and satellite dishes. *White Light Radio*, *MWTV*, *The Bellington Independent*, *BBC News* and several other media companies were represented there. Mr van Reiner's party Campaign bus was on display, too, welcoming children aboard to sample the promotional movies and educational leaflets and branded freebies.

Tom felt his heart racing as he looked over this bold display of media-power and, not for the first time this day, his insides tightened into a knot. There was a distinct buzz about

39

the place as he climbed off the bus and for the first time ever at Newlands he found himself running across the road to get to school as quickly as he could. This was the best thing that had happened to him in ages and he didn't want to miss a single second of it.

When the buzzer sounded for the start of the school day, Tom made his way with great eagerness to his English lesson, but not because he wanted to be there (he could easily have slept straight through the lesson if he hadn't been so excited). Neither was he interested in the German lesson that followed or the morning break that followed that. No, what he was eagerly awaiting was his History lesson straight after the break. Today it had nothing to do with the musty dusty past and everything to do with the very scary present and even scarier future. As Mr Harris had reminded them on Monday, when the last of the permission slips and additional questions had been handed in, today was all about them having the opportunity to have their say about the future of the country.

When the History lesson finally arrived, the classroom filled up quickly. There was much excited chatter and murmurings which only grew in the absence of their teacher. Normally punctual, Mr Harris eventually bustled in five minutes late.

"All right, all right," he said, raising his voice above the general hubbub and wrenching open his briefcase on his desk, "settle yourselves down now. We've got a lot to do. You all know what's happening straight after lunch - that's when the Question Time will start - but now is our last chance to go over what we are going to say. However," he added with a look of eager anticipation, "you might like to know that our special visitor is already on his way here - to our class - right now!"

The murmuring grew again.

"Mr van Reiner has asked to see us first," he went on quickly. "He wants to see what we've been doing in our project."

At that moment footsteps and voices came from the corridor. An excited hush fell over the class.

"Here we go," said Mr Harris, giving an encouraging wink. "Best behaviour now."

The door opened and in stepped Mr Grange, the headteacher. He asked Mr Harris if he was ready, then briefly updated him on the arrangements that would follow for Mr van Reiner. He stepped out again and there was a short pause in which the class could hardly contain itself. Then, finally, Mr van Reiner himself entered the classroom.

The MP was every bit as impressive and business-like as he had appeared on his website, Tom thought, watching him stride confidently over to Mr Harris's desk and shake the teacher heartily by the hand. Following him into the classroom came a small untidy scrum of media people which included two men with cameras on their shoulders, one man with a large hairy microphone on a short boom, another man with a rusty beard and scruffy hair who had several cameras hanging around his neck, and a smaller women with spiky tinted hair who was holding a microphone wired to a recorder attached to her belt. They all scrambled about, bumping into desks and chairs, trying to find the best positions around the room from which to record the class activities.

"*Well*," said Mr Harris as the commotion in the classroom eventually came to an end, "now that we're all ready, I'd like to introduce you to Mr van Reiner, our very own Member of Parliament."

"Hello, children!" said Mr van Reiner, adding with a playful smile, "And I do apologise for all these people who keep following me around. It's quite a party, isn't it?"

A nervous laughter went round the room.

"Mr van Reiner," said Mr Harris, "I wonder if you'd like to tell the class how you feel about today?"

"Yes, of course," he said, rubbing his hands eagerly. "I just want you to know, children, that there's nothing to be afraid of when we meet again this afternoon for the Question Time. Your teacher has already sent me a list of the questions that you're going to ask, so there'll be no surprises there. So, that means that we can all enjoy our time together! I hope I'm going to see a lot of smiling faces. I know how much *I've* been looking forwards to this ever since I received your invitation.

"You see, I care very much about your teachers here, and your school, and, of course, all of you. After all, *you* are the future! You may not realise it yet, but in a few years time it will be either you or your friends or someone else your age running the country and deciding which direction it should go in. So, you see, this is a very important time today and one that we should all make the most of.

"And now I believe I'm going to see the work you've completed on your Election Project. It sounds absolutely marvellous. And," he added with a knowing wink at the media people, "it's also a great photo-opportunity. So, let's get started straight away."

Mr Harris ushered the MP around the class, busily organising the children and their project work to be seen to their best advantage, while Mr van Reiner showed great interest in all he was shown, chatting and laughing easily with the children in a manner that had them fully engrossed. Shortly, however, a large black man in a black suit took a step inside the classroom and gave a definite look at the MP. It was time for him to move on.

Mr van Reiner said his goodbyes to the children and personally thanked Mr Harris, but as he was on his way out of the classroom, the teacher suddenly remembered the headteacher's instructions.

"Tom," said the teacher, placing a firm hand on his shoulder, "I want you to show Mr van Reiner the way to Mr Grange's office. Leave your work here, it'll be safe with me. Go on, off you go."

Tom waded through the knots of media people and children still busily recording the class's work and words, then hurried out into the corridor. Once outside, however, he came to a sudden stop. A short way along the corridor Mr van Reiner was standing talking to the black man and an equally large white man in a grey suit.

The black man, Mr Wheeler, looked even more impressive in the narrow confines of the corridor. His suit was stretched tight over his muscular frame and a wire from an earpiece coiled down inside his jacket. The white man, Mr Crane, had curly sandy hair and a nose that bent inwards halfway down and wore an identical earpiece. Tom guessed that they were bodyguards for the MP, though their presence at the school seemed strange.

"Where's Geoffrey?" said Mr van Reiner in a sharp voice. "I want him here *now*. I don't want to spend any more time hanging around in this place."

As Mr Crane reached for his mobile, the side of his jacket flapped open, revealing the thick black handle of a hand gun jutting out of his shoulder holster.

Tom drew a sharp breath.

All heads turned towards the boy.

"Oh," said Mr van Reiner, quickly returning to his warm friendly manner, "you must be the young man who was going to show us to Mr Grange's office? We were just wondering where you were." He followed the boy's frightened gaze towards Mr Crane. "Don't worry about my friends here. They're just making sure that I don't have any silly accidents." He laughed lightly, but the boy didn't respond. "Shall we go, then?"

"Sure," said Tom quietly, but at that moment another man swept round the corner of the corridor behind them.

It was Geoffrey Lions, the MP's Personal Assistant. He wore a sharp pin-stripe suit. His grey hair was slicked back and his face was a deathly pale.

"About time," said Mr van Reiner coldly, then forcing a smile waved a hand towards the boy. "We are just about to be shown to Mr Grange's office by this young man here."

But when the men looked at Tom he was no longer looking at them but staring at the floor instead, his face as white as a sheet. His shadow, basking in the burst of sunlight streaming through the windows, was boldly giving him a thumbs-up with both hands.

"*No*," he breathed.

"I beg your pardon?" said Mr van Reiner, mistaking the boy's response.

The sun caught the edge of a cloud and Tom's shadow disappeared from view. He searched frantically for it and when he spotted it again its feint grey outline was surging towards the MP like a shark beneath the water.

"*Please, don't,*" he murmured desperately, knowing what was about to happen.

"*Sir*," said Geoffrey, "we don't need this boy, but we *do* need to continue with your schedule. We'll find our own way to Mr Grange's office."

"Yes, of course," murmured Mr van Reiner, at the same time wondering what on earth was troubling the boy.

The men started back along the corridor, Geoffrey taking the lead. The shadow shimmied past the bodyguards' feet, then the MP's, brushing its playful fingers over his lacquered shoes, and then, with a final surge, stretched out and took hold of Geoffrey's ankles, wrapping its fingers tightly around his soft woollen socks. Suddenly it darkened, pulling tight, like a rope at full stretch, reaching the end of its tether.

Geoffrey crashed down with such speed that he didn't have time to cry out, only a shallow gasp escaping his lips. Mr van Reiner stuttered to a halt behind him with a look of complete astonishment. The bodyguards swung their bodies this way and that, searching for their invisible attacker.

Tom looked on in horror.

"Get him up!" Mr van Reiner snapped, adding cynically, "We *do* need to continue with our schedule."

Geoffrey shrugged off the bodyguards' helping hands and struggled to his feet by himself. Something, though, was left behind on the floor. As soon as he was on his feet he spotted it and straight away reached down to pick it up. But then a dark movement swept across the floor and the object shot away between the men's feet and straight towards Tom.

It clattered up against Tom's shoes and there was a mechanical click and a flash of gold. It spun round and round. All eyes were fixed on it. Slowly it came to rest.

It was a flick-knife.

Its gently curving ruby red handle was moulded to rest effortlessly in the grip of its owner and a small circle of pearl towards the front of it marked the automatic release button (the same that had been struck in the collision with Tom's shoe a moment before, releasing the blade). The magnificent golden blade, with its serrated edge and polished angular surfaces, winked dangerously in all directions. It was a deadly weapon, the work of a skilled craftsmen and of no small worth.

"*Get it back!*" gasped Geoffrey, glaring at the bodyguards, his eyes as sharp and lethal as any knife.

Mr Crane and Mr Wheeler started forwards, but then hesitated when the boy himself reached down for the weapon.

"*Don't touch it!*" hissed Geoffrey.

Tom froze, but the fingers of his shadow continued forwards, slipping under the weapon, picking it up, then dropping it in his fumbling grasp.

The men stared in astonishment at what appeared to have been some sort of trick of the light (and perhaps indeed it was), but the very real presence of the flick-knife now in the boy's hands was plain for all to see.

"All right, stay calm," said Mr van Reiner, putting out a steadying hand towards the others, then looked towards the boy. "That's very kind of you, young man. Thank you for picking it up. But now I'd like you to hand it over to Mr Crane, here."

The MP nodded at the bodyguard, but before he could start forwards again the door of the classroom opened and out stepped the woman journalist. Slowly, Tom stood up, while the men's gaze moved unsteadily between the flick-knife clasped to his chest and the woman staring at them.

"Wonderful! You're still here!" exclaimed Julie Marks, promptly lifting up her microphone. "Would it be all right if I just-?"

"*No*," snapped Geoffrey, "it would not be all right. You've been told what you can and can't cover and it doesn't include this. We're very busy right now, so if you *really* don't mind, go back inside the classroom and complete your *very* valuable work with the children."

"I see," she said, her eyes flicking suspiciously between the boy and the men lined up against him.

Working as a local freelance journalist, Julie had heard much about Mr van Reiner's shady dealings and relished any opportunity of getting closer to him and finding out more. But she didn't want to get on the wrong side of him, at least not before the Question Time.

"I'll see you later then," she said with a cool glance at Geoffrey, before reluctantly returning to the classroom.

"Now, Mr Crane," said Mr van Reiner, waving a hand towards the boy, "if you'd be so kind?"

The bodyguard strode forwards, his craggy face a reminder that he was the type of person who let his fists do the talking. Tom glanced down at his shadow, hoping for help, but it lay motionless on the floor.

"Hand it over, kid," said Mr Crane, thrusting out his shovel-like hand.

"Do as the good man says," urged Mr van Reiner.

"*And what good man is that?*"

All the men swung round at the sound of the voice and there, coming round the corner of the corridor, was Mr Grange.

"I hope I'm not interrupting anything," the headteacher said, casting a sharp eye over the scene in front of him, "but I was getting worried. Mr van Reiner, aren't we meant to be having a chat about the new school buildings now? I know what a tight schedule you have, but we mustn't miss this golden opportunity."

"I was just on my way," said Mr van Reiner with a nervous laugh, holding out a hand to steer the headteacher back up the corridor. "Why don't we go to your office and have that discussion. My staff will follow. They're just sorting out one or two things here."

"Of course," said Mr Grange, but remained where he was, peering curiously down the corridor. "I wonder, Mr er…?"

"Mr Crane," said the MP, introducing his bodyguard, "one of my *trusted* staff."

"I wonder, Mr Crane," said the headteacher, "if you wouldn't mind stepping aside? I believe you're standing in the way of one of my students."

The bodyguard gave a questioning glance at Mr van Reiner. The MP nodded in response and he shuffled to one side. At the same time, the hands of Tom's shadow slipped round the boy's own hands. There was a distinct click and the golden blade of the flick-knife vanished back inside its handle which was nestling comfortably inside the cup of his hands.

"Ah, Thomas Parks!" exclaimed Mr Grange with the joy of a shepherd having found a lost sheep (it wasn't for nothing that he was known as 'the human register', such was his acute memory for the names of students, past and present).

"Y-yes, Sir," said Tom, never more grateful to see the headteacher than he was now.

"Are you saying prayers?" he said with a curious smile, looking at his hands clasped together in front of his chest.

Tom peered down, his hands grey with shadow and hiding such a terrible secret. He didn't know how to answer.

"Never mind, Thomas," said Mr Grange, not wanting to embarrass him. "And where are you off to now?"

"Mr Harris told me to take Mr van Reiner to your office."

"Good, very good," he said, "but now that I'm here, of course, you can go straight back to your lesson. You don't want to miss any of the exciting things going on there, do you?"

"No, Sir."

"And Thomas," he said, shaking his head unhappily, "give those grubby hands a wash."

"Yes, I will," said Tom, then turned to go.

His hands slid down by his sides and the flick-knife slipped inside a pocket.

"We'd better be going, then," said Mr Grange, turning to Mr van Reiner and beaming broadly. "Follow me!"

The two men strode off together, disappearing round the corner of the corridor, and then the door of the classroom was pulled firmly shut.

"*Damn!*" said Geoffrey, scowling at the bodyguards. "*Damn! Damn! Damn!*"

Straight after the lunch break the main hall of the school filled up with classes from every year which had been chosen to take part in the Question Time. The buzz of expectation grew louder and louder, quietened only by the occasional shout from one of the teachers in attendance. All the seats had been turned to face the side of the hall, where a more comfortable chair was positioned on a small podium for the MP. This left the stage, alongside the seats, free for the news reporters and media people to record the event. There was an angled line of cameras on tripods facing out from the stage. At regular intervals about the hall brilliant arc lights were placed on high stands, providing the much needed lighting for the cameras. In front of the MP's chair was a cluster of microphones of various sizes and colours and a soundman waited to one side of the hall, holding a slender black microphone on a boom, ready to capture the students' questions.

Mr Harris's History class occupied pride of place on the front two rows, and with no choice in the matter Tom found himself one row back directly in front of the MP's chair. He had hardly eaten any of his lunch, he was so sick with worry, and his empty stomach groaned hungrily despite his squirming attempts to silence it. His hand played nervously with the flick-knife in his pocket, too, his sweaty fingertips running up and down its smooth cool surface. He glanced warily towards the doorways at either end of the stage, looking out for any sign of the MP's men.

His shadow, caught in the arc lights, lay splintered and beneath the seats.

A ripple of applause heralded the entrance of Mr van Reiner who was closely followed by Mr Grange then Mr Harris. The two bodyguards pushed through the double doors and took up their positions, one on either side of the doorway. Tom strained round towards the opposite doorway and felt the hairs prickle on the back of his neck as Geoffrey entered through it. The PA gave an oily smile at a teacher nearby, then turned his attention to the rows of student heads stretching across the hall. Tom quickly ducked down and twisted back towards the front, hoping that he wasn't spotted.

Mr van Reiner walked across to the chair in front of the students, acknowledging the applause with a wave of his hand and a winning smile. As soon as he was seated Mr Grange called for quiet then introduced the special assembly.

"Today," he began, "you have been selected to take part in this special Question Time. We are truly privileged to have our very own MP, Mr van Reiner, here with us. And I think you'll agree with me that he's a brave man indeed, taking all your questions! But that is what this is all about. It is your opportunity to ask questions about whatever concerns and interests *you* have. So, make the most of it! And now, without further delay, I'll hand you over to Mr Harris."

"Thank you, Mr Grange," said Mr Harris, stepping forwards and adjusting the smart tie he had put on for the occasion. "And to get us started I have a question of my own. Mr van Reiner, are you ready?"

The MP nodded, smiling assuredly.

"*If* your party wins the General Election," said Mr Harris, "what will it do to help this school *and* all the others in Bellington?"

"Thank you for your question, Mr Harris," said Mr van Reiner, "but might I correct you straight away. We *are* going to win the General Election!"

There was some nervous laughter around the hall and at least one jeer from a brave student at the back.

"I'd like to add, if I may," he said, pressing straight on, "that it is a real privilege to have this opportunity to address you here today. I'm looking forward to taking your questions and putting your minds at rest about what my party plans to do *when* it regains power. And so, in answer to the first question, I will explain what we have *already* done to improve investment in schools for the whole of the country as well as telling you about our exciting plans for the future. I know you're going to be impressed!"

Fortunately, as he rattled off his well rehearsed answers, Mr Harris interrupted at regular intervals, breaking up the lengthy responses and testing him with more pointed questions about practical details, particularly those that related to Newlands itself and the other schools in Bellington. Mr van Reiner tackled each question with great style and wit, though not always giving a straight answer, and before long the questions flowed with increasing confidence from every corner of the hall and every age group in the school.

"What's your party done to stop bullying?"

"Who's going to pay for all the old people? And how much will it cost?"

"How can you stop hackers getting onto the new on-line voting system? Is it really secure?"

"You don't live in Bellington, so how can you really help us? You don't know what it's like here!"

The bluntness of the questions and the determination of the students sometimes had the MP struggling for answers, forcing him to pause while he thought of a suitable response, sometimes pacing up and down the front of the seats, sometimes staring upwards for inspiration. Only Tom, it seemed, was not caught up in it. Instead, in his mind he was going over and over his own question, trying not to forget it - it was the one his father had chosen especially - while at the same time feeling sick at the thought of looking straight into Mr van Reiner's face once more. His fingers fiddled furiously with the flick-knife in his pocket and more than once he suddenly whipped his hand away, realising he was about to press the pearl button.

"Thomas Parks...*Tom*."

Mr Harris's voice seemed to come from a long way off and it was several seconds before Tom realised that he was being called. He looked up and saw the teacher jabbing a finger towards him, indicating to the soundman where to place his microphone. The boom swung overhead and the microphone pointed diagonally down at his head.

"Your question, Tom," urged Mr Harris.

Tom swallowed, his throat achingly dry.

"Wh-wh-what would you do," he said, his eyelids flickering as he tried to hold a steady gaze towards the MP, "if - if you had all the power in the world?"

The MP's face went blank and twitched. He gave a sharp look at Mr Harris and said in a low voice, "I don't remember this question on the list?"

"It must have slipped in afterwards," murmured Mr Harris with a vague shrug. "But it *is* a very good question, don't you think?"

"Quite," said a tight-lipped Mr van Reiner.

"Well, what *wouldn't* I do if I had all that power?" said the MP, turning back to the students and laughing woodenly as he tried to think of an appropriate answer. "Ultimate power… Well, yes, I could do a great deal with that, a *great* deal. You see," he said, regaining his momentum, "this country has grown weak, very weak indeed. It has happened so gradually, over many years, that it's been hard to spot - hard to point to any particular moment which might have caused us to stand back in horror and demand the changes we now need. But it *has* happened nonetheless. And if I had that power," he continued, casting steely glances about the hall, "I would use it, without question, to put the *Great* back in Britain. I would do that and only that. I would do it for *you*. For *your* future. And for *our* nation!"

There was a smattering of applause.

"*But first*," he went on, now focussing his sharpened gaze towards the front seats, "I would use that power in a very small but important way. That would be sensible, wouldn't it, Thomas?"

Tom felt his cheeks suddenly burning. He wanted the earth to swallow him up there and then.

"Can you think of what that might be, eh, Thomas?" the MP continued, a sinister smile playing across his lips. "No? Then, let me tell you. I'd use that power to make everyone who'd *stolen* anything give it back - *whatever* it was - and return it to their rightful owners. How about that, then?"

His head lifted back and he looked out across the sea of students, stretching out his arms in a grand gesture of friendship.

"How many of you here today have had something precious of *your* own stolen from you?" he said, his voice rising again. "How many of you have been hurt and want to see justice done? How many of you want those things that are rightfully yours returned to you? Because *that* is what *I* would do for *you*!"

As the hall erupted with cheering and applause, the MP's eyes flashed triumphantly towards Tom. Quickly Mr Harris stepped forwards to restore order, but another voice called out with a shrill urgency of its own. It was a woman's voice and it came from the back of the hall.

The noise began to subside and the students shuffled round on their seats, straining to see who it was. The woman stepped forwards into the brightness of the arc lights and Tom recognised her straight away. It was the woman journalist who Geoffrey had ordered back into the classroom that morning

"My question," said Julie Marks, boldly marching towards the front of the seats, "is about your business interests, Mr van Reiner. Are you *sure* that they won't get in the way of your plans to put the *Great* back into Britain?"

"Mr Harris!" protested Mr van Reiner, but the teacher was so captivated by the woman that he appeared not to hear him.

"You've had several *difficult* problems in the past-" she said.

53

"As you well know," he said, cutting across her, "my name has been cleared from every false accusation made against me."

"But you were only cleared of those accusations," she went on, "because the witnesses who had agreed to come forward withdrew their statements. And why did they do that, Mr van Reiner? Was it because of intimidation? Was it because they were scared off? And if they were, who was responsible for that? Who, Mr van Reiner, *who*? That is the question!"

"And this Question Time is now over!" boomed Mr Grange, suddenly striding past Mr Harris and standing in front of the students. "We cannot and will not accept general questions from the press today and now I would ask that *all* of you on the stage and working around the hall would start packing away. This was a time specifically for the students and unfortunately that time is now over."

"And now," said Mr Grange, turning to Mr Harris and lowering his voice, "if you would be so good as to conduct an orderly return of the students to their lessons, I will try to smooth over this unfortunate incident with our *very important* visitor. Let's just hope he's not too upset. Because if his party does get into power (which, granted, seems most unlikely) I would like to think that we still have a fighting chance of getting our new buildings!"

"Of course, Mr Grange," said Mr Harris, trying hard to hide his amusement at what had happened.

As Mr Harris set about his task, an apologetic Mr Grange hurried over to Mr van Reiner who was sitting moodily on his chair, looking more than a little flustered. Meanwhile, Tom kept his head down, waiting for his class be called away. As the other classes filed out, he peeped about, trying to spot the bodyguards and Geoffrey, but they were no longer standing by the doorways. He felt himself trembling, though he kept telling himself that nothing bad could happen while anyone else was there. The problem was that the hall was emptying fast and his class were going to be called away last of all.

Suddenly a hand landed on his shoulder.

"Thomas Parks," said Mr Grange as the boy almost jumped out of his skin. "There's no need to be nervous now - the Question Time is over. But I must say, that was a good question of yours, even if it was a bit *unexpected*. And," he added, lowering his voice politely for a moment, "it's good to see your hands are clean, particularly as Mr van Reiner wants a word with you now. He'd like you to stop behind. It seems he was very impressed with you and has kindly agreed to give up a few more minutes of his time. You're certainly going to have a lot to write about in your project! And don't worry about missing the start of your next lesson, I'll let the teacher know. Come on then."

As Tom stood up, the rest of his class trooped out of the hall, leaving an ominous silence behind.

"Don't be shy now," said Mr Grange, gently pushing him forwards, "you'll be quite all right."

Tom looked into the stern faces of Mr Wheeler and Mr Crane who stood shoulder to shoulder like the battlements of a castle. They drew apart as Mr Grange's last echoing footfalls left the hall. Tom's heart pounded loudly in his ears as he passed between the looming bodyguards. Geoffrey, standing behind the MP's chair, stared hatefully down at him as he approached, while Mr van Reiner now appeared relaxed, smiling smugly to himself.

"It was kind of your headteacher to let us have these few moments together to finish off our business," said Mr van Reiner. "But much as I've enjoyed this day back at school, I really don't want to spend any longer here than I have to. So, if you'd kindly return what you *stole* from Geoffrey this morning, then we can all move on and make the best of what remains of the day."

"*I'll* have it," said Geoffrey, reaching forwards.

Tom stepped back but immediately was caught by the bodyguards meaty hands clamping down on his shoulders.

"Get off!" gasped Tom, ducking and twisting, but the grip of the hands only tightened, bending him over and locking him down.

A thick clump of fingers forced themselves into one pocket, then the other, poking about and jabbing painfully into him until at last they found the flick-knife and tore it out.

Gasping, the boy was released.

"It seems we all have unfinished business here today," said Julie.

Suddenly the bodyguards swung round and clumsily tried to block her view, while Mr Crane folded the flick-knife neatly behind his wrist.

"I haven't had *my* question answered," she went on, "but first I'd like to know what's going on here. Are you ganging up on this boy again? It's Thomas, isn't it?"

The bodyguards shuffled about, but couldn't prevent her view of him.

"Why are you so interested in him, Mr van Reiner?" she said. "What exactly do you want?"

"You were told to leave," said Mr van Reiner.

"Mr Wheeler," said Geoffrey, "please escort this 'lady' from the building. And perhaps you'd show her how *grateful* we are for her little contribution today."

"Keep your hands off me, you ugly gorilla," she spat as Mr Wheeler stepped towards her. "If you touch me it'll be splashed all over the papers by tomorrow morning. *Smile!*"

She swung up the camera dangling round her neck and fired off a volley of shots, the flash blazing away.

Mr Wheeler lunged forwards, grabbing at the camera, but at the same time his feet tangled in what looked like a dark wire that suddenly stretched tight across the floor. As he fell he managed to catch hold of the camera strap and, jerking hard on it, dragged Julie down head first after him. There was a crunch of glass and metal as the camera smashed onto the wooden floor.

"What an unfortunate accident!" said Geoffrey, smiling.

A dark movement passed over the back of Mr Crane's hand and, after a distinct click, the golden blade flashed out of the flick-knife. The bodyguard stared down at it, wondering what had happened.

"Get it out of sight!" snarled Geoffrey. "And get that safety-catch on!"

"So, you've been threatening Thomas with a flick-knife," said Julie as she struggled to her feet again. "Now, *that's* going to make a good headline!"

Geoffrey snatched the flick-knife from the bodyguard's hand, pressed the pearl button, then slipped the flick-knife safely back inside his jacket pocket.

"And exactly *what* flick-knife are you talking about?" he said, smirking at the journalist. "It's your word against ours. And of course, you've lost all of those nice pretty pictures, haven't you?"

He nodded towards Mr Wheeler who was back on his feet and holding the broken camera in his hands. The bodyguard flipped it upside down, released a catch on the underside and removed the memory card. He dropped the small plastic square on the floor, then ground it beneath his heel. The useless camera was dropped down after it.

"See what I mean?" said Geoffrey.

"I think I do," she said, staring emptily at the camera.

But when she looked up again, there was a smile on her lips and a look of triumph in her eyes. She turned towards the empty stage, where the deserted cameras stood.

"Freddie," she shouted out, "how's it going over there?"

57

Nothing happened for a moment, but then came the sound of footsteps on the stage. A gangly man with shaggy red hair and a beard strode out from the wings. He was the photographer who had visited Tom's History class that morning (it was one of his cameras now lying broken on the floor of the hall). He strolled across the stage until he came to a particular camera, then leant over it and checked the viewfinder. A small red dot winked back at him.

"Yeah, Julie," he said, looking up again and giving a thumbs up, "it's cool. We can make the evening news with this one."

Suddenly Mr van Reiner was on his feet and, pushing Tom out of his way, he barked a command at the bodyguards. Immediately they turned and stormed towards the stage, but then moments later came to a shambling halt.

All at once the other camera men and journalists and floor staff strode purposefully back onto the stage and into the hall and quietly began packing up their gear. Cameras, arc lights, microphones, wires, stands, all were gathered up with a calm efficiency, while every eye kept a vigilant watch over the bodyguards. The two men, stranded in a sea of seats, dared not lift a finger against any one of them for fear of being caught on camera again.

"Thanks for waiting, guys," called out Julie, grinning broadly. "I could never have done it without you."

Several laughs echoed about the emptying hall, but none of them came from Mr van Reiner.

Chapter 4 Out in the Night

While Mr van Reiner and his men were preoccupied with Julie Marks and the rest of the media people, Tom sneaked out of the hall, then sprinted off to his next lesson. And when it came to the end of school, he hurried home, nervously glancing back, still worried that they might come after him. Although they had the flick-knife now, he was certain that they wouldn't think twice about hurting him whether he deserved it or not. He wasn't unhappy either to discover that his shadow was gone from under his feet as if it had been washed away by the drizzly rain. Yes, it had protected him against Dags, but ever since seemed to have been getting him into more and more trouble.

It was with great relief that he arrived home safely, but it wasn't that easy to escape the events of the day. As soon as the family sat down for dinner, the questions began.

"Come on, then, tell me how it went," said his father.

"Yes," said Clara with a knowing smile, "I heard you caused quite a stir. Tell us *all* about it. I just can't wait!"

So, reluctantly, he told his own version of what had happened, taking care to miss out everything about the flick-knife and his shadow.

"So, if he had 'Ultimate Power'," said his father in a mocking tone, tossing a forkful of curried chicken in his mouth, "he'd make Britain 'Great' again, would he? I'd like to see that. I don't believe it for a second! He'd line his own pockets with *our* money long before he helped anyone else. I know his type. But didn't you say the tv cameras were there? Come on, then, let's get this finished and we might just catch it on the news."

"I - I don't think-" said Tom, beginning to panic.

"Don't worry, it'll be great," said his father, getting up from the table. "I wouldn't miss it for the world!"

"Do we have to?" sighed Clara.

"Yes, we do," said her father, "and it'll do you good to see what your little brother can do."

Leaving the dirty plates piled up in the sink, the three of them gathered round the television in the front room. Their father sat in his favourite armchair, teasing that it might make the national news, while Clara and Tom sat on the sofa. Clara sat furthest away, not wanting to be there at all, which left Tom stuck in the worst position of all, directly in front of the screen.

The national news drew to a close and, after the introductory sequence for the local news, the anchorman, Tim Gedden, welcomed everyone.

"And our top story tonight," he said to the throbbing background music, "is that one of our own journalists was threatened with a knife that had been smuggled into Newlands Secondary School here in Bellington. But more on that in a minute. Our other main stories are…"

"What the-?" exclaimed Mr Parks, accidentally belching as he suddenly leaned forwards.

"Now that's what I call news!" said Clara, scrambling up close to her brother.

Tom shrank inwardly, knowing he'd just have to pick up the pieces when it was all over.

"Good evening," said Tim after the headlines, "and tonight we go straight to the startling revelation that only this afternoon in Bellington itself, at Newlands Secondary School, a knife was used to threaten our own journalist, Julie Marks. Julie was there to cover a special Question Time involving Mr van Reiner, MP for Bellington North, and it was after this that the incident occurred - an incident that involved Mr van Reiner's own staff. And thanks to the quick thinking of our own television crew it was captured on film. So, here is Julie with that film. Julie."

"Yes, thanks, Tim," said Julie, appearing on the screen. "It has been a truly extraordinary afternoon. One of our cameras was smashed and I - *I* was caught in the unenviable position of having a deadly weapon waved in my face. But first let's see the film of what actually happened."

The screen cut to the film which started with a long shot of a knot of men gathered close together at the front of the seats in the empty school hall. A scuffle broke out, the two large men fighting over something near to the floor. Several seconds later they broke apart, and then both Mr Parks and Clara gasped together, pointing at the blurred head that had popped up between the two men.

"It's you, Tom!" yelled Clara. "But you never told us about…"

Her voice trailed away as a woman came into shot, walking towards the men, her back to the camera. Suddenly the two large men swung round and then she lifted her hands in front of her and there was a burst of camera flashes. One of the two men lunged forwards, crashing to the floor and dragging her down after him.

The image froze. For a second it appeared that the film might have come to an untidy end, but then the shot zoomed in on the large man still standing, drawing closer and closer to one of his hands. The image became more grainy and blurred, but not so much that, when it finally froze again, the golden blade could not clearly be seen, gleaming coldly from the screen.

After a short pause, the shot panned upwards and sideways, passing over the man's shoulder, until it centred on a face that filled the whole screen. Even enlarged as much as it was, it was obviously that of Mr van Reiner himself. The look of anger and hatred in his eyes fixed those watching it with its intensity.

The cameras returned to Julie in the studio and she explained what had happened in her own words, describing her fall and the knife, though she was drowned out in the Park's home by the barrage of questions suddenly shot at

Tom. Both his father and sister wanted to know exactly what had happened and, more particularly, why he hadn't told them anything about this before. Tom struggled to find answers and was only saved when the distinctive voice of the MP interrupted them.

"*Clearly* there has been a terrible mistake," said the MP, talking into a microphone as he stood in front of the marble steps outside his hotel, "and I don't believe that the film your reporter has just shown helps in this matter. It is a most unfortunate incident which has cast a shadow over what has been a *fantastic* day spent with the students at Newlands Secondary School, a day in which they have found out for themselves what our party will do for them when we've won the General Election.

"But what I can tell you, is this. Yes, there was a knife. Tragic as it is, that much is true. But no, it didn't belong to any my staff, I can assure you of that. In fact, it was one of my staff who bravely intervened to take it from one of the students at the school. *That* was what you saw in that film. And there is nothing more to it than that."

"But how do you account for the smashed camera and Julie being thrown to the floor?" said the clearly frustrated reporter.

"Again," said Mr van Reiner with a light-hearted chuckle, "this is not the best reporting I have ever seen. If you analyse that film properly - and ask your reporter herself - there is absolutely no doubt that my member of staff tripped over one of the wires on the floor and *accidentally* knocked over your reporter. She was holding the camera and that, unfortunately, was broken in the fall. I'd like to add, too, that my member of staff was badly bruised in the incident, but, as I'm sure you'll be glad to hear, is recovering well this evening."

More questions were fired at the MP, then Julie was brought into the discussion, though Mr van Reiner took every opportunity to steer them towards his favourite theme of putting the *Great* back into Britain. Eventually time ran out with no clear conclusion reached. Finally, back in the studio Tim ended the report, noting sombrely that the subject of knife crime in schools had been raised again with both the Government and the local education authority, but no one from either had been available for comment.

Tom would have liked not to have been available for comment, too.

"That *was* you, wasn't it?" said his father, still barely able to believe what he had seen and heard.

Tom nodded meekly.

"And was it your knife?"

"*No*," he protested. "He's a liar. It was Geoffrey's."

"Who's Geoffrey?"

"One of his men. *He* dropped it and I picked it up. Then they threatened me and took it back. That's what you saw. It's not mine!"

"Okay, *okay*. But what was this Geoffrey doing with the knife, then? I can't imagine what he'd want with—"

"They had guns too. I saw them."

"Who had guns?" asked his father in astonishment. "*Mr van Reiner?*"

"No, his bodyguards. Mr Crane and Mr Wheeler. They had them under their jackets."

"But how do you know this?"

"I had to take them to see Mr Grange," said Tom. "I saw Mr Crane's gun when I was in the corridor."

"They must be some sort of special protection for him," said his father, thoughtfully, then added with a wry smile, "Let's face it, with the type of friends he has, he probably needs it. But," he went on in a serious tone, "why didn't you tell me this before?"

Tom chewed his bottom lip, thoughts of his shadow bubbling away furiously inside him but too afraid to speak of them.

"Because he was scared, dad," Clara said kindly. "How do you think you'd feel after being roughed up by that bunch of thugs?"

"Yeah, good point," said her father, taken aback (it never ceased to amaze him how she could come out with something so kind and mature all of a sudden, when most of his time was spent in running battles with her over the most trivial of things).

"Okay, Tom, I believe you," he said, adding with a smile, "Anyway, you certainly don't get enough pocket money for a fancy looking knife like that! But," he went on seriously, "if you get any trouble over this from the school or the press or Mr van Reiner for that matter, then you'd better tell me straight away. I can't help you if I don't know what's going on, can I? Let's get this behind us now, as quickly as we can."

"Thanks, dad," murmured Tom.

"But don't think I'm getting any nicer," said Clara with a sharp-eyed smile.

When the washing-up was over, their father changed into his tracksuit and went off to his weekly table tennis club. Tom, exhausted from the day's events, went up to his bedroom and whiled away the evening playing a basketball game on his computer (he constructed a particularly fat and ugly player who he named after the MP and then made him Captain of what he was destined to become the worst losing side ever). Afterwards, he turned in for an early night.

The trouble was that he couldn't prevent the worrying thoughts from the day rushing back into his weary mind. He smiled once, though, when he remembered the sudden look of alarm on Mr van Reiner's face after his question, but for the rest of the time the thoughts came at him like a slow merciless torture. He tossed and turned, wondering what Mr Grange might do, especially after hearing the news report and whether or not he could be excluded from school or even sent to prison. His father was said he would support him, but what if no one else believed him? Mr van Reiner had shown himself to be a persuasive liar and would have no trouble in convincing the school or the police that the flick-knife had been smuggled in by Tom.

Eventually he sat up in bed, rubbing his head in his hands, wishing he could simply forget the whole rotten day once and for all. He stayed like that for a while until he could think about what had happened no longer. And it was then that something else came into his mind, like a gift unexpectedly left at the door.

Slowly his head lifted. He blinked in the dark. "Shadow… Shadow, if you're there…"

His voice trailed away, sounding strangely hollow in the silence of the room. He was uncertain of what to say next, but then started again with a little more confidence.

"Shadow, I know you're there, so just listen. I need to know what's going on. I know Mr van Reiner's a liar - I heard him tonight on tv - and my dad says he's a crook. Are you trying to get him? If you are, I don't mind helping, but I don't want to get hurt. His bodyguards have got guns and that flick-knife is really Geoffrey's. But then you know that, don't you? Look, I'm already in a lot of trouble because of this, so why don't you tell me what it's all about?"

The room remained silent.

Reaching to one side, he turned on his bedside lamp then looked closely at his shadow cast on the wall. But it didn't move. "*Coward*," he muttered miserably, then turned the lamp off again.

But then his heart almost leapt out of his chest when his tired eyes picked out the silhouette of a figure standing by the window.

"Who-who's that?" he breathed. "I can see you. I know you're there."

At that moment there was a deep throb, then another, like the start of a mighty heartbeat. It ran through Tom's head, through his bed, through the whole house, then a voice began to wail and…and by the time the electric guitars cut through the air, he already knew that it was one of Clara's heavy metal bands launching into one of their rock ballads.

The figure reached up, slipped the catch on the window, then opened the bottom frame.

The cool night air wafted into the room.

"Shadow, wait," said Tom.

The figure started to climb out of the window.

"Speak to me. I know it's you. I want to know what's going on. *Please.*"

The figure hesitated, straddling the sill.

"*Come.*"

The word was not spoken out loud, but resonated like the note of a bell that seemed to come from some hidden place deep inside himself. It carried with it a calming peace that soaked through him.

"Okay," said Tom quietly.

The figure disappeared and Tom sprang out of bed. Looking out from the window he spotted his shadow waiting for him on the patio, caught in the light from the kitchen window. He considered the long drop down then looked at the old metal drain running down the damp wall alongside his window.

"I'll be down in a sec," he called out finally, then disappeared inside, closing the window after him.

With his heart thumping hard in his chest, Tom jumped into his clothes, dragged on his backpack and tip-toed downstairs, the wonderful peace inside him evaporating like an early morning mist. In the hallway he pulled on a coat and kicked on his trainers, then made his way to the back door. Lifting a key off the rack, he let himself out then locked the door behind him. He dropped the key in the zipped pocket inside his backpack, but when he turned and looked at the patio, his shadow was no longer there.

"Where are you?" he gasped, peering into the darkness.

The garden gate creaked opened.

"Here we go," he said nervously, crossing the garden, then, after taking a last look back, slipped into the alleyway.

The alleyway was unlit except for the glow creeping over it from the amber streetlights in the roads beyond. Dark piles of rubbish skulked along its length - rotting carpets, oil drums, plastic bags - and glassy eyed puddles peered up from the potholes. A cat yowled and a dustbin lid crashed to the ground, then Tom spotted his shadow disappearing out of the alleyway.

"This isn't going to be easy," he muttered, hurrying after it.

For the next twenty minutes he walked and trotted and ran after his shadow as it led him past houses and shops, across the park, over the railway bridge, weaving steadily towards the centre of Bellington. It danced down the middle of roads and leapt from wall to wall with the daring and skill of an acrobatic, revelling in the freedom of the night. It performed a perfect back-flip off a post-box, landing right in front of him with its arms held out, and he laughed out loud.

As they approached the civic centre the grand public buildings came into view: the town hall with its large grey dome, the college buildings with their broad steps and classical statues, and the museum with its portico entrance on fluted pillars of white stone. These were deserted, but beyond were the bright lights of the clubs and restaurants and cinemas where a steady stream of people flowed past, eager to enjoy a night out in the town.

As Tom headed on towards the lights, a police foot patrol came towards him. There was a tug at his ankles and he looked down to find his shadow urging him towards a family group nearby. He snuck in behind the family and its two children trailing behind glanced back at the strange boy, sniggering to each other. As soon as the police had passed by another tug drew him aside again.

"Now just hold on!" he said under his breath, refusing to go a step further. "Where are we going? We can't keep wandering around like this all night. My dad'll be home soon and if he finds out I'm gone, he'll go ballistic!"

His shadow, lying fractured across the cracked paving, lifted an arm, pointing across the road ahead.

Tom looked up at the tall building there. It rose up into the hazy darkness, its front lit by tapering beams. At the bottom was an arc of marbled steps leading up to a rotating glass doorway. A fixed awning bore the name of the building in blue neon lights: *Hotel Virion*.

His heart skipped a beat as he recognised the hotel entrance from the interview with Mr van Reiner on the evening news. He remembered, too, what the MP had said about the hotel during the Question Time today. Laughingly Mr van Reiner had explained to the students that, because he spent so much time in Bellington on constituency business, the Hotel Virion had become like a second home to him. It was here that Mr van Reiner was staying.

"We - we can't..." breathed Tom, but his shadow was already speeding towards it.

He hesitated, wanting to turn and run. But something held him there. Despite the dangers, he really did want to know why his shadow had gone to all the trouble of leading him here.

Taking a deep breath, he crossed the road.

Tom's shadow passed round the back of the hotel into a small car park where the cars were squeezed in at all angles. Low bushes and glowing lamps marked the path leading back to the hotel entrance. He followed his shadow across the path and through the bushes, coming to an unmarked door with no handle. His shadow slid underneath it. A second later there was a sharp bang and the door jerked open.

He peered inside. A dimly lit corridor led straight into the hotel.

Alarm lights flashed silently at various points around the hotel: on the computer screen in the office behind Reception and on the panels positioned in discrete corners on every floor as well as in the poky office of the Security Guard. John Varney, who was on duty, however, was chatting with a porter on the 8th floor. Shortly his radio crackled into life.

"The car park fire-exit, you say?" he said, confirming the message, then gave a mischievous wink at his friend, adding, "It's probably just one of those lazy porters having a fag."

The porter grinned and made a rude gesture with his hand.

"Okay, I'm on my way," said John, slipping the radio back on his belt, then with a weary sigh set off for the lifts.

On his way he remembered the crisp £50 note Geoffrey had given him earlier that evening. Geoffrey had asked to be kept informed of *anything* unusual cropping up that night - journalists creeping around, that sort of thing - because it had been a particularly difficult day for Mr van Reiner and he didn't want any more unpleasant surprises.

"And if he wants to know about a door blowing open," he said looking a little more cheerful as he pulled the mobile out of his pocket, "then who am I to disappoint?"

Along the carpeted corridor Tom passed panelled wood doors which led to various conference suites. Smart brass plates bore their upmarket names such as Wellington,

York and Windsor. The corridor ended in a spacious circular hall with a marbled stone floor and a decorative canopy like the inside of a tee-pee. Along its wall was a large double door for the main conference hall as well as tall potted plants and several deserted tables. On its opposite side were glass double doors patterned with a riverside scene of swans and willow trees.

His shadow swept across the hall.

He followed on, but halfway across heard the sound of voices coming from beyond the glass doors. He froze as two figures, their shapes distorted by the patterns on the doors, marched towards the hall.

"It's probably nothing," said John, the Security Guard. "The alarms go off a lot and most times we never find anything wrong."

The glass doors swung open.

"Looks deserted," said Mr Crane.

"Sure," said John, "there's no bookings tonight, not back here at least. But, believe me, it doesn't stop our honoured guests from wandering about wherever they like."

Their sharp footsteps echoed across the hall. Mr Crane scanned the circular wall, looking for anything out of place.

"Over here," said John, pointing towards the corridor, then both of them disappeared down it.

Sitting squashed up against one of the pot plants with his knees gripped tight against his chest, Tom released his pent up breath in a sudden gasp. His heart was beating so hard that it felt as if it was about to gallop off on its own. He had recognised Mr Crane's voice and was certain that he and the other man were already on his trail. He got up quickly and went straight over to the glass doors.

Easing them open, he peered into the main lobby beyond. It was long and gently curving, dominated on one side by the Reception desk. Behind the desk was a woman with a blonde ponytail, wearing a navy suit. She was watching three guests set off with their bags towards the lift lobby at the far end of the hall. Then, when they were far enough away, she turned smartly on her heels and disappeared into the office behind.

His shadow hesitated.

"*Where now?*" he whispered, then glanced anxiously back over his shoulder. "Hurry up! Those two won't be long."

With a nod of its head, as if it had finally made up its mind, it set off straight towards the desk.

Tom hurried after, but as he reached the desk his shadow slipped over onto the other side. There was a rustling of paper and squeaking of drawers from low down on the other side. Tom wanted to peer over to see what was happening, but dared not in case the Receptionist returned. A printer hummed into action and seconds later a sheet of paper, guided by his shadow's hand, flew out over the edge of the desk, flipping over and over, before it landed at his feet. He went to pick it up, but suddenly stopped as a hand settled on his shoulder.

"Allow me?" said a kindly man in a long overcoat, a flight-bag standing at his side, and bending down handed Tom the sheet of paper. "There," he said with some satisfaction, then standing up again, asked, "Now, how can I get some help around here?"

His hand slammed down on the bell-ring, its note chiming loud and clear.

Immediately Tom's shadow set off towards the lift lobby and as soon as he caught sight of it, he hurried after. He wanted to run straight past it and get out of sight as quickly as possible, but managed to restrain himself, keeping to its steady natural pace. Behind came the voice of the Receptionist.

"Good evening, sir," said Jenny, smiling generously, "and how can I help you?"

The man started speaking, but then noticed her distracted glances over his shoulder.

"Oh," he said, "you're wondering about the boy. He was just getting his piece of paper over here. I gave him a hand, but he seemed a bit shy, I think."

"Really," she said thoughtfully.

She had an eye for the guests - and for those who weren't - and hadn't seen the boy before on her shift. Wearing his coat and backpack he looked like any other child on its travels, but it was too late to be wandering about on his own.

Tom heard the quietening of their voices, sensed their watchfulness. The lift lobby was only metres away round the corner.

"Will you excuse me for a moment?" she said with an apologetic look. "I just want to see where he's going."

She moved towards the gate at the end of the desk, but before she reached it the glass doors to the circular hall flew open with a loud clank and Mr Crane and the Security Guard marched straight towards the desk.

"Looks like trouble," murmured the man, glancing at Jenny.

"You could be right," she replied quietly, frowning as she returned to her position.

"Jenny," said John, striding up to her, "have you seen *anyone* come this way in the last five minutes or so? Anyone at all? Anyone who *shouldn't* be here?"

"*Anyone*," growled Mr Crane.

She didn't like the MP's bodyguards, who loitered around the hotel as if they owned it, or the way John acted as if he worked for them. But she knew she must give an answer. Her eyes flicked towards the far end of the lobby and, with some relief, she saw that the boy had already gone. She smiled politely at Mr Crane, then turned to John to answer his question.

Tom's shadow leaned into one of the vacant lifts, pressed one of the buttons for the other floors, then drew itself back as the lift doors closed. Then, turning away, it slid under the panelled glass door to the stairs. Tom followed, letting the door swing shut behind him.

"That was close!" he said in a low voice, looking for his shadow in the gloomy stairwell. "But where are we go-?"

A cold hand slipped over his mouth, gagging him, and he was drawn gently back into a darkened corner.

He struggled for a moment, trying to speak, but grew still again when he saw a large dark shape moving about on the other side of the door. Seen through the patterned glass of the panels, the splintered shape (which was undoubtedly Mr Crane's) shimmered uneasily like a school of sharks hunting down its prey.

Mr Crane, shifting from foot to foot, watched the red dial above the lift as it counted through the floors, waiting for it to stop.

...3...4...

He had noticed the Receptionist's secretive glance towards the lift lobby and sensed the fear in her voice as she had attempted to casually pass off the boy as nothing of any importance. But this was a day when one boy had already caused them a great deal of trouble, so he wasn't going to take any chances. Mr van Reiner wasn't a forgiving man, Geoffrey even less so.

...5...

It stayed there. That was okay. Mr van Reiner was on 10.

He glanced across at the door to the stairs, then pushed it open and listened. There was no sound. He waited another second, then let the door swing shut and headed back to the Reception desk to find the Security Guard.

The hand dissolved away from Tom's mouth and he took several deep breaths, murmuring his thanks. Then, when

73

he was certain the bodyguard was gone, he looked at the sheet of paper hanging from his hand.

It was a bill with several lines of figures and a total amount at the bottom which made him blow out his cheeks in surprise. Mr van Reiner's name was printed in bold towards the top and directly below were his room numbers: 10.33, 10.34, 10.35. So, all his men stayed here, Tom guessed, and he was right.

His shadow started up the stairs.

"Wait!" he whispered. "We're going to his rooms, right? But why? What are we going to do when we get there?."

There was no response and reluctantly he followed on.

"If you told me what he's done wrong," he said between breaths, "then I could write a letter and complain. Mr Harris made us do one about the school buildings that need replacing. That's the proper way of sorting it out."

But his shadow was not drawn by his offer, and, over the seemingly endless ascent of the 10 flights of stairs, he learned the hard truth of one of his father's favourite sayings: 'Actions speak louder than words'. On his way up, however, he dug out some leftovers from his backpack, rapidly consuming the chewy nut bar and fruit juice. At the end of the climb his legs ached terribly, but as soon as he'd recovered his breath he opened the door from the stairs and emerged warily outside the lifts.

His shadow led him away, turning straight along the corridor marked with the sign for Rooms 10.30 - 10.45. The corridor was quiet and empty. In seconds he was standing directly outside room 10.33.

"*Let's listen first!*" Tom begged his shadow, but it passed straight under the door.

Several long moments passed before there was a gentle click and the door nudged open.

He hesitated, looking nervously back along the corridor, then, trapped between his fears of what lay beyond and behind, stepped inside.

After pulling the door quietly shut behind him, he surveyed the room. Neat and tidy, it had one double bed over which was laid a freshly pressed pin-stripe suit still in its plastic wrapper. No light came from the door of the bathroom. No one appeared to be there.

"I bet this is Geoffrey's," he murmured, quickly turning to look for his shadow.

He spotted it disappearing under a door in the wall between this room and the next. He went over and listened for any sound of voices beyond, then opened it. On the other side, past a closed door to a side room, it opened up into a spacious livingroom.

"Wow!" he breathed. "So, this is what he pays all that dosh for."

The luxurious red curtains were drawn, the lighting coming from numerous discrete fittings in the ceiling and walls. On the right a widescreen television occupied a large section of the wall. In front of the television a number of upholstered leather armchairs and a sofa were loosely arranged around a low table which held the piled up remains of an eat-in dinner. A spicy aroma still clung to the air. On the left was a large oak dining table cluttered with the paraphernalia of the MP's political campaign, including posters, leaflets, printed reports and itineraries as well as hand-written notes. As Tom passed by he noticed a sheet entitled 'Newlands Question Time', but quickly moved on.

At the far end of the livingroom were two rooms opposite each other, one the MP's own ensuite master bedroom, the other a small single-bedded room which appeared unused. Beyond these, an adjoining door led to a room which was less tidy than Geoffrey's and had two single beds, one presumably for each of the bodyguards.

Tom turned back, still not knowing what he was looking for but only too aware that the occupants of the rooms might return at any moment. He watched his shadow but even it appeared not to know what it was looking for, ranging back and forth through the rooms. He looked again over the piles of paper spread across the dining table, then, needing to get out of there, headed back the way he'd come.

Just before Geoffrey's room, however, he came to an abrupt halt. He was standing outside the door to the side room, the one place he had still not looked inside. He didn't want to stay any longer and hesitated, trying to persuade himself against it, but finally reached out and turned the handle.

For a second after opening the door an eerie glow hung at the centre of the darkened room, but then the lights, on an automatic sensor, flickered into life. Cautiously, he entered the small office. Before him was a long table at the other end of which was a chair. Facing the chair, on the table, stood an open laptop. It was from there that the glow had come.

With his heart racing, he quickly skirted the table then sat down on the chair. A glowing ball with brilliant orbiting specks coloured the screen. He tapped the spacebar. The screensaver froze, then vanished, revealing a static image. On a light blue background a powerful bronzed eagle, its wings lifted high and its talons outstretched, pounced on its unseen prey. He thought that he'd seen it recently, but unable to remember where, his attention passed on to the login box at the centre of the screen.

The username, *paulj999*, was already entered, but the password was blank, the cursor winking temptingly at the start of the line. The default password at school was always 'password', and with nothing to lose and everything to discover, he moved his finger over the letter 'p'.

At that moment the sound of voices came from the corridor.

Tom sprang up, looking for somewhere - *anywhere* - to hide, but the room had no other furniture. He ran out of the room, his head twisting to the left and to the right...

...and then the doors from the corridor opened one by one.

Chapter 5 Free Fall

After his interview for the evening news Mr van Reiner had decided to lie low. He and his men took dinner in their rooms then, by special arrangement with the management, relaxed in a private bar on the 1st floor. It was then that Mr Crane was called away to attend to a security issue, and not long after his return, they all returned to their rooms. Shortly afterwards, they gathered in the Mr van Reiner's suite. Mr van Reiner settled back in an armchair, savouring his first draws on a new expensive cigar.

"Geoffrey, get rid of these," he said, waving a hand towards the dinner plates, "and why not order up some brandies and coffee while you're at it?"

Geoffrey phoned for room service with a blunt efficiency. "They're on their way, Mr van Reiner."

The MP nodded vaguely, then with a flourish of his hand that sent wisps of cigar smoke curling round his head, said, "Sit down, sit down, everyone! I don't *think* I've got any more speeches tonight."

The bodyguards squeezed awkwardly onto the sofa, while Geoffrey eased back into an armchair.

"Well, at least we've not seen anything more of those reporters!" said Mr van Reiner brightly.

"They shouldn't be bothering us again," said Geoffrey, "not after your response tonight. And we did get some useful air-time."

"Hardly," said Mr van Reiner. "Where was the coverage of our Question Time at the school? We should have had the manifesto on prime-time tv! Instead it turned into a rearguard action with me having to explain away that knife and smashed camera. Useful? I don't think so. And in future I expect everyone to take more care in front of the cameras. But at least I managed to turn it around."

There was a knock at the door.

Mr Wheeler, struggling out of his tight fit on the sofa, answered it.

Dwarfed by the bodyguard following him in, the visitor had long sandy hair and studious gold-rimmed spectacles. Beneath his open mac he wore a casual jacket and jeans. In his hand he carried a boxy aluminium case.

"Ah, Jerry," said Mr van Reiner, "I was wondering when you'd get here. Come and sit down."

"Hi," said Jerry, nodding to Mr van Reiner and Geoffrey in turn as he slipped off his mac and settled into one of the armchairs, "and what's all this stuff I've heard about you on the evening news?"

"Never mind," said Mr van Reiner, forcing a smile, "let's stick to *your* story, shall we? Good news?"

"Sure," he said, leaning forwards eagerly, "the module has gone in successfully. It's in the live system. It had to wait for the last full upgrade to the system which was scheduled for last week, but that was postponed. The bug fixes weren't on time. It was put back to Tuesday instead. It was our last chance before the election. If it hadn't gone in, then-"

"Then we would have failed," said Mr van Reiner coolly, completing his sentence.

"Yes, exactly," said Jerry. "But it's okay now. The testing was good and it's all there, ready and waiting for the final trigger. Nobody knows about it except me."

"*Us*," said Geoffrey, underling the point, "nobody knows about it except us."

"You're *sure* it's there?" said Mr van Reiner.

"Yeah, of course."

"Then why don't you show it to us?" said Geoffrey with a sickly smile.

Jerry hesitated. "It's just not that simple. I mean-"

"Yes, Jerry," said Mr van Reiner, "tell us *exactly* what you mean."

"I mean that even if I show you the system - and that's risky enough - you don't know how it works and won't see the difference. Like I said, you can't tell it's there - no one can, that's the whole point! I could show you anything and you wouldn't know if I was lying or not."

"*Even so*," said Mr van Reiner, beginning to show his impatience, "I still want to see it."

"But the risk-"

"It's a risk *I'm* willing to take," said Mr van Reiner. "You see, I've got a lot more riding on this than you have, Jerry. I can't afford for it to go wrong. Besides, you worry too much. You said it could be done - and now it is! So, where's the harm in us just taking a quick look?"

A knock came at the door and a voice announced the arrival of the room service.

"In there," said Geoffrey, looking at Jerry and nodding towards the office, then turned to Mr Wheeler. "Wait til he's out of sight."

With a worried look Jerry collected his mac and case and retired to the office, then Mr Wheeler let in the porter with his trolley. He cleared away the dinner plates and replaced them with cafetieres of fresh coffee, a brandy decanter and clean cups and glasses. Geoffrey signed for the order, then, after Mr Wheeler had shown the porter out again, he and Mr van Reiner went into the office.

"You'll have to look over my shoulder," said Jerry, concentrating on the screen as he tapped away on the keyboard.

"Don't worry, Jerry," said Mr van Reiner, smiling as he approached him, "you just show us what you've done and then we can all enjoy a brandy together. We know how hard you've been working on this and you deserve a little treat. All I want is to see what I've got for all that money I've invested in you."

The MP's smooth talking did nothing to calm Jerry. As he logged in through the various levels of security guarding the system, he was already trying hard to think up an excuse good enough to explain away this unscheduled event. All events were logged, and the logs were checked, and if there was no good reason for an event, questions would be asked. Searching questions. Questions that he couldn't yet answer. He was already leaning towards the solution of editing the logs themselves using his privileged access rights, but that meant a lot of extra work and tricky manoeuvring to avoid detection. Not that it was anything Mr van Reiner and Geoffrey were going to lose any sleep over it, he was certain of that.

"So, who's been fiddling about in here?" he said, his eyes flickering uncertainly towards them.

"What do you mean?" said Mr van Reiner.

"*What I mean* is someone's been in here before me. It's obvious. And I can't be held responsible for what happens when people start playing around with this laptop and messing up all the good work I've-"

"But how do you know?" said Mr van Reiner.

"Before I came in," said Jerry tautly, "the lights went off. I saw it under the door. So, with the lights on a timer, someone must have been in here in the last twenty minutes."

"But we've only just got back," said Mr van Reiner, "and I've been outside the room ever since."

For several moments there was only the sound of Jerry's fingers pattering over the keyboard, then Mr van Reiner called out for Mr Crane. The sharpness of his voice brought the bodyguard hurrying into the room.

"The disturbance earlier in the lobby," said Mr van Reiner, "tell me again what happened. You mentioned a boy. "

The bodyguard gave his explanation while the MP listened intently, his frown deepening.

"So, there was a boy," said Mr van Reiner, churning all the information in his mind. "Perhaps the same boy as the one who gave us so much trouble at the school and was no doubt working with that stupid woman." He turned away, deep in thought. "But how on earth could they have got in here?"

Moments later he drew Geoffrey and the bodyguard aside, giving them instructions in a low voice, then dismissed them from the room and returned to Jerry.

"Now, let's see what you've got for me," he said with a pleasant smile, though his attention seemed to be elsewhere.

The door of the office had closed behind Tom just as Geoffrey had returned to his room. Tom watched him walk straight past the open adjoining door, waited for a moment, then turned and ran across the livingroom. His only thought was to reach the bodyguards' room before they did, but he was too late. The doors of Mr van Reiner and the bodyguards opened one after the other, and, with nowhere left to go, Tom dodged into the MP's bedroom. He passed straight through to the bathroom then scrambled down behind the patterned glass door of the shower cubicle. Hugging his legs against himself, he tried to stop himself shaking.

"Shadow, help me," he whispered, staring at its splintered shape under the penetrating lights. "You've got to do something. *Please.*"

But there was no response.

"*Why are you doing this to me? Why did you bring me here?*"

He wanted to scream and shout and cry all at the same time, but knew that to make a noise would be the end of him.

The sound of the men's voices grew, and then, realising that sooner or later he must surely be discovered, he forced himself to leave his hiding place.

He crept through the bathroom and into the bedroom but then knew that there was no way out past the men in the livingroom. Not knowing what else to do, he listened in to their conversation. When Jerry turned up he heard words such as 'system' and 'fixes' and 'online' but nothing that truly made sense to him, and when the door was knocked again he retreated back to the shower cubicle, gripped by an ever increasing terror.

Shortly the voices died away altogether. Silence returned. It was then that he forced himself out once more. If the men had left the rooms again, now was his chance to escape unnoticed.

He stepped out onto the white tiled floor.

Standing quietly in the doorway was Geoffrey.

"So, Mr van Reiner was right," said Geoffrey, toying with the flick-knife in his hand. "It *was* you downstairs. You've had a busy day, haven't you? But that's coming to an end now, isn't it?"

A mechanical click. A golden blade.

There was no way past Geoffrey and, anyway, Tom's legs didn't seem to be responding. His head felt light, then the room began to spin. The bodyguards appeared behind Geoffrey, one looming over each of his shoulders. All three men stepped forwards together, appearing to sway wildly from side to side. Tom's head tilted as he tried to straighten his vision, but then he was falling. It seemed to go on for many long seconds, the brilliant lights of the bathroom flashing past like meteorites. Then everything went blank.

The boy lay crumpled on the floor.

The three men gathered round.

"*He's not stupid*," said Geoffrey, standing in the livingroom with the others. "You said so yourself, he's been working with that journalist, and now he's broken into the hotel and our rooms. He must have heard everything we've said. And who knows what he was able to do with that laptop? I tell you, there's only one thing for it, and we should do it now, before it's too late!"

"But he can't know *everything*," said Mr van Reiner, "because only you and I do and we didn't talk about it all tonight. He hasn't met Jerry and we didn't find anything in his backpack. There are no pictures or recordings on his mobile. Nothing! So, I repeat, killing him is not an option."

"I - I've got to go," said Jerry, edging towards the door. "That's just a kid. I don't want any part of it."

"Stay where you are!" spat Geoffrey. "You're in this as deep as anyone else. We do whatever's necessary to make the plan work."

"All right, *all right*," said Mr van Reiner, glaring at Geoffrey, then, turning to Jerry, put a comforting arm round his shoulder. "We're all just a little over-excited now, as you can see. It's been a very long day and, as you well know, there's everything at stake here. I'm happy with what you've shown me. Now all we have to do now is wait. So, you can go now. We'll keep in contact as agreed. Go home to your girlfriend and forget about the boy. Whatever happens, he's our problem. Understood?"

Jerry nodded quietly, having been steered to the door. Mr van Reiner opened it.

"Just stay out of trouble," said Mr van Reiner. "We don't want anyone getting caught out at this late stage, do we? And don't look so worried! Mr Crane and Mr Wheeler are always here to tidy up our loose ends. And there aren't going to be any of those, are there, Jerry?"

"No," said Jerry, feeling a cold shiver pass through him, "of course not."

"Good," said Mr van Reiner, then closed the door behind him.

He looked thoughtfully at the others, then, when he knew that Jerry was far enough away, said:

"Now, listen very carefully. I'm as ready as the next man to do whatever's absolutely necessary. But what I need now are sensible plans to deal with the boy before he wakes up and starts creating more trouble for us. Mr Wheeler, go and check on him. Geoffrey, get me a brandy - a large one. I want cool heads and clear thinking - and I want them now!"

Mr Wheeler went into the MP's bathroom where Tom was bound with gaffer tape to one of the sturdy dining chairs. The boy's head was slumped down. The bodyguard checked the strip of tape over his mouth, making sure he wasn't gagging behind it, then listened to his breathing. It was steady.

The bodyguard walked out of the bathroom and a moment later Tom lifted his groggy head, his forehead clammy with sweat. He snorted through his nose, wanting to gasp for breath. He tried to stay calm and think straight, having heard enough to know that his life hung by a slender thread, one which Geoffrey, given half a chance, was only too happy to sever with a single sweep of his precious flick-knife.

Suddenly a dark movement swept over his face and the tape was torn from his mouth. A searing pain flashed across his lips and he only just managed to stifle his cry. He stared at his shadow as it swept up and down his sides, slicing through the tape wound round his body. In shreds the tape tumbled onto the pristine white tiles. He slumped forwards, his arms and sides aching, his skin on fire as the blood rushed back into the crushed veins. His shadow slid away towards the door of the bathroom and staggering up from the chair, he stumbled after it.

As soon as he entered the bedroom his shadow turned and tossed his backpack off the bed and into his arms. He almost dropped it, then eased his arms through the straps. His shadow moved to the window. The curtains drew apart. The pane slid aside.

"*No*," breathed Tom.

His shadow slipped outside.

With his heart hammering inside his chest, he went to the window and leaned out. Ten floors below was the car park, the damp rooves gleaming faintly. He looked across to the far end of the window. Standing on the ledge that ran beneath it was his shadow.

"*I can't,*" he murmured.

His shadow looked towards him for a moment, then seemed to lose its footing, falling backwards, its arms waving frantically over its head. But then at the last moment it reached forwards and pulled itself upright again. It gave him an innocent shrug.

"Very funny," he muttered.

But with nowhere left to go and his shadow beckoning him on, he took hold of the frame and pulled himself up.

"You could give me a hand," he gasped, hauling himself out, "but I don't want to be thrown down like all the others!"

At that moment his foot caught the side of the dressing table next to the window, jolting him forwards. The slide continued, his front and sides banging painfully against the metal frame as he writhed from side to side, trying to stop the fall. He slammed his hands down on the coarse wet ledge, but they were forced off by his own momentum, grazing the skin from his palms. Then, as he plunged out into the cool darkness, his ankles caught against the sides of the frame, bringing him to a sudden jerking halt.

As soon as he'd recovered his breath he reached round and caught hold of the ledge, dragging himself back. Only then, when he felt the solid presence of the ledge supporting him, did he slowly release the hold of his bruised ankles, drawing his legs carefully after him. Eventually and shakily, he drew himself up onto his feet.

His shadow, standing at the end of the ledge, waited.

"*Why didn't you help?*" he said crossly.

Ignoring the question, it turned to move away. Facing the wall, it lifted its hands and placed its fingers in the joints of the masonry. It started to edge away.

Tom watched, trembling with fury and fear, but then, copying its moves, followed on.

At the end of the window, his shadow looked up, then without a pause began to climb freely and easily. It was not far to the roof, but Tom unfortunately looked down first.

For one terrifying moment he started to sway uncontrollably, then, slamming his eyes shut, cringed against the side of the building. When finally he grew steady again, he peered up and saw his shadow already at the top, hanging off the edge with one hand, looking back down at him.

Little by little he edged upwards, finding a handhold, then a toehold, then drawing himself up. He started to find some sort of rhythm, keeping himself moving upwards and resisting the urge to look down again.

Soon he was at the edge of the roof, but by then his muscles were trembling badly. Then, with one last great effort, he threw both hands up over the edge and grabbed hold of whatever was there. But instead of finding a hard surface to hold on to, his hands came down on the run of three slender trip-wires that ran along the edge of the roof to prevent birds from landing there. His fingers wrapped round the wires that dug into his skin and stretched under his weight. Immediately he slid back, his feet jerking away from the side of the building.

He kicked out, trying to find a toehold, but when that failed swung from side to side, throwing first one leg then the other up towards the edge of the roof.

Suddenly, pinging loudly, first one trip-wire then a second snapped, recoiling into the darkness.

His body jerked like a broken puppet.

He slid a hand sideways, searching for a better grip. Almost immediately it struck one of the guides for the trip-wires. He wrestled his hand over it.

The third and final trip-wire snapped.

His body twisted round, facing away from the building, but kicking round with his legs he fought to turn himself back. Then, on the third attempt, he managed to throw his other hand over the guide. With the last of his strength he tried to haul himself up. His head lifted a few centimetres, every muscle in his body straining hard, but then he dropped back. He shouted at himself to try again, but his body would not respond. Slowly he slumped down, hanging limply from that single anchor at the edge of the roof.

The guide creaked, then cracked, tearing at its moorings.

Letting his head loll back, he stared into the darkness of the night sky, a single tear burning at the corner of his eye. "I hate you, shadow," he said, "I hate you."

The guide, with a final snap, broke free.

The boy fell.

The shadow, creeping out from the edge, looked down.

In the following seconds that seemed to stretch out to infinity Tom could only think how pleasant the cool night air felt against the deep throbbing in his hands. He was so relaxed, in fact, that he barely noticed the silky grip slipping down his wrists and taking hold of him. At first his arms lifted, as if in some simple act of worship, but then were pulled gently, then firmly, then strongly. The falling stopped and, after a short pause, he rose back up the side of the building. He passed the top of it and finally was gently lowered onto the damp concrete of the roof.

The midnight chimes of the town hall's clock drifted past.

Tom's shadow waited a short distance away, framed in the light of a doorway opening onto the roof.

"I can't do this anymore," said Tom, sitting slumped forwards, "not until you tell me what it's all about."

The doorway was empty. A ripple slipped through the darkness, then settled over the boy.

Tom felt his shadow's presence. "I just can't," he said again.

"Trust me, my friend, this is how it must be."

A healing warmth spread through Tom's body, then he began to sob, the tears flowing freely.

The door onto the roof led to the stairs and as Tom hurried down them his only thought was to keep his balance and avoid any further injuries to his aching body. Every step, every jolt, shot pains through his arms and legs, but finally he came out on the ground floor.

Peering round the corner of the lift lobby, he looked out towards the Reception desk. The bodyguards were talking to the Receptionist. Suddenly his shadow slipped away towards them.

Seconds later the Receptionist pointed at her screen behind the desk and then there was a commotion. The bodyguards ran off in the opposite direction, heading towards the Conference rooms. Then his shadow swept back in the opposite direction.

"Let me guess," he said with a wry smile, "you've been playing with the doors again?"

When he looked out again, the Receptionist was no longer there. He crossed straight over to the rotating glass door. Outside, he hurried down the marble steps, but halfway down his backpack was struck from behind and a black wallet slapped down at his feet.

Scooping it up, he opened it in his hands. A small colour photo sat behind the plastic window of one of the pockets. He turned it round and studied the portrait picture of Mr van Reiner and a woman.

Suddenly looking up, Tom searched for his shadow. He knew it must have stolen the wallet and put it in his backpack. A moment later he spotted his shadow leaning against a lamp post next to a lay-by on the opposite side of the road. It nodded towards the taxi in the lay-by.

Tom slid open the long pocket of the wallet, revealing a layer of crisp £20 notes. He smiled to himself.

"Been out having fun?" said the taxi driver, raising an eyebrow in surprise at his young fare.

"You could say that," said Tom with a deep sigh as he dropped down on the back seat.

"Where are you going?"

"Penrose Avenue," he said, passing forwards a £20 note, then added carelessly, "and keep the change."

"Very kind indeed," he said, and after a cheery glance in his mirror pulled away.

Tom looked out of his window and saw the bodyguards running round from the back of the hotel. They met at the entrance, then looked out, searching for where he might have gone. They spotted the taxi moving away, but by that time he was out of sight, sliding down in his seat.

Chapter 6 The Detectives and the Stolen Wallet

As soon as the taxi was out of sight of the Hotel Virion, Tom pushed himself back up on the seat. He would gladly have laid down and fallen asleep, but instead kept his eyes on the hypnotic streetlights flashing past. His hands seemed to throb in time to their passing. It was early morning and there was little traffic about and in only a few minutes he was almost home.

"Stop here, please," he said.

"Are you sure?" said the driver, glancing in his mirror. "It's just round the corner."

"It's okay," said Tom, "thanks."

The taxi pulled up and he climbed out. His backpack caught against the side of the door and something fell, he was sure, but when he peered down into the gutter he could see nothing there.

He hadn't wanted the taxi to arrive outside the house in case it alerted his father to his absence. Instead he retraced his steps along the alleyway at the back of the houses.

Cautiously he opened the garden gate. He looked at the windows. Thankfully, all were dark now, their lights extinguished. After crossing the garden, he let himself in the house, replacing the key on the rack, then as quietly as he could crept up to his bedroom. He took great care as he climbed the stairs, checking for any sign of light under the bedroom doors of his sister and father.

With his own door safely closed behind him, he dragged off his backpack and coat and, with no thought of tidiness, got into his night clothes. Then, at long last, he crawled under his duvet.

A great yawn escaped his lips as his head sank back into the pillow. A second later he was fast asleep.

The doorbell rang several times before a light came on at No.38 Penrose Avenue. The two men stood in the tiled porch, waiting patiently, occasionally looking about them for any other signs of life in the neighbourhood. It was 4am, so they weren't surprised at the delay. Not many people responded well at being woken at this time of the morning.

Eventually a light came on in the hallway and the men, looking through the panels of coloured glass in the door, saw a shapeless figure bustling towards them. A moment later the porch light came on.

"Who is it?" Mr Parks called out in a hoarse voice.

"Detective Inspector Reever and Detective Sergeant Brown," replied the taller of the two men. "From Bellington Constabulary. Can we have a word with you? "

Mr Parks peered through the spy-hole, then, after re-fastening his dressing-gown, opened the door. Shuffling out of their way, he eyed them cautiously.

DI John Reever, the taller of the two, had a sturdy frame and was balding. He offered a friendly smile as he entered. DS Jim Brown was slim and wore an open-necked shirt and jacket. He had keen searching eyes. He closed the front door behind him.

"Let me see your ID's," said Mr Parks.

The detectives reached inside their jackets for their wallets and presented them to him.

"Okay," said Mr Parks after peering at them closely. "What is it you want?"

"We need to discuss a few things," said DI Reever. "Is there anywhere we can sit down?"

"Come in here," said Mr Parks, leading them into the front room.

"Thank you," said DI Reever, while DS Brown rolled his eyes, already bored by the introductions.

DI Reever sat on the sofa opposite Mr Parks in his armchair, while DS Brown nosed discretely around the room.

"We're sorry to disturb you at this time in the morning," said DI Reever, "but we needed to act quickly on the information we've been given. This is just a standard enquiry and you shouldn't think that anyone here is in any trouble. We simply need to rule certain things out of our investigation. It shouldn't take any time at all."

"So, what's it about?" said Mr Parks, frowning.

"We've had a report-"

"An *unusual* report," interrupted DS Brown, winking at his partner.

"An unusual report," went on DI Reever patiently, "of a burglary."

"In the Avenue?"

"No," said DI Reever, shaking his head in a puzzled sort of way, "but I can't say too much about it for various reasons. I hope you'll bear with me in this. What I can tell you is that we have identified one object that was stolen. It's a wallet. There was £300 in it, all in £20 notes, and cards that identify the owner."

He watched Mr Parks, carefully, but saw no signs that he knew anything about it.

"So, why come here?" said Mr Parks.

"The people involved," said DI Reever cautiously, "have clearly stated that it was your son, Thomas Parks, who stole the wallet."

"But that's crazy!" said Mr Parks, looking at him in complete astonishment.

"It may well be," said DI Reever, "but because of the people involved and the precise nature of the information we have been given, we have to follow up the line of enquiry. I can also tell you," he went on, "that the burglary took place around midnight tonight in the centre of town."

"So, you're saying," said Mr Parks, barely able to contain himself, "that these people have told you that my son has been into town tonight and stolen their wallet? In a burglary. They must be mad! Who are these people? Why would they say such things? It's all just a very bad mistake!"

"It does seem strange, doesn't it?" said DI Reever.

"He's only twelve!" said Mr Parks.

"Yes," said DS Brown, glancing across, "but it's possible all the same."

Mr Parks looked as if he was about to explode with indignation.

"Hardly, I think," said DI Reever, ignoring DS Brown's dark frown, "but Jim has a point. We have to look at all possibilities, particularly when the victims have been so particular."

"And why can't you tell me who they are?" said Mr Parks. "Do I know them, is that it? Does Tom know them? I don't see why you can't tell me. I have a right to know, don't I?"

"Not in this case," said DI Reever. "It is particularly sensitive. We've simply been asked to complete the investigation with as little fuss as possible. But I don't think you've got anything to fear. We can clear this up quite quickly, I'm sure. I know it's very early, but would it be possible to see Thomas? That, at least, would prove he's not somewhere else."

Mr Park's hesitated for a moment, uncomfortable at the intrusion into the heart of his home, but then agreed, so long as he could see Tom first.

"Of course," said DI Reever, while DS Brown frowned suspiciously.

"And I don't want you waking him up, either," said Mr Parks.

DS Brown was about to tell Mr Parks that *they*'d make that decision, when DI Reever's stern glance silenced him.

"All we want to do is to see that he's here," said DI Reever. "Where's his room?"

Mr Parks got up and led them upstairs.

"Just wait here a second," he said, standing outside Tom's bedroom door, then slipped inside.

Shortly, he returned and signalled for them to enter.

DI Reever gave Mr Parks a reassuring smile on his way in, then went over to Tom's bed. The boy was there, just as he'd expected all along. There was the backpack, too, and as he turned away from Tom he gave a sharp nod towards DS Brown.

DS Brown stooped down next to the backpack, laying his hand over it. "Is this Thomas's backpack?" he asked, not bothering to quieten his voice.

"*Yes*," said Mr Parks, "and will you please keep the noise down. You can see that Thomas *is* here and I really don't want him woken up. He was very tired after a difficult day at school. Clara said she didn't hear a peep out of him tonight."

"That's Clara, his elder sister?" said DS Brown.

"Yes."

"And she didn't hear him? Not a peep?"

"Yes," he said, getting more agitated, not knowing where all these questions were leading.

"So, it's possible that he wasn't about, I suppose," said DS Brown innocently.

"Definitely not!" Mr Parks shouted, then quickly lowered his voice again. "*I told you he was here*."

"And where were *you*?"

Mr Park's mouth opened but nothing came out as he struggled with the question. Eventually, he answered, saying sternly, "I was only out for an hour or two. At table tennis. It's a club I go to every Wednesday. The children always stay in. They've never been out without my permission. *Never*."

"Did you see Thomas on your return from the club?" said DI Reever, looking thoughtfully at him.

"No - no, I don't suppose I did tonight. But I saw him earlier and we ate together and Clara says-"

"Yes, we know what Clara said," said DS Brown bluntly, then went straight on, "When did you get back from the club?"

"Ten - ten-thirty," said Mr Parks, "no later than that. But I don't understand why you're still asking all these questions. *He's here.* It's obvious that he hasn't been running about in the middle of town stealing wallets."

He gave an imploring look at the detectives but they remained unmoved.

"Can I look in this?" said DS Brown, tapping his fingers on the backpack, adding with a faint smile, "It's just a precaution."

"If you must," he said unhappily, "but you're wasting your time. You're not going to find that wallet in there."

"Hopefully not," lied DS Brown, unclipping the front, then worked his way through the pockets. "House key?"

Mr Parks peered forwards, then nodded. "Front door. You can check it if you like."

"That won't be necessary," said DS Brown, rummaging deeper.

Meanwhile, DI Reever moved back towards the bed. He leaned over Tom, peering at a dirty mark on the pillow where his hand was resting. He brushed the mark with his fingertip, rubbed it against another finger, then drew away again.

"I think Thomas might have cut himself," he said, mentioning it as if it wasn't anything important. "That's blood on the pillow if I'm not mistaken. Better get it checked out when he wakes up."

"Oh, yes, of course," said Mr Parks, wondering what on earth they'd discover next, "thank you, I will. You know boys, always getting into some sort of scrape."

"Yes," said DI Reever, his thoughts far away.

"Nothing else here," sighed DS Brown, standing up again.

"Then I think we'd better leave Mr Parks to enjoy what little is left of his sleep," said DI Reever and left towards the door.

Nothing was said on the way downstairs, then Mr Parks held open the front door for the detectives. DS Brown nodded politely on his way out, leaving DI Reever to finish off.

"Well, thank you again, Mr Parks," said DI Reever, "you've been most helpful. And I do apologise for this inconvenience. It couldn't be avoided, I'm afraid. If there's anything else, we'll let you know, but I don't expect we shall need to. Ah, and here's my card, just in case. The mobile's best - I'm often out and about. Good night."

"Good night," mumbled Mr Parks, taking the card, then closing the door behind them.

Two minutes later, the detectives were back in DI Reever's silver Vectra parked a short way down on the opposite side of the road. DI Reever yawned widely, while DS Brown watched the house. The porch light went out almost immediately, while the hallway light remained on.

"The backpack matched the description," said DS Brown.

"Yes," said DI Reever, adding wearily, "along with the thousands of others owned by children across Bellington."

"Ah, but this one is owned by the same boy who had a run in with Mr van Reiner today - as witnessed on the evening news - and who has been positively ID'ed by both Mr van Reiner and the Receptionist at the hotel-"

"-and who doesn't have the wallet-"

"-but *could* have been out roaming tonight and *did* have blood on him-"

"-and was *almost* sound asleep when we went into his room," said DI Reever, completing the murky picture.

"Almost?"

99

"I could've been mistaken," said DI Reever, "but didn't you notice how tightly he was wrapped up in that duvet? Boys don't sleep like that, do they? They kick their bedclothes all over the place. And he didn't move once while we were in the room, despite your repeated attempts to wake him up by raising your voice. I think he may have been listening to us all along."

"Yes, you may be right," said DS Brown.

"But it just doesn't add up," said DI Reever, stifling his next yawn. "His father was right, even if he didn't know why. How does a twelve-year-old boy - and one who *isn't* from the rougher side of Bellington - get into Mr van Reiner's rooms on the 10th floor of a hotel and then escape, despite being spotted? Mr van Reiner's thugs could easily have stopped him. But even if he escaped from them, just how could he have stolen the wallet and got away with it?"

"Fagin's little boys could 'pick a pocket or two'."

"That's a story," said DI Reever, "and this boy is not the Artful Dodger, I'm sure of that."

"But it happens," said DS Brown, "and this boy is already wrapped up in something with Mr van Reiner, we know that."

"Yes, yes," said DI Reever impatiently, struggling to make a sensible story out of the little information that he had.

"You just don't like Mr van Reiner," said DS Brown, "and that's clouding your judgement."

And you're just an ambitious upstart, thought DI Reever, but said instead, "You're right, there, I don't trust him. He's got too much history, too many black marks against his name. All the shady business deals round here over the last twenty years have got his dirty paw-prints on them."

"Not proven."

"Not in court," said DI Reever, correcting him, "but I know his type. He'll never give up his evil little ways and *that's* why I don't think this is quite as simple as it might appear."

"This is simple?" said DS Brown

The two of them laughed at the thought.

"Any action out there?" said DI Reever.

"None," said DS Brown. "He's probably making a pot of tea and wondering much the same things as we are - without the details of course."

"Well, I, for one, have done my duty," said DI Reever, releasing another great yawn, "and Mr van Reiner has had more than his money's-worth from us tonight."

"The power of politics," said DS Brown, fixing his safety-belt as DI Reever started the engine, "you just can't ignore it."

"No," said DI Reever, driving away, "and, where Mr van Reiner's involved, you dare not ignore it."

Tom had been awake, but not in the way that DI Reever had thought, not in the normal way. Yes, the detectives voices had woken him and he'd kept as still as he could, pretending that he was still fast asleep. But when they'd gone and his eyes opened, it was as if he was trapped somewhere between sleeping and waking, in a place that was neither night nor day, neither dark nor light but instead grey like the fast approaching dawn.

Like a ghost, having no fear of being discovered, he rose from his bed and went over to his backpack. He looked inside it, searching for the MP's wallet, and was surprised not to find it. He remembered having put it there after he'd paid the taxi driver and wondered where it had got to. At first he thought that the detectives might have actually found it then taken it without telling his father. But then he remembered that something had fallen out of his backpack when he'd got out of the taxi and wondered if was still lying back there at the side of the road.

Strangely, however, he wasn't worried.

Then, without any fear of bumping into his father or sister, he went to the bathroom and carefully washed the blood and dirt from his hands. He knew that the cold water would sting, but the pain felt far far away. The fine cuts and grazes soon came up pink and healthy. He knew that he'd heal quickly. He dabbed his hands dry, then returned to his bedroom.

His shadow was looking out of the window and glanced over its shoulder as he came back in. Tom said hello and smiled, then returned to bed. He heard his shadow talking to him. Its voice sounded both far away and close to at the same time. He didn't need to look at his shadow, listening seemed to be enough.

"You did well tonight," it said. "Don't worry about the wallet. It's gone now."

"Did *you* knock it out of my backpack?"

"Yes."

"Are you going to tell me what this is all about now?"

"You'll know all you need to know in good time."

"That's not a lot, I guess," he said, chuckling to himself.

"You know more than you think already. Rest now."

"Yeah, I will."

Lying on his back he felt wonderfully relaxed. The greyness felt good, very good indeed.

Chapter 7 The Voice of the Eagle

The next morning Tom's alarm sounded and he woke promptly. His eyes opened wide and he felt wonderfully refreshed, despite what he'd been through the night before. Indeed, it now seemed more like some incredible dream. But, when he started to move, his body ached terribly, even muscles that he never knew he had complaining loudly. Gingerly, he sat up. The moment his hands touched the mattress he drew them sharply away again. Those wounds, even as they healed, were real enough.

As he sat there, waiting for his body to calm again, his mind went back to that inbetween time a couple of hours ago when he had spoken with his shadow. Yes, it had been his shadow that had knocked the wallet from his backpack. It was that which had surely saved him from discovery by the two detectives. His shadow had told him that he knew more than he realised, but if that was true, it certainly wasn't clear to him. He thought of Jerry and his technical talk which he guessed was about computers, but it made no more sense to him now than it had then.

With time pressing on, he eased himself out of bed and got himself washed and dressed, taking his time as his body slowly adjusted to the new day and began to function again. By the time he was ready to go downstairs, he was moving less like an old man.

"Morning, Tom," said his father, already tucking in to his breakfast at the kitchen table.

"Hi, dad," said Tom, trying not to walk so stiffly.

"Sleep well?"

"Sure."

They ate together at the table, both saying nothing but thinking hard. His father glanced up at him from time to time, watching him closely. He was still concerned about the blood on the pillow, but had decided against mentioning the visit of the two detectives.

"Tom," he said eventually, "you'd tell me if there was anything wrong, wouldn't you? I mean, something that was making you unhappy."

"Yeah."

"Good." He paused. "No more problems with Dags, then?"

Tom smiled. "He keeps well away from me now."

"Good. But if you did get hurt - you know how these things happen - then you'd let me know straight away."

"*Yeah, dad, of course*," he said, frowning as he took his dirty bowl to the sink. "Don't worry, I'm fine."

"Okay, just checking."

"Just checking what?" said Clara, strutting in and dropping her school bag on the sideboard.

"Nothing!" they called together.

As soon as he was out of the kitchen, Tom felt a great relief that he hadn't had to lie directly about anything that had happened in the night. There had been no questions about what the detectives wanted, and even if he had got a bit hurt, he was okay now. More or less.

As he passed the phone stand under the stairs, he paused, his eye caught by the small white card lying there. After glancing back to make sure that no one was coming, he went over to it. On it were the contact details for Detective Inspector John Reever. He thought for a moment, then picked it up and slipped it inside his pocket. If he was going to get any more trouble from Mr van Reiner and his men, it might come in useful.

At midday DI Reever sat at his desk on the 3rd floor of the Police Headquarters in the centre of Bellington. He was on his third cup of coffee in the last hour which seemed to be all that was keeping him awake. The days when he would fly through a night shift then continue straight through the next day were long gone. He'd slept in this morning but even that didn't seem to have helped. Piece by piece he waded through the paperwork piled up in front of him.

The phone rang.

"Hello. Yes, this is DI Reever speaking."

It was Geoffrey on the other end of the line.

"Has there been any news on the burglary, detective? Mr van Reiner is eager to see this neatly tied up. I'm sure you understand."

"Yes," said DI Reever coldly, "I think I do. But these investigations are rarely as 'neat' as we would like them."

"*And?*"

"No, it isn't tied up, neatly or otherwise. But I can tell you that we visited the boy's home in the early hours of the morning and conducted a thorough interview and found no reason to continue with that line of enquiry at present. The wallet wasn't there, either. So, it appears there may have been some mistake on your part. As I said, it isn't always so neat."

DI Reever didn't mind omitting certain details such as the backpack and the boy's cut hands and the fact that they had not interviewed the boy himself. Whatever Mr van Reiner wanted, he was certain it had little to do with the wallet and until the whole story became clear he was not going to let the MP get anywhere near the young boy.

"A pity," said Geoffrey sourly, "because neatness is what we expect from our detectives. How about fingerprints? We couldn't help but notice what an excellent job your forensic team did this morning. They picked up plenty, it seems. That could produce a positive match, couldn't it?"

"We'll check any prints we get," said DI Reever bluntly.

"But you don't have the boy's fingerprints on record, do you?" said Geoffrey. "You'll need to get them off him, otherwise we may never find out the truth."

"Yes, that's a good point," said DI Reever pointedly, "and it's the truth - the *whole* truth - that I'm interested in. So, given that, can you explain how the boy got in and out of the 10th floors of the hotel, despite being spotted by your bodyguards? How *does* a twelve-year-old do that?"

"The Receptionist identified him too," said Geoffrey cautiously.

"Oh yes, and then there's the flick-knife," said DI Reever, ignoring the response. "Where did that go after the incident at Newlands? I'd like a look at it, if I could. You see, I don't believe it ever belonged to the boy. So, if you took it off him, where is it now?"

"As far as I know," said Geoffrey, sounding flustered, "we left it there in the school. There was no point in us keeping what wasn't ours. We were just performing a public service, taking it away from the boy. And where he got it from, I don't know. It was a distressing moment for all of us."

"Of course," said DI Reever, not believing a word, "but if you continue to pursue a conviction against the boy and nothing is found against him - and that is how it's looking presently - then this could be viewed as bullying. Bullying of an innocent child who simply dared to ask a difficult question."

"I don't think so, detective," said Geoffrey, laughing a little too loudly, "and we wouldn't want any such misunderstandings, now would we?"

"Not with a General Election so close," said DI Reever innocently, "I suppose not."

"Good then, I think we have arrived at a better understanding," said Geoffrey, hurriedly finishing, "and of course if you do find the burglar or the missing wallet, you'll let us know straight away."

"Of course," said DI Reever, smiling contentedly to himself. "Good bye."

The detective sat back, mulling over the conversation. He was certain that Geoffrey knew the location of the flick-knife and that it was likely never to be seen again. Then, picking up his mobile from the desk, he rang DS Brown. His partner was finishing off at the Hotel Virion and he wanted to know if any other details had emerged.

"Jim, how goes it?"

"Nothing much here, I'm afraid," said DS Brown. "We'll have a check against the prints tomorrow, but I'm not expecting anything, unless of course you count Mr van Reiner's thugs. I'd put good money on each of them having a string of convictions. The wallet's not turned up either, surprise, surprise, and I've checked up on the Security Guard, too. John Varney's his name. I didn't get a good feeling about him, but his story does back up the others."

"They can't all be in on this together," sighed DI Reever.

"No, I don't think so."

"But I'm not letting Mr van Reiner near the boy, even if we do dig something up," said DI Reever. "There's more to this than Mr van Reiner's letting on, and until I know what it is, we don't open it up to anyone else. Understood?"

"It's your call," said DS Brown, though DI Reever could tell he wasn't happy about it.

"I just had Geoffrey on the line," explained DI Reever. "He wanted a 'neat' ending - a noose round the boy's neck, in other words. It stank like it always does around Mr van Reiner. Any other leads?"

"Just the one, but it went cold," said DS Brown. "Yes, a taxi did leave after midnight, and I managed to trace the driver. But he says that there was no fare with him - he was just called out to get one on the north side of town."

"Okay. Let's wait for the prints," said DI Reever. "See you later."

DI Reever stared at the stain left in the bottom of his empty cup, then sighed and dragged himself back to the coffee machine.

For the next few weeks life returned to something like normal. Tom continued with his Election Project in History (even if he was distracted by troublesome thoughts about Mr van Reiner whenever he turned to it) and Dags's gang kept out of his way (on several occasions Tom tried to tempt his shadow to trip them up again, but it stubbornly ignored him, still pretending to be normal) and, by carefully avoiding Mr Denton, he managed to keep himself free of the basketball coaching on Wednesdays.

The early May Bank Holiday was spent with his mother who gladly updated him and Clara on the latest sales figures for her business - up 5% on the last quarter - while Georgie, more interestingly, cooked up a feast of pancakes, providing every sweet and delicious filling imaginable.

On Tom's return home there was only one incident of note. It occurred on a pleasant Saturday afternoon when he was sitting on the patio, tossing a tennis ball against the wall. The truth was that he was fed up again, wondering where his life was leading, and the monotonous game helped to deaden the pain of the long empty hours spent on his own. And then, on about the umpteenth throw of the ball, it suddenly stuck halfway up the wall, held there by his shadow.

He stared at it for several moments, his heart starting to race again. "So, wh-what's up?" he said when he finally found his voice.

A moment later there was a meow from the pear tree and he turned to see the tortoiseshell cat stepping from the back wall onto its topmost branch.

"Hey, it's here!" he called out excitedly.

The tennis ball bounced down and rolled across the grass towards it. Tom looked at his shadow and smiled. "I'm on my way," he said, then moved cautiously towards the pear tree.

He tried to coax the cat down with welcoming words and offers of a friendly hand, and was amazed when it responded positively. Little by little it climbed down, testing each branch carefully with its paws, often hesitating and taking another look around before advancing once more. When it was in reach, it sniffed Tom's fingers then let him stroke its neck, then continued down once more.

Tom knelt down in the grass as it stepped off the tree as cautiously as an alien landing on a far off planet. It sniffed the grass, then a daisy, then stepped gingerly towards Tom before finally letting him stroke it. It brushed its head up against him, then curled round him, trailing its tail after it. It purred loudly.

"What's your name?" he said. "Where are you from? Would you like to stay with me? Dad doesn't want you and neither does Clara, I think, but that doesn't matter. I don't have to tell them. You could stay in my room. It's up there," and, twisting round, he pointed up at his bedroom window. "I'd get food for you. We can be friends. Good friends."

The cat looked up at him and mewed, which for Tom was as good as a 'Yes', then rolled over in the grass.

"I'll call you Rolly," he said, smiling to himself, "if that's okay."

Then it sprang up from the grass and leapt back onto the tree. Quickly it clambered back on top of the wall.

"Rolly it is, then," he said, undeterred by its sudden departure. "Come again soon!"

The cat winked, then jumped down on the other side.

It was from about that time, too, that election fever began to grip the nation. Information about it poured in through television, in the news and interviews and party political broadcasts, as well as the piles of party leaflets pushed through the door almost every day. Worse still, Mr

Parks, who worked for Bellington Council and seemed to know a bit about it, kept on relaying information to Tom and Clara about the organisation required for the voting arrangements and how important it was to vote - and to vote for the right people. For once Clara and Tom were united when they delivered their ultimatum to him: no more talk of politics or the election or anything to do with voting! He looked quite shocked by their outburst and couldn't understand it from Tom whose own project was all about it. But then, after studying closely the determined look on their faces, he agreed to talk about it only when asked *or* when absolutely necessary.

But Tom could not escape the grip of the General Election quite so easily. It had been his hope that if he simply kept on pushing his pen over page after page for his Election Project then eventually it would come to a certain end. What he hadn't counted on, however, was what Mr Harris had to announce in his History class. For his Year 7 class only, and by special agreement with the headteacher, he had organised a trip to the Houses of Parliament. The class gasped with excitement and received the permission slips with trembling hands, though Tom took his with far less enthusiasm. The thought of meeting a whole house full of MP's - and Mr van Reiner, in particular - filled him with a horrible dread.

That evening, over dinner, Tom broke the news to his father and Clara.

"That sounds *so* boring!" said Clara.

"No it isn't!" protested their father, taking full advantage of this golden opportunity to enthuse about the election once more. "It's a fantastic trip. It's got a proper tour round the Houses of Parliament and there's an exhibition with films and displays and even a mock-up of the House of Commons where schools can have their own debates. And this is all happening only 3 weeks before the real General Election!"

"Yawny, yawny," said Clara, groaning as she pretended to faint over the table.

"That's enough, Clara," said her father, "and I can give you my answer right now, Tom. Here's my pen...and here's my signature. Of course you can go. You *must* go. You've worked so hard on your project and, with this, you're bound to get top marks. All right?"

"Brill," said Tom, though his face told a different story.

One week later Tom boarded the coach for London, dreading what might lie ahead. Ever since the announcement of the trip his mind had been full of images of Mr van Reiner's men waiting for him, ready to do their worst, the ghostly face of Geoffrey looming large amongst them. He had tried to think of other things, but with the coverage of the General Election only increasing it hadn't been easy, and his father hadn't helped, using the trip as an excuse to talk as much as he liked about it too. But once the journey was underway, Tom started to settle down. Mr Harris gave the class a reassuring talk, explaining the plan for the day and the usual do's and don'ts, and it wasn't long before Tom sneaked out from his backpack a packet of crisps and a drink, happily tucking into them.

Opposite him sat the gawky blond twins, Mike and Martin Marshall, who chattered and giggled away, happy with their own company. He ignored them until one of them called across to him.

"What's that?" said Tom, caught by surprise.

"That was a *bad* job you did on Dags," said Martin, grinning broadly as he leaned across the other's lap.

"Yeah!" said Mike. "You took him down. You're a hero."

"Really?"

"Yeah!" said the twins.

"Everybody knows," said Martin, "and about how you got the others. You know, Steve and - and-"

"Micky," said Mike.

"No," said Martin. "Mikey, Mike, not Micky. Yeah?"

"Yeah!"

"Steve and Mikey," said Martin.

"Mikey and Steve," said Mike

"Yeah!" they chorused together, laughing and prodding each other.

Tom smiled, both enjoying their buffoonery and pleasantly surprised at the reputation he had gained. He couldn't remember having been paid such complimentary attention and the boost to himself was so much greater than that of the occasional words of encouragement from his father. It was enough to give him the courage to try to talk to them again, though after that their attention was difficult to get back. Not that it seemed to matter so much then.

An hour or so later the coach stopped at a service station to allow for a toilet-break, then it started the long trek across London itself. A while later a cry went up - Buckingham Palace had been spotted - and a minute or so afterwards the coach pulled up. They were told to collect up their bags and coats and wait on the broad pavement. Then Mr Harris and the two other teachers led them into St James's Park where they settled down near the lake to eat their lunch.

With the warm grass beneath him and the sunshine streaming down through the leafy trees, Tom felt as if he was in a different world to the one he had left that morning. Even his marmite and cheese sandwiches were more gloriously tasty than ever he had thought possible.

"All right," said Mr Harris after what seemed far too short a time, "pack away your lunch boxes now. Our tour starts shortly and we just have time to get there if we leave now."

There was much excited chatter.

"But listen now," he said when they were all ready, "there's one more thing I want to say before we go. The guides will show us around and there will be a great deal of information to take in. Listen carefully and take notes on your clipboards - you can use them in your project. But most of all I want you to *feel* the importance of these buildings - to breathe in their long past - and to *sense* the power. The people who walk through these corridors decide our future and what could be more exciting than that?"

For a moment he held them spellbound in his gaze, then without further delay they set off.

The walk came a welcome break after the morning's journey, the children bustling happily over the broad promenades alongside the park. Soon, though, the streets became as crowded and busy as the broad multi-lane roads streaming with traffic hurrying in and out of the heart of London. The children weaved in and out of the international tourists and street traders and business people packing every square millimetre of pavement along the way.

At one point the class was diverted into the basement of a conference centre for a final toilet stop, then returned, shortly passing through the grounds of Westminster Abbey. Its great stone frontage, cluttered with sculpted figures, loomed high above. A minute later, emerging through the crowds onto a roadside pavement, the children looked up for their first sight of the Houses of Parliament.

The magnificent building, gleaming golden in the afternoon sunlight, stretched out in front of them. Its long roof was studded with grand towers and almost immediately one voice called out "Big Ben!" as the famous clock tower was spotted at the near end. Other voices groaned and pointed with greater interest to the upper crescent of the London Eye that was peeping over the roof from behind. The children were steered over the busy road and taken to the Victoria Tower at the far end of the building. There, in the Norman Porch, they were met by their two tour guides. Both middle-aged, the man and woman were dressed in smart suits with pressed green jackets. They welcomed everyone, then took them to the Robing Room where the tour was to begin.

In the next hour and a half the history of Parliament was presented through many stories, illustrated by the plentiful statues of famous figures and the epic paintings covering the walls and even the design and furnishings of the rooms themselves. The grandeur of the Royal Palace made the heads of the children spin, the sumptuous decoration stretching from the stone floors to the carved walls to the high vaulted ceilings. The House of Lords was no less splendid, dominated at the one end by the imposing golden throne rising high up to where the dark statues of ancient knights, swords locked in their hands, glowered down from their lofty stations all around. Even the corridors and lobbies, lined with yet more statues and paintings, continued the story of the nation's greatest and worst moments and those who had battled through them, friend and foe alike. Cut in stone and daubed on canvas, the nation's past was laid out before the children, reminding them of everything that had brought them to where they were today.

The House of Commons, as its name suggested, was far less opulent. It was here that the day-to-day business of Government took place and, as the guides emphasised, anyone - especially the youth of today - could listen in to the debates and decisions of the political parties. Throughout the various parts of the building there were stark reminders of the momentous turning points in the nation's past, but it was here that the turning point's of the nation's future – its fragile future – would happen.

"Our future is in the hands of men and women who are just like you and me," said the male guide with a kindly smile, "and when they're ready to make a decision they file out of here, past the Speaker's Chair, the Ayes to the right, the Noes to the left. Now, when they pass the Speaker's Chair, some still bow their heads. Why? Well, it's believed that this tradition stems from the time when the Speaker's Chair stood in front of the altar in St Stephen's Chapel. As you might know, people bow their heads before an altar in respect of God." Then he leaned closer as if to share a precious secret and whispered, "I'd like to think that's why they still do it - to remember God and ask for His help just before they make their big decisions." He stood up straight again. "And now we're going into St Stephen's Hall where the altar stood in the chapel. Our tour is almost at an end."

For the children at least the greatest attraction in St Stephen's Hall proved to be the Visitors Shop. They crowded into it, glad of the distraction after all their learning. Soon, however, they were prised away and led down a wide stone staircase into the open expanse of Westminster Hall. It stretched out before them like a gigantic barn. It had a barrelled roof of thick oak timbers with buttresses that bore straight-winged angels watching over the comings and goings below. In its plain stone walls were alcoves in which stood the crumbling statues of ancient Kings and Queens. The massive stone slabs of the floor carried the whispers of the tourists and Ministers and journalists and, so it seemed, of history itself. Mr Harris thanked the guides on behalf of the children, then turned to introduce the exhibition that stood in a corner of the hall. It was here that they would spend their last hour before setting off again to meet the coach next to the park.

The children entered a mock-up of the House of Commons and were divided into two halves, the Government and the Opposition, while Mr Harris acted as the Speaker, shouting "Order! Order!" whenever their debating looked as if it was getting out of hand. The first debate was proposed as 'A Recommendation to replace School Exclusions with Hangings' and it proved a great success, provoking much argument and laughter in equal measures. After that, the children were allowed to roam freely through the exhibition. They looked at film shows projected on the stone walls and long charts describing such things as the important events in the nation's history and the inner workings of Parliament. A popular note-wall allowed them to post up their ideas about what they wanted to change in Britain today.

Tom wandered round a display about voting. It started with a reproduction of the famous Magna Carta from 1215, and then showed how, through many centuries and hard fought battles, more and more ordinary people, men then women, were allowed to have their say in who ruled their country. Around one corner was a battered black ballot box with a pile of voting slips and instructions on how to vote. The candidates had joky names such as 'Mr I. Trouble, Spectacles Party' and 'Ms P. Soup, Vegetarian Party'. As soon as a completed voting slip was posted through the narrow slit in the top of the ballot box an automated audio recording told how voting had once been done openly but now, through the ballet box, was done in secret. This meant that today it was not so easy to threaten voters and make them vote for someone they didn't want.

Finally, at the end of the display, there was a computer, though it could hardly be seen because of the number of children flocking around it, elbowing each other out of the way. From its speakers a distinctive voice proudly announced the introduction of the new online voting system. This was to be the first General Election in the world, it said, that would be contested completely online, and it was only possible because of the years of dedicated research, design and testing from the nation's finest and most skilled technicians. At last it had been approved by Parliament, it said, its voice rising triumphantly. Great Britain was leading the world in its use of information technology. This generation would look back and tell its children of how it had been the first to elect its new Prime Minister online. Together, they were going to make history!

While the voice repeated its message, the children clicked through the screens, eager to put an 'X' in the checkbox next to the jokey name of the candidate they wanted. Then, after clicking on the 'Vote' button, there was a triumphant fanfare and a summary of the results of the mock election was flashed up. A moment later the screen returned to the start, ready for the next child.

Unable to get near the computer and with his head so full of information that it felt like an overstuffed ballot box, Tom gladly wandered out of the exhibition back into the main hall. He found himself standing alongside a small set of stone steps in front of which stood the stone statues of noble beasts - eagle, deer and lion - each presenting an heraldic shield. His eye wandered from them up the wall to one of the decaying royal statues in its alcove and up again to an oak angel in the roof. He followed the angel's blank gaze back down to the outer wall of the exhibition.

Moments later, staring at the large circular picture on the wall, a chill shiver ran down his spine.

The powerful bronzed eagle, with its wings lifted high and talons outstretched, was pouncing on its unseen prey just as it had been on the laptop in the office of Mr van Reiner's suite.

He stepped closer.

There were words printed in gold wrapped around the edge of the circle. His head turned as he read them: '*The Eagle Corporation ~ the Power for Success*'.

But what was the same picture doing here? he wondered, struggling to make sense of it through the fog of facts clogging his brain.

And then came the voice.

For one heart-stopping moment, as he stood close enough to reach out and touch it, he thought that it was actually the eagle talking to him. But the voice came from just the other side of the wall. Amongst the many other voices drifting across the hall and out of the exhibition, he recognised it instantly. The last time he had heard it was when he was in Mr van Reiner's suite.

"There, that's it fixed," said Jerry. "It was one of those kids knocking it about. It doesn't take much. I said we should've used a kiosk, but no one listened. They wanted a computer so that it would be just like the real thing."

"Well, it's working fine now," said another man, "but you'd better get away before they bust it again. Where are you off to next?"

"I've got one more call while I'm over here," said Jerry, "and I'd better get a move on. This one doesn't like to be kept waiting. Okay, see you around."

"Not too soon, I hope," said the other man with a chuckle.

Tom stood there, his heart racing, not knowing what to do. He was about to try to hide, but then realised that he had never seen Jerry and it was possible that Jerry had never seen him. It seemed unlikely, but by that time he was too late to do anything. Jerry, easily identified by the Eagle Corporation logo splashed across the back of his blue jacket, strode out of the exhibition and headed straight towards the large porchway at the end of the hall, the aluminium case swinging at his side.

There was a tap on Tom's ankles and, looking down, he saw his shadow stretching out after Jerry. It grew thinner and thinner, rushing passing the Reception Desk and on towards the sunlit porchway. It lay as thin as a hairline crack across the stone slabs of the floor, stretched almost to breaking point. For a moment Jerry was silhouetted in the porchway, then was gone.

Tom hesitated, knowing what he had to do, but scared of what might happen once he was separated from the rest of his class. He looked at his shadow again, wondering why it didn't just run off after Jerry, and then realised that it was marking the way he should go. It was so thin now that he almost couldn't see it amongst the joints between the slabs.

Then, after looking round to make sure that no teacher was watching him, he hurried off towards the porchway.

At the Reception Desk he took one last glance back. A small group of children was standing around outside the exhibition, then one of them looked across at him. It was Shelly James, easily recognised by her long chestnut hair. She started to lift her hand to point at him and he shook his head hard and gave her the biggest wink he could make. His cheeks reddened, but then, seeming to understand him, she dropped her hand down again.

Seconds later he was outside, hunting down the trail of his shadow and worrying what Shelly might do next.

Chapter 8 The Disguise and The Bear Pit

Outside Westminster Hall Tom spotted the thin line of his shadow stretching out along the path that wound out of the grounds of the Houses of Parliament. At the end of the path, pushing through the security turnstile, was Jerry. Tom ran after him, slowing to a walk a few metres before the gate and catching his breath before passing the armed police officer guarding the exit. The officer looked around, at ease in the warm sunshine. Tom pushed through the turnstile, keeping his eyes down until he was past the officer, then looked up again. Jerry was on the opposite side of the busy road.

"Wait there!" called the officer.

Tom turned slowly.

"Your badge," said the officer, pointing to the yellow sticker on Tom's coat, "put it on the board here."

Trying not to look as terrified as he felt, Tom peeled it off then hurried over to the board and slapped it down amongst the hundreds of others left there by departing visitors. He gave a nervous smile at the officer, then walked off. But Jerry was no longer in sight.

Tom crossed the road, but amongst the heaving crowds pressing against him he couldn't even see his own shadow any more. Pushing his way through he eventually came out in the grounds of Westminster Abbey. Here the crowds eased, the visitors spreading out more, ambling along the paths and relaxing in small groups over the lawns, taking in the majestic splendour of the architecture and soaking up the tranquillity and sunshine. Looking out in all directions, his heart fell with no sign of Jerry, but then his eye was caught by a silvery glint. It came from the far corner of the grounds. Scanning that area he just caught sight of the blue jacket and aluminium case as Jerry walked out through a gate.

"Gotcha!" said Tom, and after hurrying over to the gate spotted Jerry halfway across another broad busy road.

For the next few minutes Tom followed Jerry, dodging along the pavements and crossing the roads after him. They left the larger roads for smaller ones, changing directions back and forth several times, the crowds easing along the way. Tom dropped back a short way, taking care not to be spotted himself, but then after one sweeping corner lost sight of him altogether.

Tom looked ahead and behind, then across the road, but there was no sign of him anywhere. Yet he knew that Jerry could not have got away from him that fast even if he'd run off:. There hadn't been enough time. At that moment an uproar of laughter came through the windows behind him and he turned to see the front of a pub with a few sets of silver chairs and tables lined up invitingly along its front. On the sign hanging above was a snarling brown bear rearing up on its hind legs and the name of the pub, *The Bear Pit.*

There was only way to find out if Jerry had disappeared inside the pub, but Tom knew that he couldn't just stroll in on his own, not if he didn't want awkward questions from the landlord. He looked down at his shadow, hoping for inspiration, and was shocked to see that it wasn't there any more. Angry thoughts started to fill his head, but then suddenly he swung away from the door to the pub and stood facing the road, trembling all over.

Behind him, having just walked out of the pub, was the imposing figure of Mr Wheeler.

Tom gripped the straps of his backpack and got ready to launch himself across the road and run away as fast as he could, jinxing about, heading anywhere, just so long as he couldn't be caught. But just as he was about to set off, a hand caught him gently but firmly on the shoulder and swung him round, then steered him straight past the bodyguard who was looking elsewhere and into the pub.

Once inside the short entrance hall Tom pulled back and strained round to see who had taken hold of him and was almost as shocked as when he'd seen the bodyguard outside. Beneath a Panama hat tilted down and rainbow star-shaped spectacles of the sort worn by children on summer beaches and a dark red paisley neckerchief pulled up like a highwayman's mask was the dark emptiness of his shadow's head. Completing the disguise it wore a long dull mac, woollen gloves and basketball boots, both left-footed.

"Nice outfit!" whispered Tom, raising his eyebrows high, then let his shadow guide him inside before the bodyguard could return.

Like a kind eccentric grandfather with his arm around his grandson's shoulder, the shadow hurried Tom through the crowded bar to the booths at the back. With all the booths already occupied, his shadow steered him towards the one with a young couple looking deeply into each other's eyes and smiling gushingly. It wasn't a pretty sight and Tom kept his eyes well away from them as he slipped along the bench on the other side of the table. Then his shadow dropped back, disappearing amongst the crowds, heading towards the bar.

"I told you," said Jerry impatiently, "I got here as quickly as I could. I can't just drop everything and leave any time I like. I had to rig that problem at the exhibition especially so I could get here. Now, where is he? I want this over and done with as soon as possible."

Tom's head turned suddenly and he looked at the shadowy heads through the glazed glass side of the next booth. He glanced back at the young couple, now glad that they had no interest in anyone but themselves, then listened more closely to the conversation in the next booth.

"He'll be here," growled Mr Crane, "but first we need to make sure that you weren't tailed."

"Great," said Jerry unhappily, "just get a move on."

The young couple started kissing and gently caressing each other's faces, making Tom squirm inside. Then, looking across the crowded room, he saw the heads of both Mr

Wheeler and Mr van Reiner. As the two men forced their way through the squash of bodies, coming closer and closer, Tom pushed himself back into the corner of his booth. Then Mr Wheeler suddenly emerged right in front of him, looking lost and puzzled as he searched for his own booth, frowning at the young couple. For a terrifying moment Tom waited for the bodyguard to spot him, but then his shadow swept between the two of them, its mac swirling about, and slid up the bench, shielding Tom from view.

As soon as Mr Wheeler realised his mistake, he led Mr van Reiner across to the next booth. When Tom looked down again, he saw a tall glass of orange and a dark pint of beer on the table. His shadow's gloved hand slid the glass of orange towards him, the ice cubes clinking inside.

"Thanks," said Tom with a relieved smile, "for everything."

His shadow raised its drink in a silent toast and Tom returned the compliment with his. But a moment later he was astonished to see his shadow actually tip the drink down over its neckerchief. It appeared to be drinking, but where the beer was going he could only guess at. He took a long refreshing swig of his chilled orange, trying not to choke as he watched the beer spilling down inside his shadow's empty mac.

The voices started again in the next booth.

"So, Jerry, now that you've finally made it here," said Mr van Reiner with a weary sigh, "perhaps you'd be so good as to update me. There's not long to go now. So, is everything ready?"

"Of course," said Jerry edgily.

"Are you sure?"

"Yes!"

"You don't sound it," said Mr van Reiner, watching him closely. "You look nervous. Are you sure you're telling me *everything*, Jerry?"

"No - I mean, *yes*, of course I'm sure. It's just been a mad rush to get here today. You called the meeting late and I had to make special arrangements to get here and-"

"All right, all right, Jerry," said Mr van Reiner in a soothing voice, "I do understand. Unfortunately it couldn't be avoided. I have appointments I cannot miss and they can be very unexpected. But what I really want to know from you is how our preparations for the 'big day' are going?"

"Okay," said Jerry, calming himself. "There've been no problems that I know of since I last saw you."

"That you know of?" said Mr van Reiner suspiciously.

"Yes. I check the daily logs for reports of errors. There've been a few but they're minor and nothing that's going to stop us. There's no way this isn't going to happen. Eagle Corporation's already celebrating, though they're not making a big fuss about it yet. They'll do that afterwards."

"Very sensible," said Mr van Reiner, "but what about that 'final trigger' you told us about? Has that happened yet?"

"No," said Jerry, smiling to himself, "that happens at the start of the big day."

"Go on."

"There's a file," said Jerry. "Just the one. A marker file. It looks perfectly normal. It's already there in the system. It's *my* file. I'll make a change to it - one that no one else will notice - it'll have the same name, be the same size, be in the same place. But as soon as the change takes place our module kicks in and then it starts to-"

"Yes, that's quite enough about that," said Mr van Reiner, his voice rising in warning. "You must remember where we are. But tell me, how will you cover your tracks? We don't want any difficult questions afterwards, now do we?"

"I'll do it the same way as I always do," said Jerry coolly. "I'll log in remotely with my own security clearance and make the change, but I'll do a bit of housekeeping while

I'm there. Just enough to let the administrators know that I'm doing my job, keeping an eye on things, making sure everything's ticking over nicely. You see, I'm the ghost in the system."

"Good," said Mr van Reiner. "Just so long as you're not getting too clever for your own good. We don't anyone becoming suspicious."

"Like I said," said Jerry, "no one's ever going to know what's happened."

Mr van Reiner allowed himself a smile, satisfied at last. "And your account," he said, "it's all in order, I hope."

"The money's there," said Jerry, trying not to smile himself. The sight of the first payment of £250,000 when it had arrived had taken his breath away even though it was exactly as had been planned. "I'll get the other half when the job's done - when you're finally in-"

"*Shut up!*" Mr van Reiner's eyes flashed dangerously. "Careless words cost lives," he added pointedly. "You should know that by now."

Jerry nodded silently, wondering what became of the boy in the hotel.

"Now, *go*," said Mr van Reiner.

Tom watched the shadowy figures move about on the other side of the glazed glass, then Mr Wheeler accompanied Jerry across the crowded floor and out of the pub. Mr van Reiner and Mr Crane left shortly afterwards. Then, much to Tom's dismay, his shadow banged down its empty pint glass, rumbling ominously from somewhere deep inside its mac, and moved off after them. The young couple, Tom noted as he followed on, would need the pub to fall down on their heads before they took notice of anyone but themselves.

Once outside, Tom kept close behind his shadow, staying out of sight of Mr van Reiner and the bodyguards. They were led through the back streets and shortly turned off a lane and passed up a narrow brick spiral staircase, emerging on the wide pavement of a broad straight road.

When Tom peeped out from behind his shadow again he was amazed to see the coach that had brought him to London parked up on the opposite side of the road. He was first elated, then worried. Now he could rejoin his class, but surely his absence must have been noticed. But there was no time to think on it as his shadow hurried after Mr van Reiner and the bodyguards who strode across the road, passing the coach, and entered St James's Park.

On the far side of the road Tom peeled away from his shadow and joined the end of the queue of children waiting to board the coach. Then, to his astonishment, one of the teachers registered his name and waved him up the steps as if he'd never been away. Quickly he took one of the few remaining seats, then peered out of the window towards the park.

Mr van Reiner and Mr Crane were walking away alongside the lake, but then Tom spotted the other bodyguard retracing his steps, heading back towards the coach. For one awful moment Tom believed that he had been spotted himself and that Mr Wheeler was coming to get him, but, as he looked on, the bodyguard turned aside, crossing the grass towards a tree.

Mr Wheeler approached the tree with great caution. As he came close to the broad trunk he carefully slid a hand inside his jacket, then after a short pause nimbly stepped round the trunk.

Tom was smiling. He had already seen the long mac his shadow had worn hanging from the stub of a broken branch on that side of the trunk. Nudged by a gentle breeze, its hem wafted tantalisingly round the sides of the trunk.

Frowning, the bodyguard removed his hand from his jacket and looked around for the mysterious old man and his boy who he'd seen coming after him and remembered from outside the pub. He glanced up at the coach as the door closed behind the last teacher climbing on board. "Stupid kids," he muttered crossly, then stooped down to poke about amongst the belongings dumped there: a straw hat, colourful sunglasses, a neckerchief, woollen gloves and, strangest of all, two left-footed basketball boots. It was a disguise, he was certain, but where the old man had got to - and what he was now wearing - he had no idea. It was just as if he had vanished into thin air.

The coach pulled away and, leaning back in his seat, Tom let out a great sigh of relief.

There was a great buzz of excitement and much chatter from children and teachers alike as they headed for home and recounted all their stories and discoveries of the day. For Tom, however, it was his first chance to relax and breathe freely again, and there was definitely no one with whom he wished to share his experiences. Instead, as he revived, he reflected on what he'd heard in the pub and began to pull it together with all the other pieces of this intricate puzzle.

So, Jerry worked for the The Eagle Corporation which had produced the new online voting system. He was also working secretly for Mr van Reiner and, from the sound of it, getting paid a lot of money. As Tom had learned earlier at the Hotel Virion, Jerry had already made some sort of change to the system - something to do with an upgrade and a new module. But in the pub Jerry had said that it wouldn't work until he made a final change to a certain file - a 'marker file', if Tom had heard correctly - and the change was planned to take place just before the 'big day'.

Tom smiled to himself. It was obvious what the 'big day' meant. There was only one thing they could have been talking about. The online voting system was for the General Election (his own class had been playing with the demonstration version of it today!) and that would take place on Thursday 27th May - the 'big day'.

So, that was why his shadow had gone to all that trouble of revealing the truth to him about Mr van Reiner. That was why he had endured being threatened and tied up and almost plunging to his death from the roof of the hotel. That was why he had been sneaking round London with his shadow in disguise. *Mr van Reiner was trying to rig the election.* Undoubtedly he wanted the 'ultimate power' for himself.

But one important question still remained. *What did his shadow expect him to do about it now?* If he told anyone he knew about it, who would believe him? The minute he was asked to explain how he had got hold of this incredible information and he responded with tales of climbing up the side of the Hotel Virion at midnight and following his shadow about all over Bellington and London, he'd be laughed at to his face.

He considered giving an anonymous tip-off to the detectives who had visited his father, but, even if he got away with the call not being traced back to him, guessed it could only be treated as a prank call. The police didn't follow up anything unless they had some evidence to back it up.

It was impossible! He slapped a hand against the back of the seat in front and muttered crossly into the shadows at his feet.

"Hey!" called Mike Marshall from across the aisle. "What's up with you?"

"Nothing," said Tom miserably.

"But we thought you were in real trouble back there," said Martin, leering at him excitedly.

"Yeah," said Mike, "Mr Harris looked as if he was going to have a heart attack! We spent ages looking for you. We must have gone round that exhibition a hundred times.

And then you turned up with Shelly like nothing had happened. Where had you been, man?"

Tom stared at them, open-mouthed. "I - I -" he began, but didn't know what to say.

"Oh, so you've lost your memory!" said Martin, laughing as he slapped his twin on the shoulder. "Cool excuse! 'Oh, Mr Harris, I'm so sorry. I met the Prime Minister and then a statue fell on my head and now I can't remember where I've been.' Yeah, yeah, yeah, like he'll ever believe that!"

"That's stupid!" said Tom, then turned away, ignoring their jeers and laughter.

As he looked out of the window he thought hard about what might have happened back in the great hall. His absence had obviously been noticed. Perhaps Mr Harris had taken a register before leaving the Houses of Parliament, he thought. But then what had happened? Somehow Shelly must have covered for him. But *how*, when clearly he hadn't been there? Had someone else been involved, pretending to be him? It was another puzzle that needed to be cracked.

Shortly, when he was sure the twins attention was elsewhere, he cautiously stood up in his seat. He looked up and down the bus for Shelly. He was just about to give up, when, turning round once more, he saw a head pop up towards the back. It was her.

His cheeks flushed.

She gave a big wink

At that moment the twins shot up like gophers out of a hole, looking sharply from Shelly to Tom and back again, then tumbled back onto their seats, poking and prodding each other and laughing til they cried.

Chapter 9 Danger in the East

Shelly's wink and all that lay behind it was one problem. Tom could handle that later. Perhaps he'd even ask her straight about what had happened back there at the exhibition. Perhaps. But there was no way he was going to ask her in front of all those gawping eyes and wagging mouths at school, especially if the Marshall twins were around! (And, though he didn't like to admit even to himself, he was a little worried that the wink might not have anything to do with the exhibition but be one of those soppy ones which girls sometimes gave to boys.) But whatever the wink was about, it could wait for later. The real problem, the one that was raging inside him and wouldn't leave him alone, was what to do about Mr van Reiner and his plan to rig the voting for the General Election.

So, when he finally arrived home at the end of the school trip and his father, over a late and chewy dinner, pummelled him with questions about all that he'd learned, his responses were less than enthusiastic. After admitting that yes, it had been a great day out, most of his responses consisted of one word answers grunted through seemingly endless mouthfuls of the toughest meat pie he'd ever known and a rhubarb crumble that would have served better as a patio slab in the back garden. At least Clara wasn't there, he thought wearily, glad that she'd both eaten earlier and undoubtedly suffered for it.

Later, when he entered his bedroom, he let out a deep sigh and flopped back on his bed. It had been a long and eventful day, and one that seemed unwilling to end until it had the answer to that simple but perplexing question of what he should do next. "Never mind all that history," he murmured, "what about the future?"

It was May 14th. The General Election was only 13 days away. 13, that unlucky number. But who would it be unlucky for: the whole nation for being tricked or Mr van Reiner for being caught?

Again he went through the various people he might tell - his father, Mr Harris, the detectives, even the woman journalist - but the more he thought about it and went over his possible explanations, the more he realised how fanciful his story would sound.

He turned to his shadow on the wall.

"Well, what next?" he said

There was no response

After a restless sleep crowded with dark and fearful dreams, Tom gratefully blinked in the light of the new day. It was Saturday and with no rush to be anywhere else he first resolved to put aside all worries about the General Election. He knew there was nothing he could do on his own and the worrying of itself could get him nowhere. All he had to do now was to avoid his father's ceaseless rantings about all things electoral (the previous agreement for his silence on the matter now somehow forgotten or dismissed), which seemed a much smaller price to pay.

However, with little else to do, it proved more difficult than he thought to put aside the weighty and precious knowledge that he held within. He paced about the house and cycled round the park and slouched about in the back garden, the weekend dragging on interminably. His father told him to rest he looked so pale and drawn. It was probably the effects of the long day in London, he said, and taking in all that information. He didn't know how close he was to the truth.

But late on the Sunday afternoon there was a moment of quiet relief. Tom was out in the back yard, not doing anything in particular, when Rolly appeared in the branches of the pear tree.

"Oh, Rolly, get over here," he called out, stepping towards it. "It's all right. You can stay as long as you like."

Rolly watched him, then looked away again as if interested in something else, then watched him again. Finally he jumped down, landing with a soft thump on the grass. Tom crouched down next to him and immediately he rubbed his chin against his hand and curled round him in an enthusiastic display of affection. He rolled over and purred loudly.

Then Tom noticed that the hand of his shadow was stroking Rolly's soft underbelly, and for a moment he felt terribly anxious because of his shadow's appearance in front of him. Up until now such appearances had led straight on to the most challenging of times, but this time it appeared that his shadow was as relaxed as the cat and was contented enough enjoying the company of both of them. So, for quite a while afterwards, they lounged about together in the grass, at peace with each other and the world around.

Rolly certainly seemed to be enjoying himself, Tom thought, though he guessed that Rolly more than likely had other human friends he buttered up to when he wanted company or food. He had to survive somehow and this, after all, seemed as good a way as any to achieve it.

In the end Tom decided to try to coax Rolly towards the house, stroking him and leading him towards the kitchen door. Rolly followed cautiously, coming as far as the patio, but then pulled back. A second later, after several long strides and nimble jumps, he stood proudly on top of the back wall.

"Another time," said Tom smiling, then the cat was gone.

For the following week Tom remained strangely and wonderfully relaxed, sleeping well and even tackling his Election Project as if it was just another piece of school work. Meanwhile the thorny question of what to do about Mr van Reiner was put aside like a book on the shelf, waiting to be opened, if at all, at a more appropriate time. Even the announcement from his father on the Thursday evening didn't trouble Tom as it normally would have done.

His father, looking cautiously between his two children, told them that they would be spending next week with their mother. It was unusual but was necessary because of all the extra work he had been given, assisting the town council with its arrangements for the General Election. He apologised that it was at such short notice, but then suggested that it wasn't such a bad thing once in a while to spend a bit of extra time with their mother. He finished, more amazingly, by saying that he was certain that they'd have a thoroughly enjoyable time.

Clara, of course, was ecstatic, knowing that for her it meant presents and more spending money and the freedom to do much more of whatever she pleased. At the same time, Tom, who clearly preferred his father's company, could see at least one clear benefit this time around: he wouldn't have to endure any more of his father's endless talks about the election which were worsening as the day drew closer and closer. And his mother, even if she cared about the election, would be far more interested in talking about her business and friends, which, under the circumstances, was a relief to Tom. He could hopefully get through the next week in a state of perfect seclusion, letting the events of the outside world take their own unhappy course.

When Sunday came, Georgie collected the children and took them to their mother's for a slap-up 3-course dinner which no one could have failed to enjoy. Afterwards, everyone crashed out around the apartment, Tom deciding to settle down amongst the Sunday papers spread liberally over the floor of the livingroom. He stretched out his hands and fished in a colour magazine, then, turning on his back, flicked through its pages.

Suddenly his hand hesitated, holding the page open, unable to move on. It was the title of the article in large bold letters that had grabbed his attention: *The Eagle has landed! How The Eagle Corporation is running the General Election.* His stomach gurgled noisily, complaining at the rude interruption, and he flipped onto the next page, hoping to pass swiftly on. But on the next page, where the article continued, he was faced with a large picture of Mr van Reiner and another smartly dressed white-haired businessman, the two of them shaking hands outside the Headquarters of The Eagle Corporation.

In the caption for the picture Tom read that the other man was Freddie Westlake, the Chief Executive of The Eagle Corporation. It also stated that Mr van Reiner, MP for Bellington North, self-made businessman and entrepreneur, was a prime stakeholder in the corporation.

Tom whistled quietly, then, deciding he now needed to read the article, rolled onto his front, spreading it in front of him.

In the article much was made of the historic importance of the move to online voting and the critical importance of The Eagle Corporation in this. In one section questions of security were asked and answered, and in another, the technology behind the system was displayed in diagrams using pictures of computers and clouds and streaks of lightning to show how the nation would connect through the internet to the system. Towards the end of the article the commercial arrangements of The Eagle Corporation were picked over, particularly the investments of Mr van Reiner himself. But he was shown to be whiter than white, having declared his interests both publicly in articles such as this and in the House of Commons' Register as was required in the Members' Code of Conduct.

"It's a strange thing," revealed Mr van Reiner in the article, "but after all my hard work and investment in the corporation I'm still not allowed to go anywhere near the computer systems that it runs! But that just goes to show how good its security is: it's as solid as a rock. And that, by the way, is how I intend to make Britain *Great* again. I will provide rock-solid security for all its people, so that they can get on with their day-to-day business and achieve great things for themselves *and* their country!"

"Yuk!" said Tom, sick at the thought of Mr van Reiner running the country.

There was little else in the article, and Tom's eye soon strayed back to the picture of Mr van Reiner and Freddie Westlake grinning contentedly as they posed for the photograph. And it was then that, looking more closely, he noticed two things. The first, which he had already seen once before on his own computer, were the cufflinks on Mr van Reiner's shirt. This time, however, Tom could see them clearly. They carried the same representation of the pouncing eagle as that of The Eagle Corporation's logo which loomed up large in the shape of a giant sculpture standing on the trim grass mound behind the two businessmen. The second, which drew a gasp from his lips, was the display of words almost hidden from view at the bottom of the sculpture: *The Eagle Corporation Headquarters ~ Bellington East Business Park*. It was here, in Bellington itself.

Rolling onto his back again, the papers crumpling beneath him, he let all this new information sink in. Mr van Reiner wasn't just trying to rig the General Election but was also an owner of the corporation running the online voting system. So, not only was he planning to gain 'ultimate power' but also to make a killing from the success of the corporation through it. It was incredible! Not that the corporation knew about his plans, according to Jerry. And what of Jerry? Now his laptop in the hotel and his visit there made so much more sense, because he only worked a few miles away in Bellington East Business Park.

And in just over 3 days time the country would cast its first votes in the General Election.

"Thomas, darling," said his mother, delicately wading across the sea of papers in her stockinged feet, her high-heeled shoes dangling from one hand, "Georgie and I are just popping out to see a few friends. It's *business* really, but it just has to be done. Can't cancel now, it's been booked for weeks." She rolled her eyes and sighed as if it was a terrible chore, though Tom knew she'd lap up every minute of it. "Anyway, I've given Clara some spending money and here's yours" - the £10 note dangled in front of him - "and we're going to drop you both off in town so you can have some fun there. How about that, then?"

"Okay," said Tom, trying to put a brave face on it.

Soon, they were in the Mercedes, smoothly travelling towards the centre of town.

"You've got a couple of hours before the shops start to close," said their mother from the front seat, "and then you can get the bus back. Clara's got the key, haven't you, dear? We should be back before you go to bed, whatever time that is nowadays!"

She winked at them, then smiled excitably at Georgie, looking forward to their social outing. Tom glanced gloomily at Clara, noting that she couldn't stop smiling too now that she was going shopping again.

Shortly, Tom and Clara were walking towards the main shopping centre, the Mercedes driving off behind them.

"Do you *have* to take that grotty little bag with you everywhere you go?" said Clara, glancing hatefully at the grey backpack.

"It's useful," said Tom, hunching up his shoulders protectively.

"It's *ugly*," said Clara. "It's dull. It's unclean. And I don't think it's ever been washed. I bet it stinks."

"Here," said Tom, suddenly swinging it off his shoulders and towards her head, "why don't you have a sniff?"

"Get it away from me!" she cried out, fending it off with her hand. "Are you crazy? You could have injured me!"

"Second time lucky," he said, whirling it round his head ready for the next attempt, but she slapped him across the ear and he reeled backwards.

"Keep your bag to yourself!" she spat, then went to grab the £10 note out of his hand, saying, "And *I'll* look after that."

"No way!" he said, dodging her lunge, then stepped back again and followed her at a safe distance behind.

For the next hour they traipsed round the shops, wandering up and down the covered arcades and open malls, touching on what seemed like every glitzy clothes shop in town. Tom groaned and yawned and threatened to go off on his own back to their mother's *or* their father's house, anything to get away from Clara's obsessive hunt for those cheap fashion accessories. He felt duty bound to remind her how selfish he thought she was, though she largely ignored him, concentrating on the far more important work of expanding her own wardrobe. She didn't really care what he did and from time to time reminded him of this with icy clarity.

With only one hour to go and Clara well into her stride, Tom felt a familiar tug on his ankles. He knew what it was, but for several moments simply stopped and watched his sister disappearing through the crowds of shoppers, glad at last to see the back of her. However, he also knew what that tug was likely to mean and, with some trepidation, forced himself to look down.

Immediately his shadow set off towards the busy road at the end of the wide mall. Then, with his mind already made up, Tom set off after it, ready to finish off the business they had started together, whatever that might mean.

As soon as they reached the end of the mall his shadow crossed the 6 lanes of traffic, passing straight under the lorries and cars, heading towards the line of bus-stops on the far side. Tom gave a shrug of his shoulders as if to ask his shadow what it expected him to do when he was made of flesh and blood, then waited for the lights to change before crossing with the hordes of shoppers weighed down by their heavy bulging bags.

Once over the road, Tom searched for his shadow amongst the people jostling for position at the various bus-stops. A couple of buses pulled away, one after the other, then another drew up. Tom, looking round helplessly, was ready to abandon whatever crazy mission his shadow had in mind and take a ride home, but then, looking once more, he spotted his shadow at the back on the last bus to pull up.

The last passenger stepped on board and, running after him, Tom got on the bus too.

"Where are you going?" said the driver, waiting for Tom's request.

Tom stared at him blankly, then said clumsily, "Where - where are you going?"

Tom cheeks reddened and the driver, frowning, ran his hand over his stubbly chin.

"East Bellington," said the driver gruffly.

For a second Tom stared back at the driver, this time with a startled look as he realised that this bus would take him to the Bellington East Business Park and the Headquarters of The Eagle Corporation.

"Are you coming?" said the driver impatiently.

"Oh, yes," said Tom, "definitely," though he didn't look so certain.

"That's £1.90."

Tom pulled out the crumpled £10 note from his pocket and offered it to the driver, but he shook his head unhappily.

"We don't give change," said the driver, "so unless you want me to have all of that you'd better find the right amount."

Quickly thinking again, Tom twisted out of his backpack then hunted around in the inside pocket for whatever change there might be. He pulled out two £1 coins and handed them over.

"Okay," said the driver with a deep sigh, then punched a ticket out of the coin machine.

After tearing off his ticket, Tom made his way down the aisle, avoiding the frowns of the waiting passengers. When he got to the back he was surprised to see a rather large woman sitting where his shadow had been, and then he saw his shadow peeping out from behind her and waving its arms as if it was suffocating under her great weight. He smiled, but then noticed the woman scowling back at him and retreated to a bench further up the aisle where he settled down.

As the journey out of the centre of Bellington progressed he tried not to think of what might lie ahead. Instead, he looked out of the window, watching the office blocks and hotels turn into shops and then the shops turn into row after row of housing and then the houses finally dwindle down to almost nothing at all. By then the large woman had struggled up the aisle, bashing her bags against everyone she passed, and got off the bus. It wasn't long afterwards that the bus turned right at a roundabout and immediately pulled into a lay-by. Two passengers got off - the last ones except for Tom - and the driver placed his paper across the steering-wheel and started to read it. It was the end of the route.

Tom looked to the back of the bus, but his shadow was gone. Then he peered out of the window and spotted it waiting on the pavement at the end of the lay-by. He got off the bus and joined it.

"So, what now?" he said warily, and his shadow set off down the road. "Silly question," he told himself, setting off after it. "It's going to be trouble!"

Staggered along either side of the road were the entrances to various low office blocks and warehouses and industrial units. Each had its own barriers and car parks and grassy surrounds. Tom hurried along behind his shadow which was moving at quite a pace. He glanced across at the businesses on either side of the road, then, when the road was coming to a dead-end, strode across the entrance to The Eagle Corporation.

He recognised it immediately from the photograph in the colour magazine. Beyond the Security booth with its barriers he could see the sculpture of the pouncing eagle on its grassy mound and behind that the dark blue glass of the 3-storey building which was the Headquarters of the Eagle Corporation itself. The car park wrapped round both sides of the building, a small number of cars still dotted around it. Enclosing the whole of it was a circle of straight high poplar trees, standing to attention like soldiers on guard, keeping it well out of sight.

Through the shaded glass of the Security booth Tom glimpsed a movement - a man in a white shirt, he thought - and instantly looked away again. His shadow walked straight past the entrance, even though the road was coming to an end, and he hurried to catch up with it.

"You've missed it!" he gasped, but then it turned sharply to the left and started round the back of the poplar trees.

He entered the overgrown lane, then trotted after his shadow as it swept along behind the poplars. Between the trunks he glimpsed the looming dark blue building and shortly they stopped directly behind it.

"Any chance of finding out what's happening next?" said Tom, breathing hard as he tucked himself down behind a trunk.

Silence.

"I thought that might be your answer," he said, trying to raise a smile, despite the fear that was rising inside him. "I just wondered," he went on, "how you expect us to get past all that security that's in there. There's bound to be masses of it. I saw the security guard at the front as well. Any ideas?"

There was a pause, then his shadow's voice came from somewhere inside him.
"Come."

Chapter 10 Shots in the Dark

On the other side of the poplar trees was a wire fence. It was over 2 metres high and along its top edge that jutted outwards were coils of razor-wire. Any branch that had strayed too close to it had been lopped back to the trunk. Tom's shadow slid up to the fence, rose up its front, then spread out its hands and drew them straight back down to the ground. Then he watched in amazement as it peeled up the cut fence from the bottom and held it open for him.

"You need to get those finger nails cut," he whispered, then taking a deep breath, rushed out from behind the trunk and scrambled through the opening.

On the other side he squatted down on the grass verge. Directly ahead was a short road sweeping round the back of the building, passing from one side of the car park to the other. At the back of the building was the faint outline of a door made of the same dark blue glass. Then, looking up, he saw the dark glass bubbles of CCTV cameras positioned at regular intervals along the edge of the roof.

He felt himself start to panic, realising that he could be spotted at any moment, if he hadn't been already. But before he could even think of what to do, the strangest of sensations came over him.

It started like an icy chill spreading over his skin, giving him goose-bumps all over, and then the world started to turn grey before his eyes. It seemed as if the sun was being eclipsed and a great shadow was passing over the world, the temperature dropping rapidly beneath it. He cried out in alarm, but his voice was muffled as if he was under water with every sound trapped in a bubble floating off in the wrong direction.

"Don't be afraid," said his shadow, its voice now resonating close all around him. "I will carry you."

Standing up, he stared at his arms and legs. They were encased in the greyness of his shadow. He was actually inside it, the whole of him, and still able to breathe.

"Ready?"

"I think so."

Suddenly, stretched as thin as a sheet of paper, he flew across the grass, the road and in an instant snapped to a halt pressed up against the back of the building itself.

"Way to go," he said, trembling and laughing at the same time, "way to go!"

In the Surveillance Unit on the first floor of the Headquarters, Andy Stevens, the Security Manager, sat in front of a bank of 24 monitors stacked 3 rows high. He flicked down the list of security checks on his clipboard, reminding himself of the timetable for the night ahead. Dave Bryant, one of the two other Security Guards on duty, pottered about at the back of the room.

"So, do you or don't you want a cuppa?" said Dave, pulling out an electric kettle from under one of the computer desks where it was stashed in defiance of the Health and Safety reminders issued at regular intervals.

Suddenly something dark swept across one of the screens. Andy visibly stiffened, leaning forwards in his seat. "Hang on a sec," he murmured, looking from one screen to the next.

"What is it?" said Dave, pulling out a couple of mugs from a drawer and secretly hoping it was nothing at all.

"I don't know," said Andy, "but there was definitely something at the back of the building."

"A car?"

"No, I'd have picked it up on the other monitors. It could've been a shadow from something overhead, but it's not a bright day out there."

"How about one of those plastic bags floating about?" said Dave. "They can mess up the view."

"Maybe," said Andy, starting to relax again.

"Good," said Dave heartily, "because we could do with a quiet night. Now, do you want one or don't you?"

"What's that? Oh, yeah. I'll have a-"

"Yes?"

"Hang on," said Andy, leaning forwards again. "One of the screens has just blacked out."

While one of the hands of Tom's shadow smothered the glass bowl of the CCTV camera above the door at the back of the building, its other hand squeezed through the impossible gap at the edge of the door, felt up and down the wall inside, then pressed the smooth round release button. There was a clunk as the lock pulled back, then the door nudged open.

"*Now what?*" said Andy.

A green light winked beneath the blacked out screen, indicating that the door it was covering had been opened properly, then that screen came back on while another one blacked out. Meanwhile, Dave spooned a heaped teaspoon of instant coffee into one of the mugs, trying not to get distracted from what he considered was a far more important task.

"Which door?" Dave asked tentatively.

"At the rear."

"Green light?"

"Yeah. But I can't see what's going on with these screens blacking out."

"But if it's green," said Dave, dropping 4 teaspoonfuls of sugar into his mug, "then there's no problem. Right?"

Andy didn't respond, unable to accept so simplistic an explanation, and then exclaimed, "*What was that?*"

Dave frowned and shook his head, wondering how long Andy would last in this business when he was so edgy all the time.

"I saw something move," said Andy excitably, "like that shadow outside. And now look! Another screen's blacked out."

Pursing his lips, Dave concentrated on pouring the boiling water from the kettle into the mug. Everyday tasks carried their own risks and he didn't want to get distracted unnecessarily. "How many screens are down?" he asked, trying to show some interest.

"Don't ask me!" said Andy, ruffling his hair in exasperation. "They're going up and down like yo-yo's."

"Try turning the lot off," said Dave, adding a splash of milk to the mug with an artistic flourish of his hand. "It's probably an internal fault. That usually fixes it."

Andy hesitated, sighed, then reached across the desk for the master power button. All the screens blacked out together. He waited no more than a few seconds then pressed the button again. As he watched the screens, all of them came on. Not one was blacked out.

"Well, I'll be damned!" said Andy.

"Cheers," said Dave, grinning as he raised the mug to his lips.

The ground floor was like a maze with concentric rectangles of offices and workshops joined by short links. The links were the only points not covered by the CCTV cameras and it was in one of these that Tom, caught in the body of his shadow that was pressed back against a wall, now stood. He looked around from inside it with complete freedom, though everything outside was skewed and fluid, slowly pitching about and stretching in different directions. It was a dizzying effect but without the sickly feeling that would normally accompany it. There was a sound, too, that had grown rapidly from the time they had set off together. It had started like the distant beating of a drum, but now was booming so loud that he could actually feel the tremors from it. Like thunder rolling it, it felt like trouble ahead.

"Are you all right?" said Tom quietly (though he was certain that his voice could not be heard outside his shadow).

"Never felt better," said his shadow in a weak frail voice such as he'd never heard before.

"Sure?"

"Sure."

There was a pause.

"Hadn't we better get going, then?" said Tom.

A ripple of laughter bubbled up inside the greyness. "After you," said his shadow.

He laughed too.

Then suddenly, its insides raging louder than ever, they flew into the inner corridor like a streak of dark lightening,

"Oh God!" groaned Andy. "They're blacking out again."

"I can still make you one," said Dave, ever hopeful that he might be able to distract his boss and restore some calm, "the water's just boiled."

"No!" snapped Andy, then went on, "Inner North's gone. Will someone just tell me what's going on here?"

"Front or rear?"

"Rear. Why?"

"Oh, probably nothing," said Dave, laughing it off.

"*Why?*"

"Well," said Dave, sucking in a deep breath, "whatever's happening, it does seem to be working its way round the building. It's just a thought."

Andy turned back to the screens, watching them intently. One blacked out screen flickered back into life, then, a second or two later, another faded to grey before blacking out altogether. He checked their locations: they were on the same corridor.

"I think you're right," said Andy.

"Did you see a hand reaching up there?" said Dave hesitantly, squinting at the screens as he came closer.

"That shadow."

"Yeah."

Both of them, unblinking, waited for whatever would come next.

Tom's shadow, visibly trembling, stood in the entrance to a large doorway at the heart of the building. The only marking on the door was the label GF21. There was no window to see inside. On the wall was the black box of a retinal scanner, the highest level of security in the building. The shadow staggered forwards, then stretched itself up, holding its face against the scanner.

Tom felt a cold sweat beading over his forehead. The noise inside his shadow was deafening: it felt as if it was about to erupt like a volcano, blowing itself into a million pieces. It slipped down, its legs giving way, but then slowly recovered itself. Tom looked straight ahead, his eye looking through its eye, staring into the darkened glass bottom of the scanner.

A red spot lit up. The slender thread of a laser zigzagged over the shadow's eye and Tom glimpsed the faint outline of someone else's face etched in the momentary glow. A moment later a woman's disjointed voice issued a recorded message.

"Security clearance approved for - Jerry Paul."

A loud buzz and clunk signalled the unlocking of the door.

Tom's shadow, moving uncertainly, dragged open the door then staggered inside.

The door clunked shut.

The shadow collapsed on the floor.

A green light winked beneath one of the monitors in the Surveillance Unit.

"It's the Computer Centre," said Andy in the uneasy hush. "Someone's gone in."

"The light's green, though," said Dave. "It has to be one of our staff."

"Never mind that," said Andy, "I want you to go down and check who's there. Right now."

The mug stopped half-way to Dave's mouth and he frowned, but then his eyes lit up again.

"Wait a moment," he said, setting off towards the computer desks. "Let's take a look at the logs. That'll give us a name."

"Well?" said Andy impatiently.

"Hang on," said Dave. "Ah, here we are: Access log, Computer Centre…and at the end of the list…none other than…*Mister Jerry Paul!*"

"Right," said Andy. "Now get down there and give me a positive ID."

"Better still," said Dave, grinning and showing his mobile, "I'll give him a ring."

Tom spilled out onto the floor. It took him several seconds to regain his sense of balance and stand up; he felt like a spaceman returning to the heaviness of the earth's atmosphere after the weightlessness of space. He was at the edge of an expansive windowless room. Flooded with white light it had the sanitised look of a surgical theatre. Directly ahead, at its centre, was a corral of metal cupboards surrounding a suite of computer desks. Stretching out to either end of the room were row upon row of tall computer cabinets glowing from the hundreds of LED's flickering furiously inside them.

He turned and saw his shadow. It lay crumpled on the smooth vinyl floor. Except for its heavy panting, it didn't move at all. He stepped over to it and, crouching down, reached out a hand to it. Against his skin he felt the soft coolness of its body and the labouring of its heart from within.

"What's wrong?" he said. "Can't you get up? What do I do next? I need your help."

Very slowly its dark head lifted and for the first time he heard its voice out loud.

"I had to carry you," it said breathlessly, adding with a weak chuckle, "and you're quite heavy."

"I'm not that bad," he said quietly. "You should try lifting Clara."

"You must do this on your own now," it went on shortly. "I have brought you this far, but I cannot go on. You must stop this evil."

"But-"

"Go now. There isn't long."

"Okay," he said, biting his lip. "I'll try."

"He's not answering," said Dave with a weary sigh. "It's going through to his voicemail."

"Right," said Andy smartly, "get down there."

"*Yes, sir*," said Dave, flicking him a mock salute, but once outside he sauntered along, taking his time.

Just because the mobile wasn't being answered, he thought, didn't mean that Jerry wasn't in the Computer Centre. In fact, it made it even more likely that he *was* there. The only reason he wouldn't be picking up while he was on-call was because he was out of range and it was well know that the reinforced steel walls of the Computer Centre blocked all mobile reception. But with Andy as stressed as he was, it was no good arguing. This was going to be a wasted journey - much the same as the rest of his coffee was wasted - when what was actually needed was an overhaul of the CCTV cameras that were clearly playing up.

"Idiot!" he muttered, kicking at his heels.

But then, catching sight of a movement from the corner of his eye, he drew to a halt.

"Hello there, handsome," said Amy, the cleaner, lolling back against the wall of the link between the corridors. "What's bugging you, then?"

"Oh, nothing much," said Dave, smiling, then, after glancing about him, hopped across. "Taking a break, are you?"

"I've finished the Training Suites," she said. "All I've got now are the offices and toilets."

"Marvellous," he said, "someone with a plan. That's what I like to see." He stepped a little closer. "And how are *you* keeping, my pretty little thing?"

Tom didn't know what he was going to do. He didn't want to leave his shadow, either. It looked as if it might never recover. But somehow he forced himself away. It was up to him now to finish this task.

He crossed quickly to the computer desks and, sitting at one, brought up the login box. His heart raced as he typed in the same username he'd seen on the laptop at the hotel: *paulj999*. He followed this with the obvious password, 'Password', but it was rejected. He tried 'Jerry', then 'Election', guessing wildly, but before he could try again another box flashed up announcing that the account had been locked and the system administrator must be contacted for assistance.

Tom slapped his hands down on the keyboard, the rattle from the keys sounding louder than it should have in the hush of the room. "Come on, come on!" he urged himself. "You've got to work this out!"

Getting up again, he left the corral and went over to the nearest row of cabinets. They were all locked. He looked for handles on their doors, but there were none. Then, leaning his whole weight against one, he tried to force it over. But it was useless. More than a metre taller than him, it was weighed down with computer equipment and bolted to the floor. He fell back, gasping, then kicked out at it, his trainer thumping against the thick glass of its door. Rows of LED's winked back from behind the solid protection.

"Come on! Think, think, *think.*"

Skidding back to the computer desks, he pulled open the drawers, spilling out pens, paper-clips, DVD's, envelopes and other assorted stationery. Then he turned to the metal cupboards encircling the desk. The first few were locked, but soon a handle turned and the door clanged open. Inside were large boxes of paper and stacks of empty files - more stationery - and the next cupboard was no better, its shelves lined with hefty lever-arch files, the spines of which bore such riveting titles as *Computer Centre 1 Procedures Vol 3 Ver 4.5.*

The next few cupboards were locked and he was about to give up on them when one more opened. On its top shelf were plastic boxes brimming with network cables of various colours - red, blue, green, yellow - their plastic connectors poking out over the rims like snakes from a pit. On the next shelf were boxes containing power leads, adaptors and other electrical equipment. The shelf below held a variety of spares from the cabinets: thin and thick metal chassis stacked loosely as well as a scattering of motherboards and drives. Then his eyes came across a toolbox standing by itself at the bottom of the cupboard. Left lying on top of it was a plastic bag stuffed full of keys.

"*Yes!*"

He snatched up the bag and held it close to his face. The keys were labelled, each bearing its own ID. He smiled, then hauled out the toolbox. He unclipped its lid and spread open its multi-layered trays. He selected a screwdriver, wire cutters, a spanner and, feeling most useful, a weighty hammer.

Hurrying back to the cabinets, he stopped in front of one found the ID at the top of its frame. He dug into the bag until he found the right key. Trying to stop his hand shaking, he wiggled the key into the lock, then turned it and swung back the door.

The contents of the cabinet was a precise arrangement in a number of layers of sophisticated electronic and electrical equipment, their phenomenal activity shown only by the flicker of the LED's and the hum of the cooling fans. Leaving the tools and bag of keys on the floor, he ran his hands up and down the smooth hard front of the equipment, wondering how it all worked.

When his fingers touched on the ridged surface of a row of black plastic clasps, he brought his face closer, noticing how they were paired with another row directly below. Using the fingers of both hands he pulled back on one pair of clasps together. Stiffly the clasps opened, levering the motherboard they were attached to out of its slot in the chassis. He pulled again and this time the motherboard slid out completely.

LED's turned red, while others flashed intensely. The wounded system was working harder to repair itself.

The motherboard dropped to the floor. He took the hammer and hit it as hard as he could, cracking it in several places. A second strike saw sharp splinters flying off. The third was for his own personal satisfaction. This motherboard wasn't going back into service. *Ever*.

With his heart pumping hard and new visions of reporters announcing the death of the online voting system, he took hold of the next pair of clasps and rapidly freed its motherboard.

"Let's see you win the election with this then, Mr van Reiner!" he said, laughing as he dropped the motherboard to the floor then pounced on it with the hammer.

The radio on Dave's belt bleeped, crackled, then spoke. The voice was unmistakeable. "Dave. Pick this up. This is urgent."

Dave placed his forefinger gently over Amy's lips. He winked then mimed the name of his boss. Plucking the radio from his belt, he pressed the button on its side. "Andy, this is Dave. What's up?"

"Get back here straight away. Don't go near the Computer Centre."

Andy's voice sounded angry, even over the crackly line. "Is there something I should know?" said Dave cautiously. The crackling continued for some seconds before Andy answered again.

"I tried Jerry at home," he said sharply. "He's there. His mobile *was* turned off."

Dave swallowed drily. "So, who's-?"

"Never mind that! It's a lock-down. Silent - no alarms. Now get back here - *straight away*."

"Sure," said Dave, "I'm on my way."

"More troubles?" said Amy after he'd returned the radio to his belt.

"Forget the rest of the cleaning," he said, looking unusually pale as he set off out of the link, "there's been a break-in."

Andy slammed his radio down on the desk, cursing loudly. He was furious with Dave for being wrong about the mobile and because he knew that he'd never got anywhere near the Computer Centre, undoubtedly idling about the place in his usual disinterested way. But even harder to bear was the fact that his own manager, Roland Bates, had called him as soon as the lock-down was implemented and ordered him to remain where he was.

"What do you mean?" Andy had said unable to believe what he was hearing. "I've got to find out what's going on down there. There's an intruder in the Computer Centre. Anything could be happening down there!"

"Cool it!" said Roland sharply. "A specialist unit is on its way. You're job now is to keep a steady head and maintain the lock-down. You can do that, can't you?"

"Of course I can."

"Okay, then," said Roland, "and you'll need to keep the police out of it, at least until our guys have finished their business. They'll need to clear this up before the police get a whiff of it. We can't afford bad publicity at this stage. How do you think this would look if it got out only 3 days before the General Election?"

"The police must be on their way here by now," said Andy. "It's an automated response from Police Headquarters when the lock-down starts. It was the same call that you got."

"Okay, okay, I know all that," said Roland, sounding more than a little frustrated, "but you *must* hold them back. I don't care what it takes. We don't want anything messy waved in front of their faces. This could be internal - one of our own staff - and that would cause us a hell of a lot of damage. Make excuses, do whatever you have to, just keep them out of it until our guys have mopped up the mess."

"Sure," said Andy, unable to hide his disgust.

"Look," said Roland, "I know you don't like these guys muscling in on your operation, but that's just the way it has to be. Understood?"

"Sure," he said again and hung up.

Afterwards he wondered who'd been pulling Roland's strings. His boss hadn't made those decisions on his own. But he'd probably never know the answer, and so, reluctantly, continued with the lock-down procedures. It was then that he called back Dave and phoned the Security Booth at the main entrance to inform Mike, the other member of his team, of what was happening, including the arrival of the so called specialist unit.

Now the general internal phone rang out. He went over and picked it up, then listened to a garbled message from the

Development Centre asking if anyone knew why the live system was running so slow.

"Yes, yes, sure I hear what you're saying," said Andy furiously, "but what do you want *me* to do about it? I'm not a computer engineer, for God's sake, I'm the Security Manager!"

He slammed the phone down and cursed again, knowing that whoever it was down in the Computer Centre had already got to work and seemed to be putting their back into it. It took a lot to get the computer boffins so stirred up that they phoned Security for help. And here he was, ordered to stay put, waiting for the 'specialists' to arrive too late to do anything about it.

The door opened and in walked Dave.

"Sorry about the mobile," he said meekly, then ducked sharply as the mug of coffee flew straight past his head and smashed against the wall.

Tom had not only discovered what he had to do, but taken to it with an energy and passion that totally consumed him. His skill in the art of destruction was improving by the minute. Each new cabinet was torn open like a glimmering present on Christmas morning and like the best of presents each seemed to reveal something new and exciting. All the tools he had selected were put to good use. Wires, cut or ripped out, hung like loose spaghetti from top to bottom of the cabinets; motherboards, bent and broken, leaned out from their slots in the chassis or lay like so many bodies scattered across the floor, victims of the shoe or the hammer or both; unplugged power leads dangled away from their sockets; keyboards grinned toothlessly and darkened screens and LCD's, broken inwards like the sunken sockets of the blind, glared out hopelessly; whole chassis like carcasses from a wild game hunt cluttered the floor, abandoned where they had toppled::

this was an untidy graveyard in memory of the latest in hi-tec computing.

But despite his zeal and hard work, Tom had only tackled two full rows out of the ten in the room.

At one point, pausing to draw breath, he noticed a red light flashing above the entrance to the room. He guessed it was a general alarm and smiled at what was surely a measure of his success. But it also reminded him that his presence by now must have been noticed and time was fast running out.

"Shadow! Are you there?" he called out, then quickly picked his way to the end of the row of desecrated cabinets and peered towards the entrance.

His shadow was nowhere to be seen.

"Where are you?" he said, hurrying to the spot where it had laid. "We've got to get out of here! We've got to go *now*."

He hunted through the debris on the floor and around the computer desks in the corral, anywhere it might have crawled away to hide. But it could not be found. Then, thinking of his own escape, he returned to the entrance.

A sickly feeling swelled in the pit of his stomach as he looked at the black box on the wall next to the door. A retinal scanner was used to get out as well as to get in and without his shadow with him there was no way past it.

Panting hard and covered in cold sweat, he felt a furious panic start to take hold of him. It could only be a matter of minutes before the security guards came to get him. But then, as he forced himself to accept his fate, a new and stronger determination flooded through him. He turned back towards the cabinets. There was just enough time to deal one last blow to the plans of Mr van Reiner.

Collecting his tools and the bag of keys, he passed across to the next row of cabinets. But this time, instead of attacking the first cabinet he came to, he walked swiftly along the row, carefully seeking out his next victim. Then, at the far end of the row, he came across a broad grey cabinet with metal vented sides and no glass doors.

Soon he found its key and opened its double doors.

Thick black cables coiled up out of the floor beneath its base like giant snakes rising from the deep. Constrained by plastic ties, they were directed to one central box. On top of the box, on one side, was a control panel and, on the other side, twelve large black switches. Below the control panel was a printed metal sheet with red lightening bolts, text and diagrams. It described how this cabinet was the main power source for every other part of the room.

It was all he needed to know.

One by one he pushed up each switch into the 'Off' position.

Across the room more LED's lit up as the battery backups kicked in, supplying precious minutes of extra power while the whole system automatically shut itself down. Soon the room was alive with flickering lights, green melting to red, like a magical hushed firework display.

Retracing his steps to one of the fallen rows, he searched across the floor for a dismantled chassis that was neither too light nor too heavy, then carried it back to the power cabinet. Turning it in his hands he found a better grip, then lifted it above his head and hurled it forwards. The control panel shattered with a small bang and a splutter of sparks.

Stepping back out of the way, he laughed out loud.

But then, as he stood wondering what he could do next, suddenly the room was plunged into darkness

In the darkness the red light above the entrance flashed out its warning even more strongly, while the hundreds of LED's across the room died away like the scattered embers of a fire.

Tom, hiding behind the door of the power cabinet with his heart hammering hard, waited for whatever might come next.

A heavy clunk came from the door at the entrance as it unlocked. Moments later footsteps echoed across the floor and thin beams of white light strafed the room, sometimes criss-crossing each other, restlessly seeking out their prey.

"We know you're in here," said the instantly recognisable voice of Geoffrey, cutting through the tense silence. "You can't get out. There's no escape. If you give yourself up now, I promise you won't be harmed."

Tom, crouching down and breathing through his mouth, tried not to make a sound.

"But if you don't do as I say," continued Geoffrey, "then I cannot guarantee your safety."

Tom didn't believe a word. Then, as soon as the beams of light passed by the cabinet once more, he made a run for it. But as he launched out his shoulder caught against the cabinet door and, as his body twisted round, he tripped over the chassis on the floor.

The two bodyguards quickly redirected themselves towards the commotion, speaking quietly through their headsets.

"Towards you," said .Mr Crane, swinging his gun-mounted torch from side to side as he stepped cautiously down a row of cabinets, carefully avoiding the larger debris scattered about the floor.

"Roger," said Mr Wheeler. "Moving in."

But when the bodyguards reached the power cabinet, the intruder was no longer there.

Tom, having scuttled away from where he fell, now stood with his back pressed up against the cabinet at the far end of the row. With a clear view of the entrance he could see that the door was slightly ajar, the light from outside peeping in along its edge. There was no sign of Geoffrey, and the bodyguards, their torch beams sweeping from behind, were still at the power cabinet.

With every flash of the red light above the entrance, Tom's face glowed a lurid red.

Suddenly, with a loud gasp that he immediately regretted, he thrust himself away from the cabinet and made a dash for the door.

The white beams stuttered to a halt, then each flew down the sides of a separate row of cabinets. Finally they came together again across the back of the boy fleeing for his life.

Tom ran on, only a second or two from escape, glimpsing his two new shadows splashed over the wall ahead of him.

Two red dots locked on his back. The bodyguards, their orders clear, tensed, ready to shoot.

Suddenly a dark figure jumped up behind Tom.

"Two targets," growled Mr Wheeler.

"Roger," said Mr Crane.

Two shots cracked loudly, one directly after the other. Afterwards was a chilling silence.

"Moving in," said Mr Wheeler, stepping cautiously forwards, his gun still held at the ready.

"Covering you," said Mr Crane.

There was a long pause after Mr Wheeler reached the target, then his voice, strained and nervous, crackled in Mr Crane's earpiece. "There's only one here. Can't see the other. But - but this one - it's - it's-"

"It's *what*? *What's going on*?"

"It's the boy," said Mr Wheeler. "We've shot the boy."

Mr Crane, swinging his gun from side to side, hurried forwards. Then, after a final check for the other target, he told Mr Wheeler to cover him and stooped down beside the body of the boy.

The boy was lying face down, two bullet holes in his back. The bodyguard pressed two fingertips against his neck, feeling for a pulse. But there was none. The boy's flesh already felt cold. A pool of blood oozed out from beneath him.

As Mr Crane stood up again the lighting for the room flickered on once more and Geoffrey marched in through the door, brandishing the flick-knife in front of him, his eyes hungry and hateful.

"My little trap with the open door worked, then," he said, "even if you did beat me to it! So, who've we got?"

"It's that boy," said Mr Wheeler hesitantly, "the same one who was at the school and the hotel. It's him."

"Are you sure?"

Mr Wheeler stepped back from the body, making space for Geoffrey.

Geoffrey stooped down and peered at the grey blotchy face of the boy, then slowly stood up again.

"It's a shame, really," he said sadly, then suddenly started laughing and added, "because I really wanted to get him myself!"

Chapter 11 The Missing Body

"Okay, now get him out of here," said Geoffrey. "Put him in one of those computer packing boxes I've seen around and then clear up this mess."

"We saw a second target," said Mr Wheeler, but the other bodyguard cut in before Geoffrey had a chance to respond.

"It couldn't have been," said Mr Crane. "It was just a shadow. Maybe from one of those doors hanging open. We had two shots on target and if there had been someone else standing behind him they'd be lying there now. Dead."

"Okay, okay," said Geoffrey impatiently, "there clearly isn't a second target. *Fine.* Now find a box and a mop and get on with clearing this up! We have a dead boy here and unless you want to explain it to the police in person then you'd better get a move on and shift him out of here. There's to be no traces left. No blood. No cartridges. *Nothing.* And the rest of this mess," he added, winking mischievously as he waved a hand towards the wrecked rows of cabinets, "our dear friend Jerry can sort out on in the morning."

The two bodyguards, suitably roused, moved off with a quiet efficiency, while Geoffrey stepped gingerly round the body, taking care not to get any of the darkening blood on his shoes, and strode out of the Computer Centre. The flick-knife was folded away and pocketed and, once outside, he speed-dialled Andy on his mobile. The response was panicky.

"Okay, I hear you," said Geoffrey. "Stay calm. You're in charge up there, not the police. Remember that. Keep your voice steady and, if you're asked, you're speaking to one of your own men down here. Got it?"

"Yes, sure," said Andy, then, remembering the instruction, added promptly, "Thanks, Mike."

"That's much better," said Geoffrey with a sly grin. "Now, you've got to buy me at least another ten minutes. I don't care what you tell them, but if they get past you then you're going to have a lot of explaining to do. More than you'd ever want, believe me. After that bring them down yourself. There's quite a mess down here. It'll be interesting to see what they make of it Remember, ten minutes, no sooner. Understood?"

"Okay, Mike," said Andy, raising his voice for the benefit of the policemen standing near him. "Thanks for the report. Carry on with the patrol of the grounds and let me know if you do find anything."

"Ten minutes," repeated Geoffrey quietly, then cut the call.

As Andy slipped the mobile back into his pocket, one of the two detectives waiting in the Surveillance Unit spoke.

"Is that usual?" said DI Reever

"What do you mean?" said Andy, trying not to look worried.

"Is it usual," he said wearily, "for one of your guards to phone you on your mobile? Isn't that what your radios are for?"

"Oh, yes, I see what you mean," said Andy, prodding the radio on his belt as if it was a long lost friend and chuckling nervously. "No, we use mobiles, radios, land-lines, whatever's nearest to hand at the time. Whatever works, actually. The reception can be terrible around here. It's the building, you see. It has steel walls in places. For the highest security. But I'm sure you know all about that."

"We do," said DS Brown, "but we don't quite understand what's going on here. You said you initiated the lock-down then tried to cancel the automated call to Police Headquarters, believing it was all a mistake. *Your* mistake, you said."

"Yes, that's right," said Andy, leaning back against a desk but misjudging the distance and thumping into it. "I - I panicked. I admit it. There were some unusual problems with the CCTV cameras - or the monitors, I'm not sure which. Anyway, after the lock-down started, I wasn't sure about it any more."

"So, you phoned up Police Headquarters and tried to stop the call out. But by then it was already underway."

"Yes, it seems so."

"We're doing a good job then, responding so promptly!" said DS Brown, wearing a forced smile as he stepped up close and stared in his face.

"Yes, very good, detective, very good indeed."

"And then your man at the entrance turned away the officers when they arrived."

"Yes. As I told you, I thought they weren't needed."

"But now you're telling us that you *do* think the police might be needed," said DI Reever sharply, glancing back from another corner of the room as he continued his search.

"Well, perhaps," said Andy, his eyes flicking nervously between the two of them, "but we won't know until our own search of the site has been completed."

DI Reever sighed, shaking his head, then stopped alongside the bank of monitors. "Well, while we're waiting you won't mind if we take a look at the recordings from your CCTV cameras, will you? You do have recordings, don't you?"

"Yes, yes, of course," said Andy, then added in a hurry, "but I'll need to get authorisation from Mr Bates first."

"Your manager?"

"Yes."

"Okay. But do remind him that there's the small problem of the General Election this week," said DI Reever, barely able to disguise his anger, "*and this is a matter of national security.* We'd be greatly obliged by his co-operation."

"Yes, I'll call straight away. He *is* well aware of the importance of the situation."

DI Reever ignored the response from the incompetent Security Manager, instead jabbing his forefinger on the button of one of the monitors. The screen remained stubbornly blank as did a number of the others when he tried them too.

"Why aren't these working?" he said.

"I'm not sure," said Andy, pausing with his mobile half way to his ear.

"You're not sure?" barked DS Brown, looking at him in disbelief.

"I told you," said Andy, "it's these faults we've been having. I don't know what's wrong. We haven't had time to check them yet."

"Where are these cameras?" said DI Reever, indicating the screens that were blank.

"Er, at the rear of the building" said Andy, "and on the ground floor."

"Anything important there that we should know about?" said DS Brown.

"Well, there's nothing of particular interest at the rear," said Andy, pretending to think hard, "and on the ground floor there are the offices…and the store room…and…and the Computer Centre, of course."

"Oh," said DS Brown mockingly, "the Computer Centre. Not where the new voting system is kept, by any chance? Well, maybe we should take a look around there just as soon as you can let us out of here!"

"How's the search doing?" said DI Reever bluntly.

"But what about Mr Ba-?"

"The search!"

"I'll find out now," said Andy, quickly moving away from them as he called Geoffrey on the mobile.

He spoke in hushed tones, then, after ending the call, turned back towards the detectives with a look of great shock on his face.

"What's wrong?" said DI Reever.

"It *is* the Computer Centre," said Andy, the ten minutes finally over. "We'd better get down there straight away."

Andy led the detectives down to the ground floor and through the maze of corridors to the Computer Centre. As they drew closer he made sure that he was several steps ahead and when he turned the last corner into the recessed entrance was relieved to see Dave there.

"Great work, Dave!" he said in a loud voice. "Thanks for waiting for us."

"Yeah," said Dave, puzzled by Andy's unusually friendly manner, "but why did you tell me to wait outsi-?"

"That's great for now, Dave!" said Andy, slipping an arm round his shoulders and steering him away from the entrance as the detectives arrived. "I need you back upstairs now. You can take the calls coming in. The staff on site need to know what's going on."

"We'll need the names of everyone here today," said DS Brown.

"Got that, Dave?" said Andy.

"Sure," said Dave hesitantly. "But is the lock-down over? Can they go home?"

"Not just yet," said DI Reever. "We'll let them know as soon as we can, but until then nobody goes."

Dave nodded and left, then Andy went over to the retinal scanner and placed his face against it. The automated security voice spoke and the door unlocked. After taking a deep breath Andy stepped inside.

It was a shocking sight, even for the Security Manager. The normal pristine orderliness had been replaced by a trail of wreckage starting at the corral and spreading out dramatically over several rows of cabinets. It looked as if a mini-hurricane had swept through, tearing the place apart, spilling out the contents from the cabinets.

"Looks like someone got pretty angry," said DS Brown, clearly impressed by the damage. "It could cost a few quid to get this lot sorted out."

"Yes, but where are the security cameras?" said DI Reever, peering round the walls.

"There are none in here," said Andy.

"Why not?"

"The management didn't want them," he explained. "They said that this room was totally secure and having CCTV would only encourage people to spy on what was happening. They said it was safer this way."

"And they were wrong," said DI Reever, winking in a friendly way at Andy. "We'll take a look around now. You don't think your managers will mind, will they?"

"No," said Andy, at the same time wondering what the 'specialists' might have left behind, "I don't suppose they will now."

"It looks like these have all been shut down," said DS Brown, wandering between the rows of cabinets.

Andy hadn't noticed until then, but it was true that none of the LED's were on. "The power must be off," he said, wondering just how much worse this was going to become.

"It wasn't you, then?" said DI Reever, sifting through some of the computer parts strewn on the floor.

"God, no!" said Andy. "This is a 24x7 operation. It's built to keep going whatever happens."

"Except when someone pulls the plug!" called out DS Brown with a chuckle that did nothing for Andy's rapidly diminishing confidence.

For a while nothing was said as the two detectives picked through the debris and looked about the room for any clues, while Andy tried to stay calm and not think about the endless trouble this could bring him. He was beginning to think that the search would end without a fuss, when DS Brown's voice called out again, shattering his hopes.

"John, come and take a look at this."

DI Reever came across. Andy joined them, too. Then DS Brown, standing up, presented a shiny metal bullet casing on the end of his pen.

"A hand gun," said DI Reever, then glanced at Andy. "Do you keep any here?"

"None," said Andy nervously.

DI Reever looked around the room. "But why would anyone want to fire a hand gun in here?" he said. "It would only draw attention. Seen any bullet holes, Jim?"

"No," said DS Brown, and went on, "There could have been more than one of them. They might have fought."

"But over what?" said DI Reever. "It doesn't look like they were interested in stealing anything. I found a hammer and a few other tools back there. It looks as if all they were interested in was smashing up the place and they did it with a few simple tools and their bare hands. It's incredible!"

There was a long pause as they all struggled to understand what had happened.

"I think I've seen enough," said DI Reever finally, starting back towards the door. "We'll need this sealed off and the Scenes of Crime Unit in. But now, if you don't mind, Andy, I'd like to get hold of those recordings. I want to see them for myself."

Andy repeated his need for authorisation as he hurried after DI Reever, but before they could leave the room, DS Brown's voice brought them to a halt.

"Wait!" he called out as he crouched down near the entrance and looked closely at a smudge on the floor.

"What is it, Jim?" said DI Reever, waiting reluctantly.

"Oh, nothing much," he said, smiling broadly, "just a bit of blood, if I'm not mistaken."

DI Reever promptly turned back and inspected the smudge himself. "Well done," he said quietly, then looked up at Andy. "No one else is in here until our boys have finished. Understood?"

Andy nodded, the blood drained from his face.

DI Reever sniffed curiously, then ran a fingertip over the floor, taking care not to touch the smudge itself. He sniffed the finger. "It's ammonia," he said. "This has been cleaned up. I think we can be certain now where the bullet went. All we need now is the victim."

Seconds later, when the men were leaving the Computer Centre, a mobile rang and they all reached for their pockets. In the end DI Reever pulled out his mobile from under his mac and flicked it open.

"Yes, Sergeant," he said. "Yes. Good work. But who's in it?"

The Sergeant was standing next to a black Range Rover which he'd stopped at his temporary roadblock at the roundabout on the edge of the Business Park. DI Reever's idea to stop the Sergeant and his fellow officer returning straight back to Police Headquarters as requested by The Eagle Corporation and use them there had paid off.

"A Mr Geoffrey Lions," said the Sergeant, "accompanied by two other men. They told me they were called out because of the emergency at The Eagle Corporation. According to Mr Lions they all work for Mr van Reiner himself who has a legal interest in the business. They say they were told about the false alarm after they arrived and now wish to leave."

"Hold them there," said DI Reever, his eyes alight. "Search the car. Can you do that?"

"I think so," said the Sergeant, glancing once more at the two bodyguards inside the car. "But-"

"No 'buts'," said DI Reever, "just do it."

"Yes, Sir," said the Sergeant.

"And let me know what you find."

The call ended.

"And?" said DS Brown, intrigued.

"I'll tell you later," said DI Reever, not wanting to discuss anything in front of Andy, then motioned for him to lead them back upstairs.

Deep in thought, DI Reever's mind chased down the connections that he was certain would lead back to Mr van Reiner himself. Of course! Who else? The General Election, the corrupt MP and now a break-in at the same corporation that ran the online voting system - a corporation that Mr van Reiner had his own interest in! And during the break-in something had gone wrong and one of the intruders must have been shot. So, if DI Reever could pull together the pieces of the puzzle, then there was a good chance that Mr van Reiner would at last be brought to justice. It was a thought that both taxed and tempted him.

Back in the Surveillance Unit Andy contacted Mr Bates, while both detectives waited impatiently for any developments. Shortly, DI Reever's mobile rang.

"Hello?" said DI Reever. "Yes, Sergeant, how did it go?"

"They didn't like it," said the Sergeant, obviously pleased to have ruffled the feathers of someone so foul and snobbish as Geoffrey. "That Mr Lions is a *very* nasty piece of work."

"Yes, I know. And what did you-?"

"I'm sorry, sir," said the Sergeant, knowing what the question would be, "but there's nothing in the car. I've checked it thoroughly. Sergeant Redmond helped me out. We went inside, on top, underneath. We turned it over. It's clean."

"Are any of them carrying?" said DI Reever hurriedly.

"No. We shook them down as a precaution. They've not got weapons."

DI Reever thumped his fist on the desk, silently cursing.

"Shall I let them go now?" said the Sergeant. "I don't think I can hold them here any longer, not unless you're going to charge them."

"Okay," he said after a long pause, "but take their names and details. I'll want their statements later."

"Yes, Sir."

"And thank you, Sergeant," said DI Reever in a hollow voice as he folded away the mobile.

At midnight there was a single knock on the door of Mr van Reiner's suite in the Hotel Virion. Almost immediately the lock turned and the door opened. Geoffrey's face cautiously peered out.

"Get in," he said, stepping smartly aside for Mr Crane and Mr Wheeler then closed the door behind them. "Have you ditched the guns?"

Both men nodded.

"The river?"

"Better," said Mr Crane smugly. "We did an exchange with our supplier. They'll be rubbed down and the serial numbers removed. They'll never be traced back to us."

"No receipts then," said Geoffrey, smirking happily, then ushered them into the livingroom. "Come and sit down. Help yourselves to drinks. We should celebrate."

The bodyguards helped themselves to beers, while Geoffrey poured himself a large port, swirling it in the glass and sniffing it appreciatively. Soon they were talking freely.

"We certainly fooled that idiot of a Sergeant," said Geoffrey. "He looked so pleased with himself. But he never knew how close he got to the safe-box under the chassis."

"It's covered in grease and dirt," said Mr Wheeler.

"And so was he when he'd finished!" said Geoffrey.

"What do you expect from a poorly trained pig?" said Mr Crane and they all laughed together.

"So, the clean up's gone well enough," said Geoffrey. "The guns are gone and, thanks to Andy, our tame Security Manager, there's no recordings of our coming or goings. It was so good of him to turn off the CCTV cameras during our visit, don't you think?"

The bodyguards chuckled, but then Geoffrey's smile faded as he recalled the information that Andy, in another of his panics, had shared with him after their return

"It's a just a shame about the spent cartridge and the trace of blood," he said, then forced a smile back onto his lips. "But with a bit of luck we're in the clear. The guns are gone now, and they'll never know where the blood came from. There's no body and they won't have a DNA profile for the boy. *And,* if Andy has got his facts straight, they already think it was someone on the inside. That should give them enough to work on, especially interviewing every member of staff."

"But they knew we were there," said Mr Crane. "What if they come snooping around us?"

"They won't get far," said Geoffrey, "not without evidence. And Mr van Reiner is very protective of his staff. If those detectives try to cause us trouble, he'll pull a few strings and they won't know what's hit them. After all, he is an owner of The Eagle Corporation, so why would he be involved in a break-in at his own corporation? It's a crazy idea!" Chuckling to himself, Geoffrey lit up a cigarette, drawing on it deeply. "But better than that is knowing that the boy will *never* be bothering us again."

The bodyguards eyed Geoffrey warily.

"I just don't know how he managed to cause us all this trouble in the first place," Geoffrey went on, "messing up everything at the school like that, then getting in here. And how the hell did he manage to get into The Eagle

Corporation? He's a real life Spiderman! Or *was*, I should say." He blew out a long plume of smoke, watching it drift away and vanish. "All we need to do now," he continued, "is dispose of the body. And after all that's happened today, it should be a piece of cake! Talking of which, it's about time I called Andy again. It should be safe enough to pick up 'the package' now. And, if everything's going to plan, there'll be plenty of other vans just like ours arriving with replacement parts for the *terrible* damage done in the Computer Centre. So, who's going to be searching one more 'empty' box on its way out again?"

Laughing as he got up, Geoffrey waved a hand towards the drinks table, inviting the bodyguards to help themselves to more, then drew out his mobile and walked across the room, puffing contentedly on his cigarette.

"Andy," he said as soon as a voice answered, "it's Geoffrey. Okay to talk?"

"Yes," said Andy, though he sounded anything but okay himself.

Ever since Geoffrey had called to reveal his plans for the disposal of the body of the boy he had felt like a condemned man about to swing at the end of the hangman's rope. And after the call, impossible as it had seemed, the situation became worse still.

"You sound terrible," said Geoffrey, his good humour draining away fast. "Is everything all right?"

"No," said Andy, "no, it isn't. I'm just back from the store room and - and I - I can't find him."

Geoffrey's body tightened like a bow string. The bodyguards voices quietened instantly.

"*He must be there*," said Geoffrey, punching out each word with chilling clarity. "Go and look again!"

"I have," said Andy. "I've been through the boxes three times. I tell you, he's not there."

"But he's got to be! You've just missed one. There's hundreds down there. That's why we put him in the room, because it's such a good place to hide."

"*But I haven't missed him*," said Andy, his voice trembling. "That's what I'm trying to tell you. I found the box he was in. I know it's the right one - there's blood in it. There's no mistake... Are you *sure* he was dead?"

"*Yes, yes, yes!*" screamed Geoffrey, then after taking a moment to calm himself down, asked, "What about the police? Have they been down there? You were meant to stay with them?"

"I did, all the time," said Andy, "and they never went near the store room. They had no reason to. They know it's not a robbery. They're only looking for whoever smashed up the place."

"Okay, *okay*," said Geoffrey, silently pummelling the wall with his fist, "but what I need you to do now is to *find that body*. Got it? Dead people don't just get up and walk away!"

Suddenly the door to the suite clicked and Mr van Reiner strode in.

Geoffrey spun round, snapping the mobile shut. His mouth opened, but nothing came out.

"Everything all right?" said Mr van Reiner.

There was a long pause.

"Well?"

Finally Geoffrey spluttered out his answer.

"No," he said, "not exactly."

Chapter 12 The Death of Dreams

As Tom had run towards the door of the Computer Centre, he glimpsed a shadowy movement through the crack in the door. He guessed in that moment that it was Geoffrey waiting to ambush him, but ran on. Caught in the bodyguard's torch light, he had no choice but to try to get past him. Then the two shots rang out in deafening harmony.

The sound alone felt as if it could have knocked him over, but it was the double punch of the bullets in his back that actually did the job. A searing pain shot through his back and he wanted to cry out but couldn't, the breath knocked out of him. He lay still where he fell. His eyelids flickered uncertainly for a moment, then closed altogether.

An icy chill crept over him, colder than anything he'd felt before. It was nothing like the bracing cold that he'd felt when jumping straight into the sea that early in the year. Indeed it was quite the opposite of that exhilarating experience. It was as if not only his life but also his hopes and dreams were draining out of him through those unstoppable bullet holes. A dark emptiness seemed to be taking hold of him. He was alone and afraid.

But strangely, for someone passing from life to death, he was still aware of what was going on around him. At least, he could hear everything, though it sounded as if he was listening from under water in the same way as it had been for him when he was caught up inside his shadow. Geoffrey was gloating over him. "Well, there's a surprise!" he thought, smiling inwardly, knowing Geoffrey couldn't touch him now. Not even he could reach beyond death!

A minute or two later the bodyguards spoke nearby, then their strong hands took hold of him and lifted him with unusual gentleness into a large cardboard box. Rocked about inside the box, he was carried through the building. Along the way he remembered how his own shadow had carried him inside itself through these corridors. He wondered if it too was dead, overcome by its terrible exhaustion, and wondered if perhaps they might meet again in some after-life.

Then the box thumped down, dragging his thoughts back to the here and now, whatever they were (it was so confusing with his brain as cold as a block of ice and not even knowing when he'd drawn his last breath).

"I don't like it," said Mr Wheeler. "It's trouble, big trouble."

"Get over it," said Mr Crane. "It's done. Let's go."

Their footsteps passed away and a door slammed shut.

Curled up in the darkness of the box, Tom was filled with an unsettling mixture of fear and excitement, not knowing whether he was on the verge of discovering a Heaven more beautiful and amazing than anything he could ever have imagined or a Hell so terrifying and painful that even a minute spent there was unthinkable. But what came next was startling in a very different way.

Slowly the iciness that had penetrated him so deeply began to draw back and the warmth that he thought he had lost for ever took its place, starting at his core and spreading outwards, until finally the slender hairs on his skin prickled ticklishly as the capillaries just below the surface flooded afresh with hot blood. Then, as suddenly and violently as the moment a new baby is born, his whole body convulsed. His head shot back and his mouth gaped open like a beached fish and, in great wheezing gasps, he dragged down lungfuls of air, his chest heaving up and down.

As his body calmed, sensation returned to every part. He groaned, aching all over but more particularly from the acute pain across his back. "Now that *really* hurts," he murmured croakily. He wriggled round in the box, his body terribly stiff, and managed to reach a hand behind his back and under his clothes. As his fingertips travelled across the tender skin, testing it here and there, he winced from the pain, but felt no blood or open wounds.

He knew he had been shot, yet nothing seemed to make sense any more. Then, realising that sooner or later his enemies would return for the box, he set about trying to escape from it.

At first he thrashed about like a fledgling in a nest unable to get a grip on the sides of the box, but then, kicking out with his legs and rocking from side to side, managed to topple the box onto its side. He punched open the lid then crawled out into the darkness. Straight away his head bumped against the side of another box, then, steadying himself against the other boxes, he got to his feet. As he looked around he spotted the lit outline of a door against a far wall.

After clambering past a great number of boxes, eventually he reached the door. Gently he turned the handle, but the door was locked. He felt up the wall alongside the door until he found a row of switches. He squinted as the lights flashed on, then peered out across the expanse of the store room. Boxes of every shape and size were stacked up in piles that reached up to the ceiling and out to the side walls, taking up most of the available space. One central corridor led straight across the room to a broad steel roll-up door, presumably for outside access. His box, lying on its side, remained out of sight tucked away amongst the other boxes.

He knew he was on the ground floor, but was less certain about *how* he was. He ran his fingers over the dark smear of blood on the front of his coat, then, twisting round on himself, pulled out of the way his backpack, coat and shirt. Across his back were two colourful bruises, but there was no sign of the bullet wounds. Twisting back he found the skin of his stomach and chest unbroken too. He thought of pinching himself to make sure that he wasn't dreaming or, worse still, dead, but with so many aches and pains across his body needed no more convincing of how alive he truly was.

He still could not make sense of it. But the question now was how to get out of there without being discovered.

The store room appeared to be the perfect prison. The internal door was locked electronically with a swipe-card system and there were no windows on any of the walls. The roll-up door appeared to have no way of opening it from the inside - no handle or security lock or chains to pull on - but as Tom stepped back from it he spotted a cable running down from above and disappearing behind one of its metal guides. Following the cable he found it ended in a two-button controller tucked behind the guide. He pulled it out, then, watching the door closely, pressed the green button.

A motor whirred into action, the door clanked and shuddered, then jerked upwards. As soon as he saw the tarmac of the car park beyond, he ran back across the room and switched off the lights. Then, returning to the controller, he waited until the roll-up door was halfway open, then pressed the red button. The door jerked to a halt and started down again. He ducked outside. Seconds later the door clunked shut behind him.

One glance across the car park revealed the presence of only a few cars and no people. A second later he was scuttling to the back of the building, hugging the glass wall and hoping not to be noticed by the CCTV cameras positioned along the edge of the roof.

At the back of the building he paused, gathering his breath, and then, when he was certain nobody was coming, crossed the road and the grass, returning to the fence. He felt along the fence, only once retracing his steps when he thought that he must have passed the opening. But unable to find it further back he hurried on again. Finally the wire gave way beneath his hands. Kneeling down, he pushed hard with outstretched hands and crawled under it. On the other side he kicked it back into place, then fled for the trees.

Passing straight through the trees he wheeled round into the overgrown lane and shortly came back to the road that ran through the Business Park. Peering out from the lane he saw a silver Vectra pull across into the entrance of the Headquarters. As soon as it was gone he straightened his coat and backpack then stepped out and walked back along the pavement.

Keeping his head down, he tried not to walk too fast. As he passed the entrance he glanced up and saw the Security Guard standing outside his booth. The Security Guard scribbled on a clip-board and watched the Vectra cross the car park. By the time he turned round again, Tom was already gone.

As Tom approached the roundabout at the other end of the road he saw the bright markings of a police car parked up in the same lay-by used by the bus. Immediately he crossed onto the other side of the road. Then, wanting to get out of sight as soon as possible, he turned into an entrance of one of the other businesses and crossed its car park, cutting off the corner past the roundabout.

The electric window of the police car softly whirred down. "Hey!" shouted the Sergeant from inside.

Tom kept on walking, pretending not to hear.

The policeman climbed out of the car, slamming the door shut. "Stop!" he shouted. "Yes, you. You heard me."

Tom stumbled to a halt, then turned round.

"That's more like it," said the Sergeant sternly. "Now, go back and walk round the proper way. That's private property you're on. And don't be so lazy next time."

Tom quickly returned to the pavement, then hurried away round the corner of the roundabout.

"Little punk," said the Sergeant, getting back into the car. "We've got enough problems without everyone wandering wherever they like."

Tom kept up a fast pace, at the same time watching out for any cars approaching, ready to duck down a side street and run off at the first sign of danger. He passed several empty bus-stops but wasn't going to wait around in the open where he could easily be spotted. And besides he hadn't seen any buses passing by. The further he walked, the more settled he became. And then he began to think back on all he'd been through.

The Computer Centre for The Eagle Corporation was out of action, he was certain of that. The trashed cabinets would take some time to repair, but even if the work was hurried through, who would be mad enough to want to use an online voting system that wasn't working all the time and, more importantly, wasn't secure. Mr van Reiner could not succeed now. The General Election would have to go ahead with the old ballot boxes. The public would mark an 'X' next to their chosen candidates' names, fold up their ballot slips and post them, and that would be that.

Tom really had succeeded. And as that fact settled pleasantly in his mind, he managed a weary smile.

Yet inside he felt a growing emptiness, an emptiness that he hadn't felt for some time, an emptiness that he couldn't ignore. And then the awful truth came to him. It was his shadow, or rather, its absence from him. In all the frantic rush to escape from the building and get away from there he had not even looked for it. He could not see it now, not even its hazy outline, and this time knew that it had not simply gone off somewhere else to do its own thing. This time there was something far more sinister behind its disappearance.

He remembered the moment just before he had been shot. His two shadows cast against the wall had suddenly become one. It was as if the torch lights behind him had closed together. But now he realised what really had happened. Rather than the two shadows joining, they had been swallowed up by another. His shadow had jumped up behind him and taken the bullets.

Yes, he had been cold, but it had not been his cold. His shadow had wrapped him up in itself once more, protecting him from death just as its own life had drained away.

Yes, there had been blood - as his footsteps slowed, he touched again the smear of blood on his coat - but it had not been his blood. It had belonged to his shadow and been spilled for him.

No, he hadn't died, but instead had been wrapped in the shroud of his shadow's death.

And now, though he hardly dared to admit it, it was gone forever.

He came to a halt, no longer caring about himself. Tears spilled down his cheeks. "I want you back," he sobbed. "*Please* come back. I don't care about the rest of it, just *please come back.*"

At 8pm the doorbell to the apartment of Tom's mother chimed merrily.

"I'll get it!" shouted Clara, dashing out of her bedroom, but her mother was already on her way, striding across from the kitchen.

"Don't worry," said her mother, her lips smacking from the tasty spoonful of hot Moussaka Georgie had allowed her, "I'll get it."

She opened the door, then stood back with a look of shock and amazement on her face. "But - but-?" she said, staring at Tom standing before her.

"I can explain everything," said Clara, darting past her and grabbing hold of Tom, "just as soon as this little fool tells me what he's been playing around at!"

"Get off," he said, squirming under her grip.

"Not until you tell me where you've been!"

"But I - I thought," said their mother, "that Tom had come back with you, Clara. I thought he was in his room. Why didn't you say anything when we got back?"

"I was going to tell you," said Clara, struggling to hold onto Tom. "I just thought he'd be back by now. You don't know what it was like! He just kept wandering off. He said he was coming back here or going to dad's. And then he was gone! I looked *everywhere* for him. It wasn't *my* fault!"

"But that was *hours* ago," said her mother.

"Nice bangles," said Tom, helpfully pointing out the new iridescent blue rings on her wrist.

"Shut up, you!" Clara shrieked

"Clara!" shouted her mother, giving her a stern look. "Let go of him, *now*. And both of you, get inside."

Briefly their mother checked that their neighbour across the stairwell had not appeared at her door then stepped back inside, while Clara continued her explanation in a strident voice. She said that she *had* been going to tell her but hadn't wanted to disturb her from her *important* business work in the office and there seemed no sense in worrying her when he was going to turn up here or at dad's anyway - at least that was what he had told her. She was just about to continue with how difficult it was having to look after a mischievous and unhelpful little brother, when her mother's attention was caught by something else.

"What's that mark on your coat?" she said.

"Just dirt," he mumbled.

"Here," she said, stepping over to him, "take that bag off and let me see."

Trying not to wince from the pain, he wriggled out of the straps of the backpack, then let her run her fingers over the mark.

"It's blood," she said in quiet surprise, studying the dark redness on her fingertips.

He shrugged, looking tired and uncomfortable.

"You're sure you don't know where it came from?" she said, and, after he nodded, added, "And have you been crying?"

"I'm all right," he said. "I just came the long way home."

"Anyone for Moussaka?" shouted Georgie, carrying a steaming pot to the dining table. "It can't wait any longer. Come on, everyone, get stuck in or I'll eat it all myself! "

"Well, as long as *you're* not hurt," said Tom's mother, taking his hands gently in her own. "And I don't want you going off on your own again. Now go and wash your hands," she said, adding with a smile, "If we're not quick, they'll be no food left!"

The meal passed by in a sort of fog for Tom. He was truly exhausted, especially after his long march home (though he had caught a bus for the last part of the journey, using the all-day ticket he'd bought to take him to the Business Park). The mouth-watering Moussaka smelled of succulent lamb and rich spices, but he could only bring himself to eat a small portion of it. Georgie, sensing Tom's weariness, did his best to encourage him, slipping in plenty of jokes, but Tom ate nothing more, his stomach uncomfortably tight. Meanwhile, Clara, took every opportunity to show off her new bangles and ear-rings and neckerchief, soaking up Georgie's admiring glances and leaving Tom to note miserably how quickly she had turned the situation in her favour.

As soon as he could Tom excused himself from the table. No one objected - even Clara managed to hold her tongue: all of them could see how tired and sad he looked. "Straight to bed tonight," said his mother and he certainly wasn't going to argue with that.

Minutes later he lay in bed, his clothes cast down across the floor. The television, mounted on the wall, was turned on more for the comfort of its noise rather than the programmes it offered. It helped to blot out the deep loneliness he now felt. And as its images changed over and over again and it droned on, he drifted off to sleep.

A terrible nightmare took hold of him. In it he tumbled over and over, falling into a black bottomless chasm, and after what seemed like many hours a voice started calling to him from somewhere nearby. His head twisted round, trying to see where it was coming from, and then suddenly he was awake again. He blinked through the darkness at the glow from the opposite wall.

It was the television.

He heard a familiar voice.

"Yes, Tim," said Julie Marks, clutching a large microphone in front of her as she stood outside, lit up against the darkness, "this is an incredible story breaking right here in Bellington tonight and it has everything to do with the General Election now only days away. You can probably just see the road behind me" - she waved a hand towards it - "that leads to The Eagle Corporation's Headquarters here on East Bellington Business Park. I can now inform you that a break-in took place here earlier this evening. But let me explain why that is so important. What you have to understand is that it is here at The Eagle Corporation's Headquarters that the new online voting system is kept. That means that the break-in took place in the same building that houses the computers holding the whole of the UK voters' registration details. And *this Thursday* it is going to process every vote cast in the General Election. It is here," she ended emphatically, "that the result of who is going to lead our nation for the next five years will be determined."

"But is the information itself at risk?" asked Tim, looking particularly worried behind his desk in the television studio.

"I believe the answer is yes," she said. "I have been told by a reliable source that not only was there a break-in but that the intruders managed to cause significant damage to the computers themselves. It looks as if someone was trying to stop the new online voting system, though the extent of the damage has not yet been verified. As you can see I'm quite a way from the Headquarters itself and the police are not letting anyone in or out for obvious reasons. But *someone* got into this building today and, despite its supposedly high levels of security, managed to penetrate to the very heart of it."

"Thank you, Julie," said Tim, then turned to introduce a recorded briefing from the police.

DS Brown stood outside the Police Headquarters, speaking into a tight collection of microphones. "I can confirm," he announced briefly, "that there was a break-in to The Eagle Corporation Headquarters today and that the police are carrying out a full investigation. There is nothing further to report presently."

A number of questions were shouted out at the same time, but he only repeated that he had nothing further to report and that as soon as there *was* something, an update would be issued.

"Well, not much there," said Tim, turning back, "but Julie, I believe you've already spoken to the Chief Executive of The Eagle Corporation, Freddie Westlake." Julie nodded. "And now we'll hear what he had to say."

The businessman, wearing an open-necked shirt and casual jacket, looked completely unruffled as he stood outside the palatial wrought-iron gates of his luxurious home tucked well out of view behind tall trees.

"I can well understand your concerns," he said, "and you must know that my Corporation will do everything in its power to understand how its exceptional security systems were overcome today and then prevent it ever happening again. This is a situation we cannot and will not tolerate."

"But how good is your security," said Julie, "when it was overcome so easily?"

"Firstly, I cannot respond to your provocative question until I know how the break-in took place and that is now the subject of a full police investigation. And secondly, you don't have to take my word for the fact that we have exceptional security systems because they are regularly and independently inspected as required by Her Majesty's Government. The Eagle Corporation has had a clean bill of health and was awarded one of the highest grades of security. It couldn't operate without it. It needs it to protect this information of national importance.

"And that is why you should know," he went on, smiling generously, "that at no time today has any information been improperly accessed or lost. In fact, the online voting system has not stopped functioning even for a second. Yes, there was a report of some damage inside the building (which is only to be expected after a break-in), but The Eagle Corporation has already invested heavily in a second Computer Centre at a secret location. This exactly mirrors the operation in Bellington. So, even if the one in Bellington was completely destroyed - and that would be remarkable in itself" - he laughed dismissively - "then our second one would take over, and vice versa. You see, we have thought of everything and there is nothing that the public - or the Government for that matter - needs to worry about! No one has rung in to complain, because no one has noticed a difference. And that's because there isn't one! Our business is good and no attack on *my* Corporation, however clever, is going to stop it! Thank you."

The businessman turned as if to go, but Jackie was already firing off her next question.

"Why did you say 'attack'?" she said. "Wasn't this just a break-in?"

Freddie continued through the gates, unwilling to be drawn.

"And where exactly is this second Computer Centre?" she called after him, but then the recording ended, returning to the studio.

"Thank you, Julie," said Tim, smiling contentedly. "A very revealing interview. And now I believe we can go to a briefing just in. It's from Mr van Reiner, MP for Bellington North who's here in Bellington for the run-up to the General Election. And this is what *he* had to say."

The MP stood on the steps at the entrance to the Hotel Virion.

"I don't want to say much," said Mr van Reiner with a triumphant look, "particularly, as is well known, because I have an interest in this company. But what I can say is that I'm glad to be a part of any British business showing such resilience as this. It is the type of business I am proud of and will always back - as will any Government I have the honour of playing a part in. It is the type of business that is going to put the *Great* back into Britain once more!"

His voice droned on from the television, the familiar speech unfolding once more, but Tom was no longer listening. In fact he had barely heard a word since Freddie Westlake had revealed the news about the second Computer Centre. As the news had sunk in he had rolled over and with a whimpering moan buried his head under the pillow.

His fingertips clawed at the pillow. He didn't care if he never breathed again. His hopes, his dreams were over. Dead. Like his shadow. Everything he had done had come to nothing. And there was no one left to help.

Chapter 13 The Eve of Battle

The next morning was the start of the new week, but it felt like the end of the world for Tom. He struggled to get up then wandered through the apartment like a ghost. Everyone else busied themselves with breakfast and getting ready for work or school and thankfully had little time for him. He didn't want to be noticed, just left alone, preferably for ever.

Only at one point was he roused from this morbid state, though afterwards everyone wished he'd stayed as he was. It happened when he was looking for his coat which for some reason was no longer in his room. He remembered dropping it on the bedroom floor the night before, but it definitely wasn't there. Eventually he discovered it on a rack in the small utility room. As he entered the room he smarted from the powerful reek of detergent, and then, approaching his coat, saw that the smear of blood had been cleaned from it.

The smear of blood that had been the last remaining trace of his shadow.

No one had seen him cry out in the way he did - not even when he was a little boy - and no one understood the reason for the fury and tears that suddenly exploded from inside him. And all because his coat had been cleaned! It made no sense, and his mother, for one, was in no mood for any sort of tantrums with a busy day already upon her.

"First, you run off by yourself," she scolded, "and now you're yelling at me for cleaning your coat. This behaviour isn't good enough and when I get home I expect to see a change...*for the better.*"

Clara stared at him as if he was out of his mind and Georgie stood back in silence, not knowing how to help. No one understood the wound that had pierced him so deeply, and for the rest of the day he carried it in silence on his own.

School was no better.

Dags steered clear of him after seeing his dark wounded look (though, as Tom knew, he needn't have feared him because his shadow was no longer there). Mr Harris was tremendously excited now that the General Election was only three days away. This was the great moment for their Election Project, he told them, and he'd especially brought in newspapers and recordings of news bulletins so that they could see the latest polls and make their own forecasts for the final results. Tom said as little as possible in one of the most exciting history lessons the class had ever known, and it was only afterwards that the teacher, puzzling to himself, tried to remember if Tom had been there at all.

At the end of school he drifted out with the droves of other children, and crossed the road, heading for the bus-stop a short distance away. His head hung down gloomily and he didn't notice the black Range Rover parked up ahead of him. Hidden behind the darkened glass of the car, the three men tensed, watching him come towards them. This was the miracle boy who had cheated death on more than one occasion and they were under strict orders *never* to let the same mistake happen again. It was their own necks on the line this time.

"We wait for the right moment," said Geoffrey icily, "when he's on his own. And then *I'll* cut his throat. No one else. Understood? I'll show you how it's done *properly*."

Mr Crane and Mr Wheeler nodded in stony silence.

As the bus weaved into town the Ranger Rover kept on its tail. Every bus-stop was watched for the boy getting off, but he remained on board almost to the end of the route on the far side of town. Eventually the bus pulled over in the pleasant suburb of Cedarwoods and no more than a hundred metres from the apartments where Tom's mother lived. The Ranger Rover pulled up behind the bus, while a silver Vectra cruised slowly by.

A girl wearing a black skirt and white blouse (the standard uniform of Newlands) got off first and walked away in the opposite direction to the apartments, then a white-haired old woman with spectacles stepped down sideways onto the pavement, carrying a stick in one hand and a heavy bag of shopping in the other. As soon as she was out of his way, Tom got off the bus and strode past her.

The kerbside doors of the Range Rover, standing only metres ahead of him, gently clicked open.

"Well, I don't know!" said the old woman in a cross sounding voice, causing Tom to glance round. "Oh, it's not you, Tom," she said, smiling and waving her stick as if he should carry on, "it's just me being a very silly old woman who doesn't know *what* she's doing any more!"

He hesitated, wondering how she knew his name.

"Oh, of course, silly me," she said, pausing for breath, "you don't recognise me, do you? I'm your neighbour! I live opposite your mother in apartment 5b. Right then," she said, setting off again at a slow pace, "now that's settled, we'd both better be on our way. And do remember that if you ever want to get out and just *be* somewhere else, then you're most welcome to come and visit me."

"Thanks," mumbled Tom, feeling awkward as he watched her struggle on with such determination. Then, finding it impossible just to leave her, he offered to help with the bag.

The old woman looked up in surprise. "Oh, how kind!" she said. "That would be a *great* help. And by the way, I'm Mrs Dennis, *but you can call me May*."

As he took the bag from her he almost dropped it, it was so heavy, and he looked again at her, amazed that she had been able to carry it at all on her own. But now, relieved of her burden, she was now hobbling away and leaving him behind.

"Such a kind little boy," she muttered to herself. "I must remember to have a word with Marie."

Tom waddled after her, the bag dangling from both arms in front of him. Then, remembering what she'd first said, he called out, "*What* don't you know?"

"What's that, my dear?" she said, pausing to look round.

"What don't you know?" he puffed as he caught up with her and rested his load for a moment. "You said it back there."

"Oh, did I?" she said with a curiously secretive look, then gave him a twinkling smile. "Well, whatever it was, I was right, because I really don't know!"

Moving on again, they passed the Range Rover, then crossed the road, and the doors of the Range Rover pulled shut again.

The silver Vectra belonging to DI Reever had pulled up a short distance after the bus-stop, far enough away not to be obvious yet near enough to keep a watchful eye over everything that unfolded. He had been following the Range Rover ever since its location had been picked up early that morning, certain that Mr van Reiner and his men were involved up to their necks in the break-in and hoping that the Range Rover would lead him to more answers before the trail went cold again. He and DS Brown had taken it in turns tailing the car back and forth across Bellington.

In the afternoon it had led them to Newlands Secondary School where Tom got on the bus and the Range Rover followed behind Once again the connection was made with this unremarkable boy. But what did Mr van Reiner want with him? Whatever the reason it would be very different from his own desire to talk to the boy. It was something DI Reever had to get to the bottom of, and soon, if the boy was to come to no harm.

Parked up in Cedarwoods, he had watched in his mirrors as the passengers got off the bus, the Range Rover clearly visible in the background. He was sure Mr van Reiner's men would make a move on the boy there and then and thought he glimpsed the doors of the Range Rover starting to open. He nudged open his own door, ready to run back, but then the old woman had started talking to Tom and the two walked off together.

"Well done, lad," he said, watching him struggling with the bag. "That little act of kindness may have done you more good than you'll ever know."

And now, with Tom and the old woman safely inside the apartment block, he decided to make his own move. He hadn't wanted to reveal his presence so early, but now that Tom was involved, the game-plan had changed. Tom's safety was at risk, he was certain, and he didn't want Mr van Reiner's men getting to him first. So, it was time to show them just who was watching who. After a brief call to DS Brown, he left the car and strode back along the road.

He walked straight towards the Range Rover, staring at the windscreen, the leafy reflections from the overhanging trees hiding all behind it. He drew closer and closer, then the engine growled and suddenly the wheels skidded in the debris of the gutter and it roared away, narrowly missing him.

He smiled to himself, glancing after it. DS Brown was tucked round the end of the road, waiting in his BMW. He would pick up their tail again. DI Reever set off across the road, heading towards the apartments.

At the entrance he ran his finger over the name-plates until he found 'Ms M. Selly', knowing that was the maiden name Tom's mother had reverted to after her divorce. He pressed the button. Shortly the intercom crackled and a man's voice asked who was there.

"Hello. This is Detective Inspector John Reever. Can I come in, please?"

There was a moment's pause, then Georgie replied, "Yes, of course. Come up to the 5th floor. Okay?"

"Thank you."

A buzzer sounded and the door clicked open. DI Reever entered the lobby and went to the lift. When he arrived at the 5th floor, Georgie was waiting in the open doorway of the apartment.

"Hello," said Georgie, looking slightly nervous, "I hope that nothing is wrong, Detective."

"Call me John," said DI Reever, smiling reassuringly, "and I hope so too."

Georgie led him into the livingroom.

"Is Ms Selly here?"

"No, not yet," said Georgie, offering him a chair. "She's at work. She's a busy woman, you understand. Maybe I can help."

"Well, it's Tom I'd like to talk to, if that's all right," said DI Reever, remaining standing. "I just need to ask him some questions relating to a line of enquiry that I'm following up. I spoke to his father about a month ago, but there have been some new developments. Yesterday, in fact. Tom may be able to help us with them. That's all."

"Oh, I see," said Georgie, who didn't really but wanted to help. "He's only just got back from school, but I'm sure it's okay."

"You should stay with us," said DI Reever, "for Tom."

"Oh yes, of course," said Georgie, then went to find him.

A minute later he returned then introduced Tom to the detective.

"Hello, Tom," said DI Reever, pulling out a small wallet that he flicked open in front of him. "This is my ID. Now, if it's all right with you, I'd like to ask you a few questions. I'm hoping you can help me with some enquiries that I'm making. Let's sit down?"

Silently Tom sat on the sofa and DI Reever took the armchair directly opposite him. Georgie leaned back against a window sill, watching over the two of them.

"Oh, by the way," said DI Reever, dragging something out of his pocket, "I found this in the car and wondered if you'd like it."

Without warning he tossed the small can of soft drink at Tom who only just managed to catch it in time.

"It can be thirsty work, all this talking," said DI Reever, winking at him in a friendly way. "But now I'd better explain what this is about."

Tom turned the can over in his hands, keeping his eyes lowered. He had no doubts about why the detective was there.

"I don't know if you saw the news last night," said DI Reever, "but there was a break-in yesterday at The Eagle Corporation on East Bellington Business Park. It happened at about 6pm. Anyway, I've been looking at the recordings from the security cameras, trying to find out what happened, but it hasn't been easy. Even our experts have struggled to see what was going on. We found *something* and thought you might be able to help. Here, I've got some photos. Would you have a look for me? Maybe your young eyes can make it out."

Georgie frowned, wondering what this had to do with Tom, but the detective had already pulled out the photographs from under his jacket and, leaning forwards, offered them to Tom.

Tom took them. He flicked through them, trying not to show any interest. The images were murky and muddy in tone. One looked like a close-up of fingers holding the lens of the camera. In the background was a shape. It was stretched out and grey but clear enough to reveal the outline of a small person with a bag on their back.

Tom's cheeks reddened. Shaking his head, he handed back the photographs.

"No," said DI Reever, trying to catch his evasive gaze, "nothing there? The pictures are not very good, I know, but don't you think this one looks like a boy with a bag on his back? A boy about your size with a bag just like yours?"

"Hey, give me those!" said Georgie crossly, stepping over to the detective.

"Of course," said DI Reever, offering them up. "Tell me what you think."

Georgie studied them closely, then laughed, shaking his head. "These could be anything!" he said. "For sure, I can see something here, but it could be a shadow or a smudge or almost anything. And anyway, what has this got to do with Tom? Why are you asking *him* these questions?"

"Today," said DI Reever in a more serious tone, "we followed a car that was involved in the break-in at The Eagle Corporation. It came here. It was following Tom. And yesterday evening one of our men at the Business Park spotted a boy - a boy with a bag on his back. He thought nothing of it at the time. But after examining these photos we believe it's the same boy who was inside The Eagle Corporation at the time of the break-in." He paused, concentrating on Tom. "I need to ask you, Tom, where were you early yesterday evening."

Tom kept his eyes lowered.

"Hey, just wait a minute!" said Georgie, slapping the photograph back into the detective's hands and dropping down on the sofa next to Tom. "If you want to accuse Tom of anything, then you'd better stop right where you are."

"I'm not accusing Tom," said DI Reever calmly. "I just need to rule him out of my enquiries. I wouldn't be here if it wasn't entirely necessary. And you need to know that he may be in danger. Those men who followed him here today are not fooling around. Someone was shot and wounded in that break-in. These men are 'professionals' and I, for my part, don't want Tom coming to any harm."

"Okay, *okay*," said Georgie, holding up his hands in exasperation, "but I still don't see how Tom is a part of this."

"Tom?" said DI Reever, waiting patiently. "Where were you?"

"I - I was in town with Clara," he said, staring at the can as he flipped it over in his hands. "She was shopping and I got bored. Then I walked home."

"On your own?"

Tom nodded.

"Did you go straight home?"

"No," he said after a pause. "I wandered round for a bit."

"And did you go to The Eagle Corporation?"

There was a long silence before he answered, tears welling up in his eyes as he met the detective's cold clear gaze. "*Why would I ever go there?*" he said in a trembling voice, then looked down again.

"That's enough," said Georgie, wrapping an arm round Tom's shoulders. "No more questions, okay?"

"Just one more thing," said DI Reever, "*please.*"

Georgie frowned, then nodded sharply and said, "Just one more and then it's over. Then, you go, yes?"

"Yes, and thank you," said DI Reever, turning to the boy again. "Tom, I think you know why I'm here. I think you know that I want to help you in what ever way I can. But I need you to promise me one thing. If you're ever in trouble, you must let me know straight away. I'll leave my card here and you can phone me. I don't know how you're wrapped up in all this, but I really don't want you getting hurt. Okay, Tom?"

Tom nodded.

"Good," he said, getting up and handing one of his cards to Georgie. "And thank you both for your time. Oh," he added, glancing back, "and if you're not having that drink, Tom, I'll take it for my boy."

Tom got up and handed it back, then returned to the sofa.

"Great," said DI Reever, pocketing the can, then Georgie showed him to the door.

As soon as the door to the apartment closed behind DI Reever he went over to the window on the 5th floor landing and searched up and down the road for any sign of unwelcome visitors. After a couple of minutes he was satisfied that no one was hanging around and left the building. As soon as he was back in his car he pulled out his mobile and called DS Brown.

"Jim, it's me," he said. "Where are you now?"

"The usual," said Jim in bored voice. "Hotel Virion. They came straight here. How about you?"

"I drew a blank," said DI Reever. "Young Tom wasn't playing ball. I'm sure he knew what was going on in the photos, but he didn't let on. It ended up in tears."

"You big bully," joked DS Brown.

"Yeah, yeah," sighed DI Reever, "that's what you get for trying to help. Anyway, I've got a present for you, my boy."

"*My boy?*" said Jim in disgust. "I prefer the insults. Anyway, what is it?"

"A drink," said DI Reever, carefully extracting the can from his pocket and inspecting it against the light.

"Now you're talking!"

"No, not for you," said DI Reever, chuckling. "It's for forensics. I'll drop off the can on my way over and you can get them to check it for fingerprints. It's plastered with Tom's. If he's not going to admit that he and his backpack have been travelling to all the hotspots in town, then I'll prove it this way. You remember the fingerprints we got in Mr van Reiner's suite? What's the betting that those small ones are going to match the ones on the can?"

"I'll put a tenner on it," said DS Brown.

"And I'll put another on them matching some of the ones we get from The Eagle Corporation."

"And then we can have another chat with the boy," said DS Brown, "and hopefully get the evidence to put an end to whatever's going on around here."

"That's the idea," said DI Reever, starting the car, "that's the idea."

It was two days later almost to the hour when the phone call that DI Reever had been waiting for finally came through at Police Headquarters. He answered it, listened carefully, then replaced the phone, smiling to himself. Then he stretched back wearily in his chair, trying to focus his thoughts once more.

"So, Tom," he said quietly to himself, "now we know that you were at the Hotel Virion *and* The Eagle Corporation."

He paused, collecting his thoughts that were already racing ahead, then decided to review each location in turn.

"So, you *were* in Mr van Reiner's suite and the receptionist *did* see you and, of course, you *were* wearing that backpack. But then," he went on, frowning, "where did Mr van Reiner's wallet get to in the end? Perhaps you didn't take it. Or maybe you did and hid it on the way home. Or maybe you did get a lift from that taxi driver but he took more from you than you'd expected. Jim can check again. We don't want any loose ends."

He smoothed away the creases from his forehead, then peered out across the open-plan office. Most of the desks were empty. He preferred the quietness at the end of the day, even if it was a struggle to pull his thoughts together.

"So, then, what about The Eagle Corporation?" he went on. "You were there too. Your fingerprints were all over the Computer Centre! But whose blood was it? You didn't look injured when I saw you at home. But if there's no DNA match I'll want a blood sample all the same. And then there were those recordings," he said, blowing out his cheeks and tossing his pencil across the desk.

The Security Manager had told him that there had been problems with the CCTV cameras, but it was too much of a coincidence that it was only those covering the car parks and the ground floor that stopped working from shortly after the break-in until later that evening. The man had definitely been trying to hide something. Why else would he have stalled the detectives for so long after their arrival? DI Reever's guess was that he had been covering up for whatever Mr van Reiner's men had been doing while they were there. But what exactly was that?

He looked into his empty coffee cup, then across to the coffee machine, but decided it was too late for a refill.

"Okay," he said, summoning his thoughts one last time, "let's say that Mr van Reiner's men caught you, Tom, while you were wrecking the Computer Centre. But then how on earth did you get away from them? Was there someone else involved? Was it their blood that we found? *And why did you want to wreck all those computers anyway?*"

It didn't add up, whichever way he looked at it. There were too many pieces of the puzzle still missing.

"So, Tom," he murmured, collecting his mac and briefcase and setting off for home, "you'd better get a good night's sleep. I've got a lot of questions that I want to ask you tomorrow and this time there won't be anywhere left to hide."

Tom did indeed sleep well that night. The gloom that had taken hold of him at the start of the week was still painfully acute and he was thoroughly drained of all life and energy. His only hope was that after tomorrow, when the General Election was over and he could finally complete his project, then he could forget about this whole sorry episode and start to rebuild his life.

The last thing he would have wanted that night was a visitor to wake him up and remind him of all that he'd been through, so it was just as well that the dark figure standing at his bedroom window made no sound at all.

The figure was thinking about the momentous day ahead when the whole of the country would chose its next Government and its next Prime Minister. The figure remembered all that Tom had come through already and the great victory he had so nearly won when he had delivered that blow to the heart of The Eagle Corporation. Yet tomorrow, it knew, would be an even greater day for him. It would be the most important day of his life: the day of the General Election.

The figure sighed. It glanced across at Tom who lay peacefully asleep, then drew its eyes away again, knowing it had to let go of him. It looked out over the lights of Bellington, but its thoughts remained fixed on him. Tomorrow he would face a greater challenge than ever before, but this time, on his own.

The figure, despite its own uneasiness, remained there for the rest of the night, standing like a sentinel on guard before the day of battle. It stayed until the break of dawn, when the first sunlight burst over the horizon and rested over the apartment.

For a second it stood there, grey as smoke except for the two thin beams of sunlight piercing straight through it and emerging from the holes in its back, then vanished from sight altogether.

Chapter 14 A Moment of Madness

Thursday 27th May. It was the day of the General Election. Voting online started from 6am with the Great British public logging on to the official website from computers at home or work or in libraries or internet cafes or from specially adapted polling stations in schools and village halls and council buildings where computers had been set up for this particular day. Even those on the move used their mobile devices to gain access through the internet to the online system. The wires of the country soon began to heat up and glow from the streams of digital votes passing in milliseconds from the tapping of fingertips on computer keyboards to the Computer Centres of The Eagle Corporation. The contest had started and it was going to be an extraordinary day.

DI Reever had been bombarded for months with instructions about how to vote online in the General Election. Like everyone else in the country he had been sent leaflets in the post and endured the Government's childish advertising campaign on television and billboards that had used cute farmyard animals to act out step by step what was expected of every voter. There had been the instructions at work, too, explaining how and when to use their computers to vote. On and on it had gone, like one of those terrible computer viruses spreading out of control throughout the nation, jamming up the works. And on top of all that, of course, there was the avalanche of leaflets and emails and other pieces of advertising from the prospective candidates and political parties vying for his allegiance. In total it had done a pretty good job of putting him off voting ever again.

And then Moira, his wife, called after him as he was about to leave the house: "Don't forget, darling. It's the big day. Who did you say you were going to vote for?"

"I didn't," he mumbled to himself, grabbing a buttered slice of toast as he almost ran from the kitchen, not wanting to get caught up in any political discussions before the day had even started. Today his mind was on other things. In particular he had his sights set on his meeting with Tom and didn't want to miss him before the start of the school day.

The Vectra pulled up a short distance from the entrance to Newlands just before 8am. DI Reever was surprised to see that a number of children were already there, hanging around in front of the entrance and in the yard just beyond. He was certain Tom wouldn't have made the trip across town yet, but in case he was wrong or Tom was back with his father, got out of the car and had a good look for him amongst those already there. At last, satisfied he hadn't missed him, he went back to the car.

For a minute he toyed with the idea of contacting the headteacher to ask if he could wait inside the school, but was then distracted by the slice of toast starting to curl up at the edges on the dashboard. He grabbed it and took a large bite, letting the butter ooze out onto his tongue, at the same time keeping a careful eye on the steadily increasing number of students arriving outside.

Tom sat at the front of the top deck of the bus. Usually it was a good place to look down on the world, but today as the bus crossed town he kept his head down, his expression as troubled as the grey clouds scudding across the sky. All he wanted was to get through this one day, the day he had been dreading all week, knowing as little as possible about the General Election. A discarded newspaper lay beneath his feet which he had purposefully placed over the colour pictures of the leaders of the main political parties splashed across its front page. The very presence of it there unsettled him, but as the bus crossed the centre of town and neared the Hotel Virion he forced himself to keep his eyes fixed down.

Yet as he held his head in that position and closed his eyes against the world around, he could not blot out the memories of his shadow saving his life at the hotel and later giving up its own life, taking the bullets meant for him. And a nagging inner voice kept on at him, asking if he couldn't have done more - if he still couldn't do something to stop Mr van Reiner from finally gaining ultimate power. He argued back inside his head then tried to will it away, but in the end, unable to win, suddenly threw up his head like a diver bursting from the water, gasping for much needed breath.

And then two things he saw stopped him dead. The first was the blue neon sign for the Hotel Virion directly across the road. The second was Jerry, hurrying up the steps at its entrance.

Although Jerry was not wearing his uniform for The Eagle Corporation or carrying his aluminium case, Tom clearly saw his face as he glanced back. There was a look of deepest concern on his face, and then Tom remembered that he had to make one more change to the online voting system before it would work in the way that Mr van Reiner had planned. A change he could make remotely from the laptop he kept hidden away in Mr van Reiner's suite. A change that would secure him the second half of that great sum of money Mr van Reiner had promised.

The bell on the bus sounded and moments later it pulled over.

DI Reever watched the next bus arrive with keen interest, trying not to let his impatience get the better of him. The bus was from the south side of town where Tom's mother lived and he was certain that he'd be on it. He watched as the usual scrum of school children emerged from it, chattering away and knocking into each other before wandering off towards the school gates. He checked the faces, re-checked them. He looked for Tom's backpack, then looked back at the bus to see if any more children were getting off. But then the bus pulled away and he knew that Tom had not been amongst them. He flicked open his mobile and speed-dialled DS Brown.

"Hello, Jim. No, he's not here yet. He should be though. Another bus has just gone. How's things with you?"

"Mr van Reiner and the rest of them are here at the constituency office," said DS Brown, then paused, his attention caught by something. "In fact, they're just coming out now. Looks like it was a last pow-wow for the party faithful. Now they're waving him off. Oh, my God, it's heart breaking! Where are my tissues?"

"All right, all right," said DI Reever, "I get the message. So, now where's he heading?"

DS Brown watched the black Audi carrying Mr van Reiner and Geoffrey accelerate away along the road, closely followed by the Range Rover carrying the bodyguards.

"Well, at a guess," said DS Brown, "I'd say they're going back into town. There was talk of a press conference, but I don't know where. I'll let you know. Got to go."

"Okay, keep in touch," said DI Reever, then folded the mobile away. "So, where the hell are you, Tom. Late for school?"

At least, he thought, Mr van Reiner's men were no longer hunting him down. But why wasn't he here by now? He had a bad feeling about this, but, like the school children milling restlessly outside, could only wait for the start of the school day before making the next move.

It was a moment of madness for Tom. Madness, because all those bottled up emotions which had plagued him since Sunday suddenly erupted from within and propelled him straight off the bus at the first bus-stop after the Hotel Virion. Madness, because his thoughts were in complete turmoil, spinning and shouting at him and making no sense at all. Madness, because he was heading straight back into the eye of the storm without the help of his shadow or a carefully made plan or a shred of hope of stopping Mr van Reiner in his battle for ultimate power.

But in his own way he wanted to vote.

Yes, after resisting so resolutely all the election propaganda, he was now determined in a way he had never been before to make a difference and do it himself, come what may. He might be about to make an utter fool of himself and achieve nothing and even die, but in those moments of extreme passion it no longer seemed to matter. What he did know was that he had to do something to make sense of everything that had gone before. The slogan of the election's advertising campaign urged the public to go online and let their fingers do the voting, but he was doing it the old fashioned way, voting with his feet.

This madness (if madness it really was) raged inside him like a blazing fire. The heat of it surged through his limbs as he marched up the road, heading straight for the hotel entrance. The fire burned up his fears, their blackened remains blowing away behind him, and without any hesitation he latched on to a middle-aged couple, flashing them a sweet smile as they entered the hotel. The Doorman nodded politely, watching them pass by.

On their way to the lifts the couple, charmed by Tom's appearance, asked if he was staying there for long. Using them to shield him from the Reception Desk he told them he was only there for a short visit, at the same time looking out for any familiar faces behind. Neither Jenny nor the Security Guard nor Mr van Reiner and his men were there, but he knew he must remain vigilant. He might bump into them at any time.

The couple left the lift on the 4th floor, parting with a final fond goodbye. Tom smiled and waved in reply, then as soon as the door was shut again, took a deep breath and watched the LED for the floor numbers count upwards.

On the 10th floor he walked straight out and, at the end of the lift lobby, turned into the corridor that led to Mr van Reiner's suite. Ahead was a large metal trolley stacked high with sheets and towels and toiletries and everything the hotel staff needed to clean and refresh the rooms ready for the next guests. The door to the room next to it was open and he heard the sound of someone busying about inside. He walked straight past, a look of absolute determination on his face. He was about to confront whoever was in Mr van Reiner's suite and do whatever he could to stop them. And without his shadow there was only one way in.

He stopped outside Mr van Reiner's door. His fist lifted up, ready to knock loudly.

"I wouldn't do that," said a woman's voice in gentle warning.

His hand stopped millimetres from the door and he turned sharply. A maid, wearing black slacks and a white blouse, looked across at him from where she stood next to the trolley.

"The man in there looked very cross," she said, keeping her voice down, "and he told me that *no one* was to go into those rooms today. He doesn't want them to be disturbed. Not by anyone. Not even me," she added with a sad frown, waving her security card uselessly and shrugging her shoulders.

"But I need to get in," said Tom. "It's important."

"Are you his boy?"

"Definitely not!" said Tom crossly, the fire inside raging again.

"Then I can't help you," she said. "But remember my warning."

The sound of someone's voice came from inside the suite. Footsteps approached the door. A second later the door opened and Jerry stepped out, talking earnestly on his mobile.

"Yes, yes, I'm on my way now," he said. "I'll be down in just a minute. *Okay.*"

As soon as he was gone the maid signalled for Tom to come out of the room she was cleaning. "I told you," she said, "he is not a happy man. So, what will you do now?"

"I don't know," said Tom as if it didn't matter, "but thanks for the warning."

"It's okay," she said, smiling kindly. "But now I must get on with my work. Please excuse me."

After collecting a pile of fresh linen and towels she disappeared inside the room. Tom glanced after her, making sure she was not coming back, then trailed a hand over the top of the trolley until his fingertips came upon a square piece of plastic. It was the security card that he'd seen her leave there. Immediately he pulled it down and walked on to Mr van Reiner's suite.

Without missing a beat he slotted the card into the lock of the door, waited for the green light, then turned the handle. Once inside, he closed the door quietly behind himself, then listened for any sounds inside the suite. He heard nothing, while the stale smell of food and the dimness of the curtained room seemed even worse than on his last visit

Quickly he made his way through the livingroom to the office where the laptop was kept. The lights of the office were still on from when Jerry had been in there. He went round the table and sat down in front of the laptop.

This time it was not lying idle. Instead its lights flickered and it hummed softly. The screen looked quite different, too, and not like anything he'd seen before on a computer. It was entirely black except for a number of rows composed of symbols and unusual truncated words. The last line, though, he understood. There was a command: 'show number votes'. Next to it was a number counter that was climbing so rapidly that its lower digits were just a blur before his eyes. It was already well over four million.

The nation was voting.

Slowly Tom got to his feet, then picked up the chair. He lifted it over his head, ready to smash it down on the laptop. His arms trembled, a look of pure rage over his face. He wanted so much to destroy whatever evil Mr van Reiner had planned. He wanted to stop the country being tricked out of its power. And he wanted revenge for the murder of his shadow.

But as the chair hung above his head, another thought entered his mind, one that stopped him from completing the task. He remembered how The Eagle Corporation had protected itself with a second Computer Centre and at that moment realised that whatever he did to the laptop in front of him it was never going to stop what had already been set in motion.

The chair was lowered down again and he sat on it, slumping over the table. He bit his lip so hard that it drew blood. The fire inside him was flickering weakly as if about to burn out.

The number counter passed five million.

He had failed once more.

"Hello, Mr van Reiner," said Jerry, walking up to him and his men in the lobby, "there really is nothing to worry about. It's all going exactly as planned."

"*Not here,*" he hissed, at the same time forcing a smile in case anyone else was watching. "Anyway," he continued a more relaxed voice, "I want to go up and have a look at how everything is progressing."

Jerry looked as if he was about to protest, but was swept away towards the lifts, a bodyguard at each shoulder.

"This is the 'big day'," Mr van Reiner went on, "and *our* big moment. I wouldn't want to miss any part of it. There's no problem, is there, Jerry?"

"No, of course not."

"Good. But I need to be quick. I have another appointment. It's a busy day. I haven't even voted myself yet!"

It was an irresistible smile, thought Jerry, until you knew what lurked beneath it.

As they came out on the 10th floor Jerry was pleased to see that the maid's trolley had not moved from where it was. The last thing Jerry needed at this moment in time was an eager maid tidying up his laptop.

"Jerry, you really need get some fresh air in here," said Mr van Reiner as he entered the livingroom. "I let you stay here and you treat it like a rubbish tip. Let's open up those curtains, too. No one overlooks us here."

The bodyguards attended to the curtains, while Geoffrey nodded towards the office. "*You're* needed in there, Jerry," he said.

As Jerry entered the office he found Mr van Reiner sitting in front of the laptop, smiling contentedly.

"All these votes for me!" he said with a gleeful clap of his hands.

"Not quite," said Jerry, coming round behind him, "that would be a little too obvious. No, that's the total number of votes cast so far. But if I bring up *this* window" - he reached round him and pressed a couple of keys simultaneously - "then you can see what's actually happening. There," he said pointing, "that column shows the total number of transfers. And these ones show who they've come from and gone to."

"But they're all coming to me, aren't they?"

"No. Again it would be too obvious. We had to balance it out. Muddy the waters a little. Stop any of the other candidates getting suspicious. Just so long as you win in the end."

Mr van Reiner nodded approvingly, though a frown remained. "I thought you said there would be no trail left behind.

"There won't," said Jerry, "at least not where anyone else can find it. All the transfers are happening in the Computer Centres and this summary information is only stored here on my laptop. It's not even saved."

"And it mustn't be," said Mr van Reiner, staring directly at him.

"Sure," said Jerry. "I'll lose it today. I just thought you'd want to know what was happening."

"I do," said Mr van Reiner, "but no one else should."

"No, of course not."

Mr van Reiner eased himself back on the chair. "So, my party will have a landslide victory that will be confirmed later today. There may be complaints - we should expect them, of course - but the voting system will be checked and nothing will be found out of order."

He waited for Jerry to agree.

"No, there'll be nothing out of order," said Jerry, nodding vigorously. "And at the end of today I'll make sure the log files tell our version of the story. Then, if anyone's suspicious enough to want to check it out, they'll see that I've just been doing my job as normal. There's no way we'll be discovered."

"I don't pretend to understand the complexities of what you've done," said Mr van Reiner with a satisfied look, "but I do know that it's going to hand me the election on a plate. And when that happens you will receive the second half of your payment."

Jerry smiled with a look of great relief.

"All right, everyone, it's time we were getting along," said Mr van Reiner in a hearty voice as he emerged from the office.

Jerry stepped out behind him.

"Is everything as it should be?" enquired Geoffrey, keeping a careful eye on Jerry.

"The voting, I would say, is going exceptionally well," said Mr van Reiner, chuckling to himself, "but now it's time I was off to do my bit. Come along, Geoffrey, I think we can leave it to Jerry now. Have you got everything lined up for the photo-shoot?"

"Yes," said Geoffrey, "we've got the local media as well as our own photographers and cameramen. There'll be plenty of footage ready for your victory tonight!"

Both men were laughing as they left the suite, the bodyguards following close behind.

"Thank God for that!" said Jerry, puffing out his cheeks. "And now for a 'light snack' thanks to my loving sponsor."

A call was made to Room Service in which the 'light snack' was more fully described. It consisted of a full English breakfast with trimmings as well as toast and coffee and a selection of French pastries. It arrived soon afterwards and he tucked into it while watching the election coverage on television.

As soon as Tom was certain that only Jerry remained and he was fully occupied with his slap-up breakfast, his fingers tensed round the edge of the cupboard door in the spare bedroom and pulled it closed on himself. Then, shut in the darkness, he wriggled round, slipping off his backpack. He unzipped it and felt around the inside pocket until he found his mobile. It bleeped as it came on, startling him for a second, then glowed a ghostly green. From the inside pocket he then pulled out a card, the one that Georgie had handed him after DI Reever had visited his mother's apartment. *If you're ever in trouble, you must let me know straight away.* That time had now come. Reading the number on the card, he punched it in.

As soon as Jerry finished his breakfast (or what he could eat of it at his first attempt) he flicked off the television and returned to the office to check on the progress of the voting. He noted with increasing excitement the number of votes transferred from other candidates to Mr van Reiner's party. It was such a clever pattern, so difficult to spot and impossible to trace. He imagined the voters making their choices, tapping away on the keyboards, putting their confidence in all the assurances that had been given them about the security of the new system. He imagined them meekly accepting the results, unable to question them, blind to the processes beyond their screens and the robbery of power that was taking place under their noses. He imagined with even greater pleasure the already healthy figure in his off-shore bank account doubling just as Mr van Reiner, the new Prime Minister of Great Britain, waved to his jubilant supporters from the window of No.10 Downing Street. Then, setting the screen of the laptop back to the vote counter, he left the office.

But then, as he crossed the livingroom and was about to turn on the television again, he heard a small sound from the spare bedroom. Taking care not to make any noise, he went over and found the door ajar. He thought he heard a whisper from inside, but then all was quiet.

Very carefully he opened the door fully, glancing warily ahead, then stepped quietly inside. Everything was as it should be, untouched, unused. He could see nothing out of place. He went round the small room then knelt down to look under the bed. Nothing was there. Finally his eyes settled on the cupboard, but instead of opening it he deliberately walked back towards the door.

The door shut.

There was complete silence for several long seconds before there was another sound. It came from inside the cupboard. It sounded like the muffled bleep of a mobile phone, then there was a gentle shuffling about inside.

The cupboard door clicked open. A second or two later Tom's head slowly appeared, peeping out.

"*You!*" shouted Jerry.

Suddenly he darted forwards from where he'd been standing next to the door and grabbed hold of the cupboard door before it could be pulled shut again. Then Tom was hauled out and thrown to the floor.

"Stay there and don't move!" panted Jerry, standing over him as he pulled out his mobile.

Glancing anxiously down, Jerry waited until a voice crackled on the other end of the line.

"*What is it now?*" said Geoffrey, obviously unhappy with the interruption.

"You'd better get back here," said Jerry, "*now*."

"We can't! The vote is taking place. *Mr van Reiner is busy.*"

"The boy's here," said Jerry, his voice trembling.

There was a long silence at the other end, then Geoffrey spoke again.

"*Don't let him go*," he said, his voice heavy with threat. "I'm on my way."

There was a squeal of tyres as the black Range Rover skidded to a halt outside the Hotel Virion. Geoffrey and the two bodyguards jumped out and the keys were tossed at the startled Doorman as they stormed past.

Glancing across the lobby Geoffrey spotted the Security Guard hovering about in his usual dreamy fashion. Their eyes met for a moment, Geoffrey's glinting dangerously, then Geoffrey and the bodyguards ran on to lift lobby, leaving any pleasantries for later.

Mr Crane took the stairs, making sure no one escaped that way. Geoffrey and Mr Wheeler reached the 10th floor before him and pressed on ahead. The corridor leading to Mr van Reiner's suite was empty. Mr Wheeler swiped the door card and they marched straight into the livingroom.

Geoffrey carefully closed the door behind him, then turned to find the boy, in the middle of the floor, taped to one of the dining chairs. A strip of gaffer tape covered his mouth.

"Get Jerry," he snapped irritably, waving Mr Wheeler away, then stepped closer to Tom.

Tom's cheeks puffed out as he struggled for breath. A look of fear filled his eyes.

"Tom Parks," he said, "you seem to have led a charmed life. When we tie you up, you escape. When we shoot you, you come alive! But this time," he said, slipping out the flick-knife from his pocket and releasing the golden blade, "this time there won't be any mistakes. This time, my little friend here" - the blade flashed only millimetres away from Tom's face - "will take care of everything. I'll guarantee it. *Personally.*"

Geoffrey glanced towards the office, looking for Mr Wheeler, but then decided to carry on.

"Maybe it's better that we're alone for our last few moments together," he said with a hateful smile. "After all, the less witnesses, the better. Wouldn't you agree? No interruptions either. And now, from you, there will be no more meddling either."

The blade flashed across Tom's cheek and the blood began to flow.

Suddenly Tom cried out through a cut in the tape over his mouth.

Startled and confused, Geoffrey stepped back and stared at the boy. A second later he was knocked to the floor by the full weight of DS Brown.

"Tom! Tom!" cried out DI Reever, running out from spare bedroom. "What's he done? Why didn't you shout out earlier?"

At that moment a scuffle broke out in the office. Bodies thumped against the walls and there were breathless shouts from inside, then Mr Wheeler stormed out, closely followed by Jerry with the laptop under his arm. The two ran straight out of the suite and along the corridor, shortly followed in some disarray by the pair of policemen they'd overpowered.

DI Reever pulled out a handkerchief and pressed it firmly against Tom's cut cheek. "Don't worry, they're not going anywhere," he said, listening to the shouts in the distance. "We've got officers covering all the exits."

"Thanks," said Tom, taking hold of the handkerchief, the previously cut tape hanging in ribbons from his body. "I waited as long as I could, like you said."

"A bit too long for my liking," said DI Reever, "but you're safe now."

"It's a set up!" shouted Geoffrey, writhing beneath DS Brown. "We've been framed! *You'll never prove a thing.*"

"Maybe," said DS Brown through gritted teeth, grabbing him by the hair and thumping his head down on the floor, "and maybe not. *But we'll have a bloody good try.*"

Chapter 15 A Whole Lot of Questions

At midday DS Brown stood in the courtyard at the back of Police Headquarters. He had spent the rest of the morning making sure Geoffrey and the bodyguards were securely locked up and there were no mistakes in the processing of the paperwork for their arrests. He'd taken a keen interest in the recovery of the laptop and finding out what evidence it might provide in the case against Mr van Reiner. Now, though, he was awaiting the return of DI Reever and the walking wounded from the Accident and Emergency Unit at Bellington General Hospital. He and DI Reever had been in regular contact on the mobiles, exchanging any scraps of information as they came to light, and the last call informed him that he was on his way.

A couple of minutes later the silver Vectra pulled up in the courtyard. Inside was DI Reever, Tom and Sergeant Mike O'Conner, one of the policemen involved in the arrests at the Hotel Virion. The Sergeant got out of the back seat, his arm in a sling and one eye heavily bruised.

"Nice one, Mike," said DS Brown, grinning. "You're going to be popular at home."

"I know," said the Sergeant. "No jobs for a month and I'll be waited on hand and foot. It'll be tough but I think I can handle it."

"You'll be glad to hear that we got the lot of them, no little thanks to you," said DS Brown.

"What about the monster that ran me down?"

"Him too."

"Great."

"And how's our other wounded soldier?" said DS Brown, turning back towards the car.

Tom climbed out of the front passenger seat, a clean white dressing taped neatly over his cheek.

"I think you'll live, won't you?" said DI Reever, getting out on his side of the car.

Tom tried to smile but winced from the pain.

"Come on, let's get you inside," said DI Reever, leading them up the steps to the back entrance of the building. "I think there's some people inside you'd like to see."

Interview Room No.3 was on the 1st floor of the Police Headquarters and there were loud voices coming from inside.

"But if you knew that Thomas was in trouble, then why didn't you tell me?" said Marie, his mother, her voice rising to a shrill peak. "I just don't understand you! A detective comes to the house and you don't think that's important enough to give me a call."

"*No*," said Alan, his father. "As I've told you a hundred times already there wasn't a problem. *It was a mistake*. The detective was following up an enquiry and after he'd asked his questions and taken a look in Tom's room then there was nothing more to it."

"*You let him into Thomas's room?*"

"*Yes*," said Alan, trying to stay calm. "What's wrong with that?"

"But *why*?"

"He was looking for a stolen wallet. It wasn't there. It was nonsense. Someone thought Tom had been out in the night on his own and had stolen it. But he hadn't. He was at home. Asleep. *Got it?*"

"*No*," she said tearfully, pacing about the room which, although designed for cheerful comfort, was giving her none presently.

"And what about the police coming to see you?" said Alan crossly. "This is the first *I've* heard about it. Don't you think it would've helped if you'd told me about that?"

"Georgie was there," she explained, "he dealt with it."

"*And?*"

"*And I've told you,*" she said, "there was nothing to it. The detective asked questions about that break-in at The Eagle Corporation, then showed them some fuzzy pictures. Georgie said it was crazy - they could have been anything. Then the detective left. That was it. Nothing more. There was nothing to tell you. But of course, *if I'd known what had happened before then I might have done something more about it!*"

And with that there were more heated exchanges between them which only ended when the door opened and in stepped DI Reever.

"Hello, I'm sorry to interrupt," he said, "but I think there's someone here you'd like to see."

Tom entered the room and for a moment there was a hushed silence as his parents looked at his bandaged face and he looked back at them, trying unsuccessfully to smile.

"Oh, Thomas!" his mother called out eventually, rushing over to embrace him.

"Are you all right, Tom?" said his father, drawing close and putting a hand on his shoulder.

"Of course he isn't!" she said. "Just look at him."

"But I'm okay," mumbled Tom, feeling his own eyes moistening as his mother and father huddled around him for the first time in more than two years. There was pain from a wound much deeper than the one on his cheek.

DS Brown excused himself, closing the door quietly behind him, then DI Reever waited for the family to compose itself again. He invited everyone to sit down on the comfortable chairs. Tom chose the sofa, his mother and father settling either side of him.

"Thank you," said DI Reever, taking an armchair opposite them. "Now perhaps I'd better explain what's been happening. Especially as your Tom, here, is finding it a little difficult to speak at the moment."

"I'm okay," mumbled Tom, then winced again.

"What happened?" said Marie, directing her question at the detective. "Will he be all right? Will there be a scar?"

"The cut is from a knife," said DI Reever, "and it's fortunate it wasn't any deeper. We took him to A&E at Bellington General - along with our own Sergeant who was wounded - and the doctor said it was a clean wound, no dirt, no fuss. He used butterfly stitches on it and said it should heal well, hopefully without a scar. I've got the anti-biotics," he added, pulling a box of pills from his pocket and passing it over.

Marie gasped tearfully and squeezed Tom to herself, kissing the top of his head.

"Who did it?" said his father, a knot of anger twisting inside.

"We've arrested the man," said DI Reever. "His name is Geoffrey Lions. He's the personal assistant for Mr van Reiner. I think you'll have heard of *him*. He's the MP for Bellington North. Your MP, I believe."

"Not mine," said Marie in a detestful voice. "He's on the wrong side of town and I'd never vote for him anyway."

"I knew he was corrupt," said Alan, adding gladly, "and he never had my vote."

"We've arrested three other men who were involved," DI Reever went on, "all working in one way or another for Mr van Reiner. But let me explain…"

For the next few minutes he went over the investigation, starting with the complaint of a burglary at the MP's suite in the Hotel Virion and the accusation against Tom. He then moved on to the far more serious incident of the break-in and vandalism at the Headquarters of The Eagle Corporation on East Bellington Business Park. He described the MP's links with the corporation as well as the presence of his men there that same evening. It was these men that had led him back to Tom at his mother's house the day after the break-in.

Both parents shifted uncomfortably as the story unfolded, casting momentary glances at their son and each other, not knowing what to say as so many questions piled up inside them.

"And then today," DI Reever continued, "Tom called me on his mobile. You see, I'd been waiting for him at his school because I had a few questions of my own that I needed to ask him. But he didn't arrive. Did you, Tom?"

Tom's eyes lowered secretively.

"Why ever not?" said Marie, twisting round to confront her son directly.

"I saw Jerry," he mumbled, trying not to stretch his mouth too much. "He's *bad*."

"I don't understand," said Marie tearfully, as upset by seeing her son struggling to speak as she was by the lack of a complete explanation.

"We all have a lot of questions that we want answered," said DI Reever with a sympathetic look, "and I don't think we'll get too many from Tom until he feels a little better. But let me tell you the rest of what I do know. There have already been some major developments since the arrests today. I *can* tell you that Jerry Paul, who Tom just mentioned, works for The Eagle Corporation and played a key part in Mr van Reiner's plans. You see, amazing as it sounds, what Tom helped to uncover today was a plot to rig the General Election. He called me from Mr van Reiner's suite in the Hotel Virion where Jerry was using a computer to access the online voting system. The votes were being transferred from one candidate to another. In that way, we believe, Mr van Reiner and his party could be assured of victory today. They would have gained power and formed the next Government, whatever the public had voted. But Tom got in their way and helped stop the plan succeeding. Fortunately we got to the hotel before Mr van Reiner's men got to Tom and had just enough time to set a trap for them."

"And that's when Tom was hurt?" said Alan, an angry glint in his eye.

"Yes," said the detective, " and I'm sorry for that."

"But *you* put my son in terrible danger," said Alan, shaking his head in disbelief.

"I think you'll find," said DI Reever plainly, "that not only did we rescue your son today, but that he's been in a lot of danger for some time."

"Oh, I'm just *so* glad you're safe now," said Marie, smothering Tom with affection, but her hand accidentally brushed his cheek and he yelped with pain. "Oh, I'm so *so* sorry, my poor brave little Thomas!"

"I think there's something else you might like to see," said the detective, "if you'll just wait here a moment. I'll have some drinks brought in too. It has been a very traumatic time."

DI Reever left the room, returning not long after with DS Brown. He introduced DS Brown and announced that the drinks were on their way, then everyone watched with interest as DS Brown sat down and opened up the laptop he was carrying. When he was ready he placed it on the table in front of the sofa and angled it towards Tom and his parents.

"This isn't the computer we found today," he explained, "but we've copied over some *very* interesting movies. Here, have a look at this. Can you all see all right?"

The others nodded, leaning closer. At first there was only the view of an empty chair and the wall behind. It was so still that it might have been a single picture. But then came the muffled sound of voices in the background. Suddenly a distinctive, refined voice spoke from much closer and the image trembled as if the camera had been knocked. And then a man in a suit swept into view, turning to take up the chair. It was Mr van Reiner.

Staring straight towards the camera, he leaned forwards with as much anticipation as his present audience, then gave a smile of great satisfaction.

Tom, trying hard to keep his face still, smiled on the inside, while the detectives looked on with their own deep sense of satisfaction. It was a moment to treasure.

Then Jerry appeared on the screen, and, leaning over Mr van Reiner's shoulder, explained what was happening. Occasionally he reached past him, fiddling with something below the view of the camera.

"They're looking at a laptop," explained DS Brown. "Jerry's changing what they can see on the screen. I can show you that too afterwards. Thanks to Tom we've got the lot."

Jerry and Mr van Reiner were speaking again, then an awesome hush fell over the Interview Room as the MP said his final words. *"But I do know that it's going to hand me the election on a plate. And when that happens you will receive the second half of your payment "*

Marie gasped.

Alan swore.

The movie stopped and DI Reever took over.

"This will form a key part of the evidence we will present in court," he said, "and I think it will prove beyond any reasonable doubt that Mr van Reiner planned to deceive the whole nation to gain power for himself and his party. But it's only thanks to Tom that we have the evidence. It was he who had the presence of mind to turn on the laptop's webcam to record everything in front of it. Even what was happening on the screen was captured too. He did it just before he hid away and called me, and if he hadn't, then this country would have suffered perhaps the greatest fraud in its long history. "

The wound on Tom's cheek throbbed deeply, but now for a moment, as his other cheek flushed hotly too, the pain was forgotten. He looked up at each of his parents in turn and was pleased to see their faces full of admiration and amazement and love. It had been worth it all just for this, just to have the two of them back together again, with him, and happy.

The drinks arrived accompanied by a plate of chocolate biscuits. Marie and Alan accepted the cups of tea, while Tom sucked on the straw poking out of his glass of squash and nibbled enthusiastically on the biscuits, pressing them in at the corner of his mouth. Meanwhile DS Brown went on to show the screens that Jerry and Mr van Reiner had seen on the laptop, giving a running commentary on how cleverly the votes were transferred between the many candidates of the various parties.

"But what's going to happen to the election now?" said Alan who had been picked up from one of the new polling stations where he'd been assisting. "Won't they have to do it all again? No one's going to trust these computers now. It's a complete mess!"

"I don't know what'll happen," said DS Brown, "but we've got The Eagle Corporation and our best IT people working on a solution right now - and some pretty anxious Government people watching over everything, too. Apparently they've found some important log files and all the information appears to be there, but we won't know what they can do with it until later. It's beyond me when it gets into the technical details."

"They should lock up Mr van Reiner, along with the others, and throw away the key," said Alan bitterly.

DS Brown gave a sympathetic nod, then went to close down the laptop.

"I'd like to thank you for your help," said DI Reever, "all of you. But especially Tom. I think we all know how important this day has been for our country and I hope that one day you'll get the recognition for what you've done. But for now," he said, winding up, "I think we've done all we can here. Of course we'll need to talk to Tom again as soon as he can talk more easily, though we might need to contact him in the meantime if there's anything he can help us with. Now, DS Brown will show you out - as soon as he's stopped playing with his toy" - he winked at Jim who rolled his eyes in response - "and he can introduce you to the two Constables who will be accompanying you for the next few days."

A look of alarm spread over the faces of both parents.

"I know," DI Reever said, responding to their looks, "it may sound a little dramatic. But these people were trying to kill your son and we don't know yet if any others were involved. They could have powerful allies and we can't take any chances. It's just a precaution. The Constables will make sure you're comfortable and safe. But you will need to stay in one house. Just until we can be sure that you're no longer in danger."

Looks passed between Alan and Marie, uncomfortable awkward looks. But before they could raise their voices in complaint DI Reever, reading their minds, explained:

"It has to be the one house, though it doesn't matter which. I just don't have the staff to cover both. Hopefully it won't be for long. I know it's an inconvenience, but your safety is my priority. And it's either that or the cells in the basement here. And I think I know what you're answer to that would be!"

His smile was met by frosty looks from both parents.

"But how long do you think this'll go on for?" said Alan, breaking the difficult silence.

"A week, maybe two," said DI Reever. "No more, I hope."

While both parents struggled internally with their deep concerns about sharing the same house again, Tom's eyes sparkled happily, telling a different story.

"Stay at Dad's," he mumbled, looking up hopefully.

"Well, while you're deciding that," said DI Reever, "you can meet the two Constables. They can help you with moving any belongings you need. I'm sure you'll find them most helpful. But there is one other thing," he said, pausing before he opened the door for them. "Under no circumstances should you speak to anyone else about what you've seen or heard here today or, for that matter, anything else to do with this case. Until we've finished our enquiries we mustn't have news of this getting out. You'd be surprised how quickly stories spread and then the next thing to happen is that someone we need to find disappears, or later, in court, we're accused of corrupting evidence or misleading the jury. This is very important and I hope I'll have your help in this."

He looked straight into each of their eyes in turn and they all nodded their heads in response. Then he let them out.

"And Tom," he said in a heartfelt voice as the boy walked past him, "thank you."

Later that afternoon, as the rain that had been threatening all day made itself known, DS Brown steered his BMW along a winding country road in the next county, heading towards Mr van Reiner's private residence. It had not been difficult to track the MP down; his public itinerary for the day was well advertised on his web-site and, ever since the arrests that morning, an unmarked police car had been following him and keeping the detectives informed of his whereabouts.

"Tom's parents didn't look too happy at having to stay under the same roof again," said DI Reever.

"Yes," chuckled DS Brown. "I thought they were going to have a bust up there and then. And then they would've ended up staying in the cells!"

DI Reever smiled. "At least her new boyfriend isn't going to be around. That really would've set the cat amongst the pigeons. It's much better that he's at her apartment, looking after her business or whatever he does, while they're at his father's house. And Tom got his way, after all!"

"Good for him," said DS Brown.

"You can say that again," said DI Reever, then frowned. "It's just a shame he got that cut. There's so much more he's got to tell us. But that won't be happening for a day or two, now."

"You did tell him to call out as soon as he was in danger - any danger at all," DS Brown reminded him. "He just waited far too long. It was almost as if he wanted to take that first cut. But it wasn't necessary. We had more than enough evidence against Geoffrey and the others and Tom knew that better than we did. He knew about the laptop, too."

"Yes," said DI Reever thoughtfully. "It's something we can put to him later. That and what he was doing in Mr van Reiner's suite the first time, not to mention how he got in and out of there."

"And the same for The Eagle Corporation," said DS Brown. "I'd like to hear how he got in and out of there!"

"And what he knew about Jerry Paul."

"And what *really* happened when Mr van Reiner visited his school," said DS Brown. "That's a bit of a mystery too."

"Yes," said DI Reever, "I'm looking forward to our first real interview with Tom. But before that we've got unfinished business with Mr van Reiner himself."

"Yes," said DS Brown eagerly, his grip tightening on the steering-wheel, "it's time to haul in the big fish."

The BMW came to a halt at a T-junction, indicated right, then pulled round the corner. Not long after it had passed out of sight, a muddy Volvo estate came to the same junction and, without stopping, swept round the corner, following straight after it.

Sitting in the stone-walled livingroom of his luxurious country home, Mr van Reiner eased back in a leather armchair, trying to get himself to relax. But despite having every modern convenience to hand, he couldn't get comfortable. *And this the day when his party was assured victory in the General Election!* And not only that, but the results were going to

231

reveal the 'unexpected' defeat of his party's present leader. The obvious successors would be weakened by their slim margins of victory, whereas his victory would be by a massive majority. There would be no contest for the position of the new leader: he would be the clear and outright winner. So, as the new Prime Minister of Great Britain, ultimate power finally would be his.

Yet, still, he remained uneasy.

The ice clinked in the whisky glass in his hand and he glanced irritably at the last few rusty drops remaining at the bottom of it. Usually he would have a glass or two to loosen himself up after the working day, but today he hadn't been able to hold back and had already, at this early hour, drunk too much. Nothing, it seemed, would calm his nerves until he heard the announcement of those final results.

A widescreen television, standing in an alcove in the stone wall, droned on. The endless chatter and speculation of the all day Election Special had plodded nowhere in particular for the last hour in which he had been watching it. It had been padded out with live links to all parts of the country where desperate interviewers had swooped down on pubs and cafes or hung about in shopping malls and at railway stations, asking the public for its opinions on the outcome of the day. Clever graphics popped up and spun round and changed shape, displaying the minute by minute changes in the predictions for the voting. Words, words and more words came out of the speakers, but none of it added up to the real result that everyone wanted to know (Mr van Reiner, most of all).

He slammed his hand down impatiently on the arm of the chair, then went over to the drinks cabinet and refilled his glass. His hand trembled and he cursed, then he paced about the room, going over the day: the party meeting in the Bellington office that had gone well enough; the final check with Jerry at the hotel; and then the photo-shoot when he had cast his vote online (at the time he remembered thinking with amusement that it didn't matter who he voted for, not with Jerry's module moving the votes around in the background). But after that, when Geoffrey had whispered in his ear about the appearance of the boy once again, then his nerves had really started to jangle. And they hadn't stopped ever since.

That boy! How could it be that he was still alive, still causing them problems, still popping up everywhere they went? How was he able to move about like a ghost, getting in and out of anywhere he pleased, and even escaping from bullets? There had to be some simple explanation, not that it mattered now. Geoffrey was disposing of the problem once and for all, personally. And that was why, he supposed, he hadn't heard back from him since the morning.

Pulling out his mobile, he checked for messages and missed calls, but there were none. It was unusual not to have any contact from Geoffrey for so long and it must be this, he assumed, that was adding to his nervousness.

"And just in we have some breaking news," said the long-suffering chairman of the Election Special, wearing a puzzled frown, "though it's probably not what our audience has been expecting. It certainly surprised us here in the studio when we received it a minute or two ago."

Mr van Reiner spun round on his heel, almost spilling his whisky. His eyes sharpened towards the television.

"Yes," the chairman went on, "while you were listening to those varied and fascinating opinions from the great British public in every corner of the land-"

"Yes, yes," Mr van Reiner said through gritted teeth, "just get on with it!"

"-we have been given an announcement from the Government," said the chairman, holding the printed note in his hand. "It says here that there is likely to be a delay in the issuing of the results from the General Election today, but it is only to be expected with the bedding in of any new process of this scale and importance. This, it says, will ensure the security and safe outcome of the nation's voting. Well, all I can say," he went on, looking up and raising his eyebrows in astonishment, "is that this clearly *wasn't* expected, If anything, I, for one, would have expected the results of the voting from an online computer system to reach us far more quickly. Anyway, we can discuss that in more detail with our learned studio panel in just a minute. But before that, if you'll bear with us, we have a link to Bellington and our reporter, Julie Marks, who is standing outside the Headquarters of The Eagle Corporation. It is there, if you weren't already aware, that the new online voting system is hosted. Julie, what can you tell us?"

Mr van Reiner took a step closer, biting his lip.

"Thanks, Martin," said Julie, clutching her microphone as she stood in the rain outside the main entrance to The Eagle Corporation, "and I hope that those questions can be answered by Freddie Westlake, the Chief Executive of The Eagle Corporation, who's kindly agreed to talk to us now. Freddie, what can you tell us about these problems today?"

The shot swung round, bringing the unruffled white-haired businessman into view.

"Hello, Julie," said Freddie, smiling bravely as he glanced up past the rim of his umbrella at the dark sky, "and might I say that, on a day like this, isn't it good to have an online voting system!"

"That might be true," persisted Julie, "if it weren't for the *problems* you're having on, this, the very day of the nation's General Election. So, can you explain why the Government has just made this announcement about a delay in the issuing of the results?"

Freddie chuckled amiably. "Well, I'd be lying if I said there weren't *any* problems. After all, this is the first time this has been done for any nation. But the one or two glitches haven't been anything that we weren't well prepared to deal with and certainly won't put this election in jeopardy. The Eagle Corporation has placed enormous investment in the production and testing of the new online voting system and, I repeat, *nothing* will stop us from getting those results today."

"*Today?*" said Julie, pouncing on the remark. "Are you sure? The Government doesn't seem to know when the results will be out. And why has this announcement been released in the last hour? If this was so well organised, then why wasn't this type of delay factored in? After all, a whole nation is waiting for the results!"

"I couldn't possibly comment on the timing of the Government's announcement," he said, his smile nailed in place. "I can only imagine that it's being cautious. And sensibly so. As I've said already, this is a new process, and everyone wants to be absolutely certain that the end result is the right result. Now, that's worth waiting for, isn't it?"

"Of course," said Julie, "but what about the other incident this week. There was the break-in on Sunday. Does that have any links to the 'glitches' you're experiencing today?"

"No, I can assure that it doesn't," said Freddie, "and as I told you before it didn't even scratch the surface of our operation here. We were able to carry on as if it had never happened and all it goes to show is the outstanding strength and resilience of our workmanship here at The Eagle Corporation. Thank you and now I must return to my business on what is one of the most important and historic days for our country."

As Freddie walked away, the Election Special returned to the studio discussion with its panel of political and technical experts, but Mr van Reiner had already grabbed hold of the remote control and turned off the television.

"For God's sake, *what's going on?*" he spat, pulling out his mobile.

The doorbell rang.

Striding out of the livingroom he called to his housekeeper that he would answer the door. As he crossed the square hallway many troubling thoughts rushed through his mind. Why hadn't Freddie called him directly to let him know about the delay? What *was* the reason for the delay when the voting had been progressing so well that morning? And where the hell was Geoffrey after all this time? All of these he hoped to have an answer to when, expecting to find Geoffrey standing before him, he flung back the oak door.

"Hello, Mr van Reiner," said DI Reever.

"Yes, yes," said the MP, staring in bemusement at the two men in his doorway, "and just who are you?"

"You don't remember us?" said DI Reever. "Perhaps you've forgotten. We attended your suite at the Hotel Virion after a burglary was reported. I'm DI Reever and this is DS Brown. Can we come inside?"

"Oh, yes, of course I remember," said the MP, forcing a smile, "but I'm afraid this is a very inconvenient time for a visit. You obviously know that this is no ordinary day and I have a great deal of business to attend to. Whatever you want to report about the burglary I'll be happy to accept a written explanation by post, but I really must insist-"

"I think it's we who'll have to insist on this occasion," said DI Reever, looking him straight in the eye and stepping forwards.

The MP held up his hand, bringing DI Reever to a sudden halt.

"This is *my* house," said the MP, his eyes now sharp and dangerous, "and unless you have a warrant to proceed, you're coming no further. I don't like to insist on my rights, but if necessary I will do so."

"I see," said DI Reever, taking a step back.

"And I think you'll find you're outside your jurisdiction, Detective Inspector," said the MP, his smile returning. "Bellington is in the *next* county or perhaps you didn't realise that."

In response the two detectives moved apart to reveal the Volvo parked across the entrance to the circular driveway. The front passenger window slid down and a hand appeared, waving a scroll of paper.

"That's Detective Inspector Jennings," explained DI Reever. "He *is* from this county. And that's the warrant in his hand. I hope you don't mind him not getting out, but he didn't want to get wet. So, now, if it's all right with you, Mr van Reiner, we'll come inside. We've a few questions we'd like to ask you."

Chapter 16 The Return of a Friend

The next day it rained and rained and rained. Not that Tom knew much about it, because he slept and slept and slept. It was midday before he made his first appearance downstairs and even then he looked terrible. Alan, who had been checking on him every hour, rustled up eggs on toast for both of them, but Tom only managed a few difficult mouthfuls before excusing himself and returning to bed.

"How's the cheek?," said Alan, following him upstairs.

"It hurts," mumbled Tom.

"I'm not surprised. I've got painkillers, if you want them."

Tom nodded and gratefully accepted the two pills and glass of water that his father brought him. Then, with his head throbbing and his legs feeling as if they might give way at any moment, he slumped back into his bed.

Not long after, DI Reever stopped by the house to give the news that Mr van Reiner had been arrested and charged.

"There's no way out for him this time," he said with great satisfaction. "He's managed to get away with it all these years, but the evidence against him is too great this time. We showed him the movie from the laptop and he went as white as a sheet. He got quite angry when we offered to show it to him again! And then, after he'd calmed down, he even offered to cooperate with us. You could have knocked us down with a feather! Anyway, there's a lot more work to be done yet. I just wanted you to know how well it was going and that we should be able to step down your protection soon. We don't think there's anyone else involved now, but don't want to be taking any chances just yet. I'll keep you updated."

Tom's father thanked him for all his help and offered him a cup of tea, but he couldn't stop and dashed out through the pouring rain. Then, with Tom's mother at work and Clara at school, Alan made the most of his time stuck at home, watching without disturbance the results of the election. They were finally being released almost twelve hours later than was normal prior to the introduction of the online voting system. There was much debate about the delay and what was behind it, with talk of cover-ups and bungling by Government officials and modern technology that could never truly be trusted. But all of that subsided when at last the results were announced for each of the constituencies around the country.

The television panel, looking more than a little ragged around the edges, hauled themselves into action once more, and graphic displays popped up to map out the results as they emerged. And finally came the results everyone had been waiting for. Shortly Alan sank back in his armchair, a contented grin spreading across his face. Mr van Reiner had lost his seat for Bellington North. It was all he needed to know for now.

When Tom woke again in the late afternoon, Alan took him a soft drink and some biscuits and let him know the result of the election for Mr van Reiner as well as the news from DI Reever. His words and the deep sleep seemed to revive him and he was even pleased to see Clara when she popped in on her return from school. She declined the offer of peeping at his wound, however, and seemed quite put out by all the fuss he was attracting.

"It just all seems a bit much," she said, fidgeting on his bed, "when you've been running off all over the place and getting yourself into a whole load of trouble. It would've been better if they'd given you a good clip round the ear and a severe warning, then left the rest of us in peace. How do you think it feels having one of those Constables looking up at *my* bedroom window all night and just because *you* can't be trusted any more? The world's gone mad - *as usual* - and no one's listening to me!"

Tom was quite glad he couldn't talk properly and simply let her words drift past him until she got bored and left him alone again. He dozed off and only woke an hour or so later when a noise in the room disturbed him.

His eyes blinked open, dry and sore from so much sleep in the warmth of the house. He propped himself up on his elbows. He thought he'd heard the click of the bedroom door, but when he looked it was shut. His head turned slowly, looking one way then the other across the shadowy curtained room, but no one was there. Yet still he felt as if another presence was there in the room with him.

"Dad?" he mumbled, then reeled as the same hot pain rose and fell in his cheek once more.

There was no answer.

"Who's there?" he said, then with a great effort threw back the duvet and swung his legs out of bed.

His bare feet struck something bony that wriggled away and with a frightened gasp he immediately dragged himself back across the bed. A moment later, as he lay spread-eagled on his back over the mattress, he received several sharp stabs across his stomach. In terror he struck out with a sudden swipe of his arm and hit whatever it was that was attacking him. A body flew across the room, thudding down on the wooden floor and skidding into the wall beneath the window.

When he scrambled upright again, clutching his duvet to himself and peering out across the room, he then saw the shadowy outline of his attacker as it paced nervously back and forth in the corner beneath the window. And suddenly, his fear replaced with worry, he reached for his bedside light and called out to it.

"Oh, Rolly, Rolly," he said, fighting off the violent heat in his cheek as he flicked the light on, "I'm so sorry! *I didn't know*. Forgive me, Rolly. Please don't go!"

He started to get out of bed again, but then stopped. The cat was arching its back, its tail twitching warily.

"Please," said Tom his insides in turmoil, "I won't hurt you again."

The cat looked from the window to the door and back again, needing to find a way out.

"Okay," said Tom in a sad voice as he carefully climbed out of bed and moved towards the door, "you can go if you want to."

The door clicked open, then he returned to his bed.

"It's up to you," he said quietly.

Rolly looked at him, then the door, then shot out.

Tom thumped his mattress, feeling the tears welling up in his eyes, then slumped down on the bed. He was so angry with himself for having hurt the only friend he had left.

A footstep sounded in the doorway.

Tom looked up, quickly wiping away his eyes.

"Well, he seems to like me," said Alan, stroking Rolly's soft furry belly as the cat lay purring loudly upside-down in his arms, "and I'm sure he might even get to like you too eventually. He certainly keeps on turning up in the garden and I can't seem to get rid of him. You did say once that you'd like a cat, didn't you?"

Tom nodded, a smile forming on his lips. He wanted to say a massive thank you, but the words just wouldn't come out.

By the next afternoon the rest of the family, relaxing in the livingroom, were commenting on how much Tom had improved.

"Well, he did sleep through almost the whole of yesterday," said Alan, a mug of coffee in his hand. "I've never seen him like that before. He was completely wiped out. He only started to pick up in the evening and that wasn't for long."

"He probably felt better when you told him he could keep that mangy old cat," said Clara with a look of utter disgust. "Why did you do that, dad? *You* don't like cats. Who's going to feed it? And what about all those hairs it'll leave around the house? *I'm* not going to clean up after it and it's definitely not coming in my bedroom!"

"I don't think that's very kind," said Marie, watching her daughter cautiously after this rare criticism of her behaviour. "Tom's been through an awful time and he's not had a pet since Robbie died."

"He's not had a friend since then," said Clara cruelly, then glancing at her mother replied, "And that's fine for you to say, but what are *you* going to do to look after it?"

"Don't talk to your mother like that," said Alan sternly, while inwardly agreeing that Marie was unlikely ever to help with the cat. "It's my decision. If Tom wants the cat, it can stay. He can feed it and help brush up the hairs."

"Anyway," said Clara, giving up her protest for an easier target, "if I had a day off school lazing around then I think I'd be feeling a whole lot better too!"

"I thought he was talking a little better this morning too," said Alan, ignoring her comment. "Yesterday he was in a lot of pain - it was easy to see. But it seems a lot less today."

"You did remember the antibiotics," said Marie.

"Yes, yes," said Alan, "of course."

"Good," said Marie, though she kept a troubled frown. "It's the scar I'm worried about. Won't it be awful if he has one?"

"I don't think he will," said Alan. "The doctor seemed confident enough and we've got to go back and get it checked out in a couple of days."

"Let's hope he's right," said Marie, nodding purposefully.

The doorbell rang.

"That'll be Georgie," she said, brightening up again as she got to her feet. "I'll see you all later. Things to do, clothes to buy. Chow!"

Alan muttered something darkly and Clara looked alarmed, shaking her head disapprovingly, but Marie was already out of the room. They heard the front door open and the sound of voices, then a few seconds later Marie returned, followed by one of the Constables assigned to watch over the household.

"Constable Lake needs to see Tom before she goes off duty," said Marie. "I'll just get him."

She disappeared again, calling for him several times then trotting upstairs. She came down again then went into the kitchen before finally returning to the livingroom once more. She looked at everyone, including Constable Lake, with a puzzled expression.

"I can't find him anywhere," she said. "I don't think he's here."

No one had actually told Tom that he couldn't leave the house. He had sort of guessed it, what with the Constables popping in and out at regular intervals, but everyone had been so pleased to see him out of bed and walking about and trying to smile at them that the words had never been said. So, when he had slipped past the livingroom where everyone was talking and sneaked out into the back garden and grabbed his bike from the shed and left through the back gate, he hadn't felt too guilty. On the contrary, he was so pleased to get out into the fresh air now the clouds had broken and the sun was shining, that he felt wonderfully free, like a new person.

Fortunately the Constables were not so vigilant that they had the alleyway covered (or perhaps he just got lucky as they changed positions at the end of their shift), but either way he had a clear run to the park.

He did feel a hundred times better than yesterday and his speed of recovery amazed even him. The sleep had done its job well as had the news that Mr van Reiner had been caught and locked up with the rest of his men and that the General Election finally had been completed in good order. The nation might not like who was in power today, but at least it was who it had voted for. The gift of Rolly, too, had lifted his spirit. All these things had played a part in his swift healing, but none as much as one other thing that no one else yet knew about.

Ever since he had been shot at in the Computer Centre at The Eagle Corporation, a part of him had been torn away. He felt the loss of his shadow in his very soul. It was a deeper wound than the one on his cheek could ever be, whether it left a scar or not. And the loss of his shadow had left him weaker and more vulnerable than he would ever care to be. He had been left without an incredible friend.

But what he had thought was true - the loss of his shadow for ever more - proved not to be so.

Astonishing as it had seemed to him, when he had woken this morning the first thing he laid eyes on was his shadow standing at the window, the curtains drawn back, looking as if it had never been gone.

He spoke with it, his joy almost uncontainable. His cheek hurt almost as much as it had the day before, such was his enthusiasm to talk, and yet he had to restrain himself for fear of attracting attention from the rest of the household and as a result having to part with it again as it hid away from prying eyes. The morning had been almost unbearable because he could not share this most precious of news with anyone else, and yet everyone was commenting on how marvellous he looked and how quickly he was improving! The love for his shadow burned within him and the fire lit his eyes, and in this small unspoken way everyone around him shared in its presence with him.

It was a part of him that could never be revealed, not in the final words of his Election Project nor in the witness statements he would have to make in the court cases against Mr van Reiner and his men. Anyway, who would believe him if he did? It was a mystery which only he could know, and much as he would like otherwise, could never share.

The bike cut through puddles left from the previous day and night's heavy downpours. He slalomed from side to side of the park's smooth wet tarmac paths, leaving a snaking trail where his tyres passed. He and the bike felt as one, slicing through the sharp fresh air, circling round and round the park.

He sat back and spread his arms out, releasing the handlebars. His arms lifted as if in triumph, as if in praise, and he gave a double thumbs-up. A gentle smile spread over his lips, the dull throb of his cheek's pain ignored.

His shadow rippled over the tarmac behind. Its arms were lifted and its thumbs raised, too. It was glad to be back.

Nothing looked extraordinary between the boy and his shadow. Not unless you looked closely. And then, if you knew what to look for, you would have seen the two holes in the shadow.

Two holes, letting the light shine through.